Possession Of My Soul

Possession Of My Soul

The Three Immortal Blades

Kia Carrington-Russell

Crystal Publishing Books

CRYSTAL PUBLISHING

Published by Crystal Publishing (Australia)

Copyright © Kia Carrington-Russell 2014

ISBN 978-0-6483370-7-2

Dedication

A huge thanks you to my family and friends who have been supportive of my endeavors. It has been a long windy path over the last few years and I thank you all for the hours you have spent listening to my long rants and enduring the bizarre dances I come up with as I am taken over by excitement. Thank you to the test dummies who read chapter after chapter, edit after edit.

A special thanks to my best friend, Keeley, who has experienced every step and detail of my writing before it was even on paper, during and after.

I have made many professional friends along the way who have helped me every step, I thank you all.

I thank all of my supporters and readers. I will always be thankful and smile at the progress of this fantastic book that we have created and shared.

Prologue

"Hello?" I croaked. My kidney felt like it had frozen; shards of ice stabbed me from the inside. My knees buckled, and I fell tumbling to the pavement. I managed to keep a firm grip on the phone that was now clutched to my stomach. I opened my lips to release a scream—the pain was horrific—but no noise left my mouth, leaving the tension locked inside my body.

"Karla, where are you?" Mum's voice was panicked and teary; my dear mother that had always taken care of me. My body felt like it was decomposing under the force of a hundred spears. My wrist shook with the intensity of supporting my weight against the pavement. It felt like a good time to tell Mum that I loved her and that this may be goodbye—because that's what my body was telling me.

"Karla?" I could hear the pain in her voice. "Karla, you need to get home. Now." I heard my dad in the background telling Mum to ask where I was and where he could pick me up. It ripped me to shreds to imagine how heartbroken they would be to know how much pain I was in. I braced myself and yelped as I raised myself, only for my feet to sink once again beneath my weight.

"Karla, I'm so sorry, baby!" Mum started crying and I heard the shifting of the phone. My body felt like it was drifting—panic swept over me making my pain unbearable.

"Karla? Karla?" Dad's voice was as frantic as Mum's. "Karla, get home now. We have things to discuss." He sounded jumpy and tearful. I took one step back, and my leg buckled again. I tried dragging the other leg under my body but they could no longer move. *My body is shutting down on me.*

My eyesight was blurring into blotches of black, and then blotches of green. The pain was like venom triggering every nerve of my body to shut down. *I can't handle it anymore.* "I love you," I gasped into the phone, while tears replaced the stream of rain drenching my face.

"What? Are they there? Don't become what they want you to, Sweetie. Please!" my dad shouted. I heard Mum scream in the background and I felt her pain layer on top of mine. *I can't breathe. Don't become what they want me to? What is Dad talking about?*

"What who wants me to be?" I whispered, wincing as I felt myself slipping in and out of consciousness. A loud ring echoed through my head, blocking out the noise of my father and the rain. Then silence. All noise was lost. My knees collapsed at the same time as the world around me. *I can't breathe. I can't breathe*. I thudded to the ground again, barely able to see my hands in front of my face. My lungs wouldn't accept any air now.

My body had completely stopped. My mouth filled with blood, and I could feel it trickle onto the road below my face. Relief and fear was all that functioned in my mind. *Relief to know that the pain will go away; fear to know that I'm dying.*

I felt ice-cold hands lifting me off the ground from the waist, while another hand cradled my head. My eyesight could only determine the outline of his shadowy face. The sadness it contained reflected my own. Rain washed over his face and dripped onto mine. His lips moved as if he were shouting, but I heard none of his rage or fury. Only bliss. My face was cradled in his chest; he was embracing me in his arms. My eyesight was slowly taken away from me, leaving me in the dark. *I can't breathe.*

1

Awakened Curse

The burden of self-discovery
is to find not who you are,
but what you are.
Finding out what you're capable of is another matter to
dwell on;
but when paranormal ability is profound, self-discovery
turns into the unspeakable capability of one's actions,
understood only by those who use it, inflicting the
insecurity and burden of those who cannot.

Chapter One - Appearance

"*Y*ou've been talking about this for the last two weeks. Why don't you save yourself all the suspense and go ask him?" I asked, yawning into my hand.

"What do you think, Karla?" Sarah pondered, her head tilted to one side. During the past five minutes she still hadn't realized I was actually answering her questions, or talking at all for that matter. Sarah was my best friend. I loved her, but in our ten years of friendship, she had never really stopped to listen to my opinions on her ever-changing love life. In this past year she had tried far too many times to involve herself in my own love life—trying to start a romance between Greg and me. He was an absolute dork but he offered me quiet companionship in the library, and great advice on assignments.

Sarah continued talking. I knew that after discussing her romantic interests, her mind would invariably fix on her competition with her archrival: the mean-hearted, blonde and bouncing Courtney, daughter of the town's mayor. Roperia was only a small town with a population of just over two thousand people, and Courtney acted like her family was royalty here.

"What if he asks Courtney to the Tuxedo Ball instead of me? Do you think she has a better chance? Oh my goodness, *of course* she does. I didn't even think of Courtney. Karla, look at me. I have no chance! She's *so* pretty with her bouncy, blonde curls and her perfectly manicured nails and her—..."

"Don't you mean her *fake* bouncy, blonde curls and her *fake* nails?" I asked, interrupting her as I've already heard all of this before.

Although she acted as though she didn't compare, Sarah *was* beautiful, and we both knew it. Her icy-blue eyes sparkled against any color she wore. She even made the tacky grey jumper we wore for school look like it was designed especially for her. Her snow-white hair was in a different style every day. She tried to avoid wearing the same hairstyle within the same month. *"It always shows you're incapable of being creative, and, the more natural it looks, the more attention you get,"* she would say with a sly wink each time I questioned some of her bizarre hairstyles.

I looked down at my flat chest and folded my arms self-consciously. I was fair skinned with green eyes, and in my own opinion, quite average. I was of medium height, and I longed for long legs like Sarah. But instead, I was left with a tomboy figure with very little curves.

"Stop spacing out and listen to me," Sarah demanded, waving her hand in front of me. "I reckon that nerd you hang out with at the library will ask you. I guess he could look cute with his dorky glasses off and maybe if he dropped the encyclopedia vocabulary once in a while."

I hated it when she talked about Greg that way. He was a friend.

We reached the school gates and I saw Greg huddled up in the corner reading. I couldn't see what he was reading, but I guess it was the latest issue of his anime magazine. Or maybe his new cheat book for a game he was telling me about yesterday. I forgot what the game was, but it was something about him slaying dragons, 'Epic Sin', I think.

We were late for class, again, and as we neared our room, Sarah reapplied her lip-gloss and moved her fringe to the side, tucking it stylishly behind her ear. Although the conversation had subsided, she was still waiting for my response to the idea of me going with Greg to the Tuxedo Ball.

"His name's Greg. He's not a dork, he's just really intelligent and that makes it hard for him to relate to other people," I hissed, as we reached our tables just in time. Miss Simons was starting the first lesson of the day, Math.

"Besides..." I continued, "I'm not going to the ball. It's just an excuse for your date to hold you around the waist, making you lightheaded and feverish at the thought of their touch... and then, BAM!" I flicked my fingers apart making a flashing action. "He's got you outside, alone." I was so absorbed in my theatrics that I hadn't realized the whole class was listening.

I didn't even realize Courtney was sitting in front of me, but nobody could miss her evil cackle and, apparently, she was laughing at me. "Well yes! I guess that's what a frigid would say, isn't it? Oh Karla, you should get out more. I almost feel sorry for you," she said smugly. Her hazel eyes were narrowed as if it was painful for her to stare directly at me. She flicked her hair over her shoulder so that everyone got a whiff of her strawberry shampoo.

I shriveled into my seat, looking out through the window in embarrassment. I could see my reflection in the window: pouted lips, saddened eyes and flustered cheeks. I twirled my finger through my light brown hair, disheartened.

Sarah, oblivious, tugged on my arm lightly until I finally gave her an annoyed glance of acknowledgment. "How come you're not coming to the ball? It's going to be so awesome! Everyone's going to be there. You have to come. We can go shopping together and go pick out each other's dresses," she said, clapping her hands together and letting out a little shriek of excitement. "It'll be great. Oh my, I know the perfect—…"

"Miss Sloan. Perhaps you would like to share with the class what you're obviously dying to tell Miss Grey?" Miss Simons said, with her arms across her chest. We haven't even been in the classroom for five minutes. Only a few people raised their heads to watch the drama, but knowing Sarah, she wouldn't settle for that. She'd want to be heard and seen. *Especially by Paul. And who's sitting in front of us, next to Courtney? Of course, Paul is.*

"I was just saying to Miss Grrrreeeeey…" She rolled the 'Grey' out way too long. *Here she goes* I thought, cringing. "…that this class is so boring, same as your dress. Or is that by any chance your shower curtain? Because those stains are not working wonders for you, Miss Simons."

The whole class sprayed their spit across the room, laughing at her. With the only exception, me. I trailed my eyes back to the window, unamused.

"How dare you speak to Miss Simons that way?" Courtney asked, giving a polite smile to Miss Simons. "I myself think that dress looks delightful. Do they have it in my size Miss?"

"Give it a break, Courts. Your sucking up isn't that flattering," Paul said, with a small smile on his face.

There you have it: the attention Sarah was after, from Paul. I could see him in the corner of my eye—his big, bulky frame. His shirt looked way too small for him; it hugged him tightly, showing off the big muscled arms he was so proud of. He had dark brown—almost black— hair that contrasted well against his tanned skin. He had a new bandage over his hand. Although I assumed it was gained in some stupid fight when I first saw it yesterday, I was told later, by an elderly customer at work, that he had hurt his hand while fixing her fence. She had many kind things to say about 'the young chap', as she put it. It sounded like a very different Paul to the one I heard stories about at school.

He stretched around and gave Sarah the tiniest of smirks. She ate that up with the hugest smile that could stretch across her face.

Then, his eyes trailed to me. I could see him in the corner of my eyes just staring at me. I will admit he does have nice green eyes—*for a class clown*. It was kind of awkward having him stare at me, so I gave him a side glance to tell him, *"Yes, I know you exist."* He smirked at the gesture. Maybe I had made it too obvious.

Throughout all the laughter, I could hear Miss Simons yelling at everyone to shut up. Her dress wasn't even that bad, bohemian even—I personally found nothing wrong with the style.

"Perhaps, if everyone finds it so funny, they might enjoy a call home. Miss Sloan? Office, now! Karla, Paul, and Courtney! Afternoon detention, tomorrow!" Miss Simons was screeching, expanding her lungs as much as I think they possibly could and making her face as red as her hair.

"But I didn't even do anything," I whined. It was hopeless. *She's hated me from day one*. Unfortunately, this was term three and she has yet to warm up to me.

"You will learn to take responsibility the hard way, Miss Grey. If a bunch of seventeen-year-olds such as yourselves find it funny to disrespect your elders, then you will all stay for detention," Miss Simons said, flushed. She was tucking her short bob cut behind her ears self-consciously. Everyone silenced quickly and ducked their heads back into their books as if they were angels. Of course, Greg already had his head in a book, laughing to himself at some drawing that was displayed on the page. He was probably oblivious that everyone else was even laughing at all.

Sarah had already packed up her stuff and was reapplying her lip-gloss, even though it already looked like her lips had seven coats of 'Hot Pink' plastered on them. "Sorry. You know what she's like, though. So over the top," she said, resting her hand on my shoulder with a sympathetic smile. Then she walked past Paul, giving him a big cheesy grin as she sashayed past him. *She is going to be the end of me.*

"Miss Simons, I can't do detention that afternoon. My father has a gathering tomorrow night and I must attend. And Paul must attend as well," Courtney said. She had the reputation of being able to get her out of anything. Well, her daddy could.

"I see Courtney. You have the detention off, but Paul is not avoiding the detention. He is required to stay," Miss Simons replied calmly. *How is she so calm now after she just blew my head off?*

Of course, Courtney pleaded and whined, but it didn't work. I was kind of hoping it would though, because now I would be stuck with Paul. Miss Simons didn't budge, though.

Paul stretched back and turned to face me. "Looks like you're stuck with me Friday afternoon, darling," he remarked with a sly wink. I smacked my head on the desk in a show of annoyance.

Wow! A whole afternoon with the class clown! It's sad to know any girl in this room would swap places with me in an instant just to be with him. Courtney didn't like that thought either, and begged Miss Simons to let him do it some other time. But like I said, Miss Simons hated me, and so, she wouldn't budge—not even for Courtney.

Chapter Two - Collided Paths

That lunch, I studied in the library with Greg. An English assignment on Shakespeare was due within a few weeks, just before the term finished. I wanted to get to it in nice and early, plus, I was hiding from Sarah.

"Don't worry; she isn't going to sneak up on us. One: the library is like the last place Sarah would enter. She would pretty much shrivel up and die," Greg remarked, as he flicked through his Biology book. He held two fingers up without raising his head from the book. "Two: she's been suspended."

"What! Are you serious? Who told you that? For how long?" I asked, shocked.

"Four days. It's intriguing what you can overhear from the lunch ladies' conversations, isn't it?" His face was emotionless, but I could tell he was smug about it. He glanced at me and pushed his glasses up from the bottom of his nose, even though they slid back down into their usual position straight away. That was the only conversation I had that lunch. Greg and I never really indulged in conversation. It was more of a 'working side by side in the library' thing, but we both enjoyed the company.

Despite my lunch with Greg, I still felt extremely distracted. *I can't understand why Sarah would want to be suspended simply so she could get attention from Paul. And I most certainly can't grasp why I keep thinking of Paul.* Every thought I had led to the vision of his green eyes during my last period in class. I continued looking from his broad back in my mind to my textbook in front of me, annoyed with myself. I tried pushing the image away every time it resurfaced, confused as to why it was all I could think about. Finally school finished and I left in a hurry, flustered by my bickering thoughts.

Work wasn't any better. I was all over the place: I broke the mugs, forgot a few customers' orders, and charged them the wrong amounts. I was hopeless. I was a worse waitress now than I was on my very first shift. My boss decided it was best if I just took orders. That way, he wouldn't lose any more of his mugs or plates. Somehow though, I still managed to break a metal spoon. I looked up at the clock. It was almost nine, meaning my shift was over in about half an hour. The realization brought me the only relief I had felt the whole day.

I walked outside to serve the remaining customers in the trendy outdoors area. The fresh air outside was so much better than the air-con inside. The wind tangled in my hair and tickled my neck, sending a shiver down my spine. Looking over the exterior of the café, it really did look better now since it had been renovated after the fire at the end of 2013. I was proud to work in the coolest café in town, and we were often busy even at this time of the night.

I walked over to the busy tables, ready to serve the last two men. One guy was drinking his coffee near the door, talking on his phone. I couldn't see his face, but I saw the white cup in his hand and knew he'd already been served. I went to the other guy, who was sitting in one of the fashionable wicker chairs. Pen to paper, I put my happy smile on as if I haven't a care in the world. He was a large-framed guy, and from behind, his muscles tensed. He looked a little like… *"Paul?"*

"Hey Karla," Paul said, waving nervously before shoving his hands into his pockets.

"What are you doing here?" I asked, placing my hands on my hips, annoyed.

"I saw you walking home last night in the dark. I didn't like it, so I thought if you had no lift tonight I could give you one," Paul smiled shyly, as he rubbed the back of his neck looking down.

"I'm fine with walking," I replied, a little surprised.

"I know it might be weird, with me turning up like this, but you really shouldn't walk home so late at night," he lectured me in a concerned tone of voice.

"I will be alright. I walk every night. But thank you for the offer," I said, stunned. I held my notebook tighter and turned to walk away. I frowned, confused as to why Paul had really come. *Why would he want to drive me home?*

Paul caught my hand, making me look back at him in surprise, his large hand covering mine. He dropped it in an instant after realizing what he had done while red spread across his cheeks. He opened his mouth to say something, but a stranger who now walked over to us interrupted him.

"Is everything ok?" the man asked, joining the already awkward conversation. He was about my age, maybe a year or two older, with sandy blonde hair, deep brown eyes, and he had a very well built body, not as big as Paul's, but enough to show he was well equipped and fit. His voice was placid but it had a rough grind to it, proving he wasn't a boy, but a young man. The lamp behind him kept flickering its light on and off. It sent flashes of gold and then dull brown through his hair.

"Is your boyfriend harassing you?" the stranger continued when there was no reply.

I found my voice at last: "He's not my boyfriend, and no, he's not harassing me, he was just leaving." I was embarrassed. *Paul is not my boyfriend and why has this stranger come over?*

Annoyance deepened Paul's tone: "This is none of your business mate walk—..."

"How about you leave her alone so she can get back to work?" The guy was quick to interrupt, and, as an afterthought, he added with a smirk: "mate."

"I don't know who you are but that won't concern me when I shove my fist into that pretty little face of yours," Paul threatened. He was known for his excellent skills in boxing. Unfortunately, I heard he had become accustomed to using his talents outside of the boxing ring.

"Hey guys, that's enough," I said, confused as to how this escalated so quickly. Paul's stance was uneasy and his hands were tensed into shaking fists at his sides. I could feel the mounting tension. "Stop it, both of you, enough is enough," I hissed, holding my hands between them. "Paul, I finish in thirty minutes. Go drive or something until then."

"Why doesn't he have to leave as well?" Paul asked angrily.

"Because I'm the customer," the stranger retorted with a smirk, as he raised his mug to his mouth and took a casual sip.

Mr. Richard stepped out of the café. "Is everything okay out here?" he asked, squinting at the boys.

"Everything is fine. Paul was just leaving, and I'm about to pay for my coffee," the young man said, gesturing to his coffee as he took another sip.

"Karla, is everything okay?" Mr. Richard repeated, concerned.

"Ah, yes. Everything is fine, like, ah..." I had raised my hand to the stranger who was still slurping on his coffee. I didn't even know his name.

"Lucas" he said with a smile.

"Like Lucas said, Paul was just leaving." Paul gave me a hurt look and without saying anything he paced around the corner to the car park.

"Karla, can you please charge this young man for his coffee then bring the chairs and tables in," Mr. Richard said, glancing over Lucas disapprovingly and vanishing back into the store.

"What was that?" I asked Lucas, pointing in the direction Paul had left.

"It's a mocha, two sugars," Lucas answered nonchalantly. He spoke thoughtfully as if what he'd ordered was an important matter.

This didn't deter me from confronting him. "I didn't need defending. I think I can talk to him myself, thanks," I said, strapping my arms across my chest in annoyance.

"How much?" he asked, concentrating on his mug.

"How much is what?" I spat out angrily.

"Is the coffee? Look I'm pretty busy, I only had a few minutes to meet you, but I am sure I will be seeing you very soon," Lucas said mysteriously. He then grabbed my hand and placed money into it. "Keep the change. See you around, Karla. Look after yourself until then."

I kept staring at him in disbelief until I could only see the outline of his muscular frame through the dark.

Paul drove out of the narrow alleyway behind the café with his new green Ute. He gave me an awkward smile and opened the door for me from the inside. He dipped his head in shame as he rubbed the back of his neck with his hand.

"I'm sorry about before," he began. "I know I was out of line and it was weird that I came to pick you up."

"It's okay. I don't know who he was though," I said, looking back at the shop through the side mirror and thinking of Lucas. I had never seen him around here before. "Thank you for offering me a ride," I added shyly, as I fiddled with my hands.

No one had ever really put themselves out for me like this. I looked back at Paul as he focused on the road. His eyes were still a beautiful green, even in the darkness of night. His muscled arms that gripped the steering wheel tensed as he noticed I was looking at him. I dipped my head with red spreading across my cheeks.

All too soon he pulled into my driveway. I thanked Paul once more and closed the car door without hesitation. I hurried across my lawn as my heart raced. *Am I flustered? No, that can't be it, I must be coming down with the flu*, I reasoned, raising my hand to my cheek.

I inserted my key in the door and twisted it slowly so that I didn't wake up my parents. I waited quietly for the response of the door that would give me permission to enter. The door made the little click and I slowly took my key out and pressed gently on the door, edging it slightly inwards every time. The door decided not to cooperate and made a huge screeching whine from the hinges. I froze in my awkward stance, feeling like a burglar, even though it was my house.

"Stupid door," I hissed under my breath. I hated this door. It might as well have barked at me. I heard the harsh noise of Dad's rumbling snore, and went on inside, relieved I didn't wake them.

I slid through what little gap there was between the door and its frame. I gently pressed against the door and it reacted to my touch, just as I reacted to its noise. There was a loud bang and I was spitting through my teeth. *Stupid door can't help itself being a troublemaker.*

"Karla?" a low moan escaped from my parent's room. "Is that you, hun?"

"Yes, Mum. It's just me," I sighed in defeat. "Go back to sleep." The door had once again won.

I turned off the lamp Mum had left for me on the side table and walked over to the kitchen to grab a glass of water. I walked down the hall to my room and flopped onto the mattress, not bothering to switch on the light. I tried to drag my head up to my pillow, but decided it was too much exertion.

I was surprised at how exhausted I was, and yet my mind was completely awake. It pounded with thoughts: *Why did Paul come and pick me up from work today? And why do I seem so immature around him?* I thought of Lucas and Paul's argument, frowning in confusion. *Who was to blame? Did Lucas have a right to intervene?* I didn't think Paul was being argumentative or aggressive towards me. And Lucas did seem to antagonise Paul a lot. However, Paul clung to his every word, deeply and angrily. *Was Lucas really concerned for me or was he simply trying to cause an argument with Paul?* I burrowed my head deeper into the pillow, growling in frustration.

It was one of those weird nights. I was confused, but also tired. My mind took the hint of what my body was pleading for, and I eventually fell into a deep and satisfying sleep.

Chapter Three - A Fresh Start

I growled and hit at the ringing alarm that woke me from my satisfied sleep; desperate for it to stop. Eventually it did, but the clashing noises from the kitchen didn't subside, which was giving me the same grief. I took a big, tense stretch and curled back into a ball, resting my head in a damp patch on my pillow. A little embarrassed, I rolled over onto the other half of the pillow and lay there instead. I hadn't drooled on my pillow since I was eight. *How embarrassing.*

A little hint of syrup and melted butter passed my nose, prompting me into my usual reaction. *Pancakes!* I jumped from my bed excitedly and jogged to the kitchen: my quick morning run.

"Good Morning, Karla," Mum said with her back towards me, but I could tell she had a gentle smile, kind and loving as always. Her red hair was wavier than usual, meaning I wasn't the only one that had a good sleep.

"Good Morning, Mum," I said, smiling as she started putting more pancakes on the plate. "I got an interesting call from your teacher yesterday," she muttered calmly. "So you have detention today?"

"It's not my fault. You know what she's like..." I said, beginning to pick at the edge of my pancakes in annoyance. *It wasn't even my fault.* Whenever my mother received a call from the school, it was always because Sarah had done something bad and I had gotten caught somewhere in the middle of it all. I groaned again; I felt a little stupid for somehow always getting involved.

"I know. I'm not lecturing you. It makes me a little *proud*, actually."

I coughed and spluttered as I wiped away the juice I had tried to gulp down. Mum had never tried this sort of guilt-method on me before. Now, after seventeen years, she decides to try a different technique for parenting. She glanced up at my bewildered face, amused. "Not because you're getting detention, silly." She swung the fork at me, swinging it around in circles. "It just means my little girl's opening up from her shell. Obviously talking and making friends if she's getting detention."

"Mum…" I said, moaning in embarrassment. I hated it when she still called me her 'baby girl'. It was embarrassing and I didn't even have to have Sarah here to tell me that.

I lowered my eyes to the big portion of food she had given me this morning and realized there was only one plate on the table. Now that I thought of it, Dad would have come screeching down the hall at the smell of pancakes long before I did, and, if I stood in his way in the process, he'd run me over not even realising I was even there.

"Where's Dad?" I asked, picking at my breakfast.

"He's… ah… working overtime," she said, sighing with a hint of guilt in her tone. "We're not doing too well, baby. He's trying to earn as much as he can, so we're not in even more debt." She sighed even more quietly this time and patted my hand. "We'll get through this," she reassured me, but I could see she was trying to convince herself in the process. I hated seeing my Mum like this. It made me feel bad for accepting the plate of food she'd gotten up to cook me. We've been in debt for a while, but nothing made Mum cringe this badly, as she sighed out the word 'debt'.

"I'll ask for more hours at work. I get paid next Monday. I—…"

Mum interrupted me and squeezed my hand tightly. "No. Your father and I will deal with this, Karla. It has nothing to do with you," she said sternly. Either way, I was giving her that money and she knew it.

I shrugged my shoulders casually. "I know. But I want to know what it's like to be an adult, having to keep your money lined up for more important things. It can be… ah… like a little learning experience," I said with a smile. Her face was motionless and she let out a frustrated sigh as she took her hand from mine, dropping it to her side in an exhausted fashion.

"And besides," I continued, "when I'm a millionaire, don't be expecting to get money from me. I'll give you some now while I'm not experienced." I was joking. She gave me a weak smile back—a fake smile.

"Well. I've got to go to work." She perked up as if she was excited about work—excitement she faked everyday—before continuing: "Your father and I will be late tonight. I'll be back at eight and your father will be home at ten."

"Okay."

I heard the scraping of the keys against the coffee table in the lounge-room and then the irritating squeak of the door shutting behind her.

I arrived at school on time for once, and I enjoyed the peace and quiet of Sarah's absence. I didn't see Greg either, but I knew he was roaming somewhere near our class. I walked past a few of the other kids, younger than me, playing soccer.

I dawdled to my classroom, wasting time so that I didn't have to wait for too long. My classroom was first on the right across from the library; so it never took me long to get to my destination and hide. I trailed up the stairs slowly, thinking about Paul: *I wonder why he came to see me last night?*

I reached the top of the stairs where Miss Simons noticed me. We both exchanged a mutually disappointed sigh and she gestured me in. Hesitantly, I slowly crept one step closer to her room—her territory—and looked down, examining the carpet.

"Close the door," she quietly murmured, while shuffling through some paperwork. She got out of her chair as I reached her desk so she could look down at me; showing who had the authority and the power. An image pinched inside my head; of me throwing her coffee in her face, letting the mug slip as well, and then running out of her class giggling like a little mischievous fairy. In reality though, that was a stupid thought. This dragon could see that image flicker through my eyes and she casually grabbed her mug from the table and whirled her other finger around the rim.

"It's not that I don't like you, Karla," she insisted. I wasn't sure if she was trying to convince me, or herself. "I think you're quite a bright girl. It's just you choose the wrong people to sit with." She gave me a quick glance and continued with her lecture, not caring if I was listening: "I mean Sarah, Courtney, and Paul."

If Sarah were in the room, she would point out the fact that I hate Courtney and that I still wasn't sure about Paul. I faded in and out of her conversation with, "Uh huh" and "I know." I jolted in relief when the bell rang. "Do you see what I'm getting at?" she asked, while slurping away at her coffee.

"Perfectly clear," I lied. The last ten minutes of my life was wasted. We both knew it was pointless.

The class piled in and I stepped out for a breath of fresh air as I placed my bag down and grabbed my books. *English. Great.* I looked over to where the young bunch were still playing soccer and watched contentedly as Mr. Powell came up and scolded them.

"Hey," Paul said startling me. I dropped one of my books and clumsily tried to pick it up, hitting my head on the port rack as I raised my head back up.

"Hey," I replied, embarrassed as I rubbed the bump I had just gotten. *Why am I so shy around Paul after last night?*

He opened the door for me and everyone glanced my way, giving me a second look when they realized Paul was with me. Courtney perked her chest up high and scrunched her hair up, with a big smile. A little disturbing, having her focus directed towards me, however indirectly. At least she wasn't looking at me with her usual contempt. I shuffled between the desks and took my usual seat. This time, thankfully, Courtney wasn't sitting in front. Greg was in his usual spot as well, two seats behind me, and busily reading his new book.

I set my desk up the usual way and glanced out the window. It was a cloudy day; it would rain this afternoon. I heard a hissing noise and felt a cold shiver trail up my body, making my hands shake for a couple of seconds. Before I could even look up, I felt someone's eyes glaring at me with hatred. Courtney gave me a dirty look with her lips pursed together. Her eyebrows fused above her eyes, and as she sat alone. Then, I realized why she was so angry.

"Are you kidding me?" I whispered in a hushed tone.

"What?" Paul asked, confused.

Paul made Sarah's desk look tiny. I was used to a petite frame sitting in that chair instead of a massively built, almost adult one. People were staring, as was Courtney, her peering eyes now threatening death. I shrivelled in my chair and looked back into his innocent eyes.

"Why aren't you sitting with Courtney?" I hissed through my light brown hair, looking out to the side so he didn't see the discomfort in my face, although it was conveyed by my tone.

"Because I felt bad about yesterday and I wanted a fresh start."

I looked at him in childish confusion. "A fresh *start*?" I acknowledged the words he spoke and repeated them back to him, hoping he'd hear how silly they sounded.

"The name's Paul." He raised his hand out to me. I looked at his massive hand and then at his beaming face. I was about to confess to him how stupid his gesture was, until I got interrupted.

"Karla. Paul. If you cannot restrain yourself enough to keep your mouth shut, then you will be more than welcome to another detention!" the Devil woman called Miss Simons announced.

I looked away and out the window. I surveyed the outside area with a fiery blaze. *Nothing. Nothing. Road. Tree. Road. Flowerbed. Statue of Courtney's dad.* I rolled my eyes at the statue of her tall father with his hairless face and head. *Mr. Powell's car, and a black car.* I wasn't good with cars so I had no idea what kind they were, but the black car looked more expensive and faster than Mr. Powell's little green buggy. Somebody was in it, but I couldn't see through the tinted windows. *Road. Tree...*

"Look, I know this sounds stupid, but—..." Paul was interrupted by my intimidating glare. I gave him a harsh frown with pouted lips. I didn't want another detention. He put his head down in defeat. I could still feel Courtney's daggered eyes trying to see through me into my soul. I worked busily for the next two lessons, trying to avoid eye contact with Paul. He constantly looked at me intently as if he were examining me. I didn't know why, and I didn't like that. *Why has Paul Stuart taken a sudden interest in me?*

Chapter Four - Black Shadows

*T*he dark clouds that had surrounded us this morning finally delivered as the rain began to heavily pour. Our punishment was to clean and scrub the room. After that, I would be able to leave. As planned, I took the tables and chairs outside and scrubbed them repeatedly. As soon as my mind began to wander, my face flushed red once again—I was thinking of Paul. His attention made me feel special, almost. I blushed at my stupidity and left the chairs out to be rinsed off by the rain that had started to wash over the land.

I dawdled back through the door clutching and releasing my fingers trying to get what little feeling I could back, and watched the blood slowly return to them taking away some of the redness. I gazed out the window as I normally did and let my mind focus. I wanted to remember the roaring sky so I could sketch and paint it later. I loved art and my mother was very supportive of my passion. It was also a way to make some money on the side. As of late I didn't have the time to do anything but work, study, and attend school. The dark clouds and heavy rain was a magnificent view. Such anger was beautiful, although, that idea didn't stick with me for very long.

What if Paul is crushing on me? How will I deal with it? I don't even know if I like him. He's not my type of guy. I have been told his fists speak before his intelligence.

However, after last night, I didn't picture him as badly as I once had. I guess now when I look back on it, he had always tried to approach me throughout our time at school together. I was simply too shy and looked away when he had tried to make eye contact. *Why all of a sudden was he trying exceptionally hard to get my attention?* I let my head take a wild spin and tried to grasp onto reality once again.

My hearing was being drowned out by the thunder and rain, and I let my eyes focus once again outside of the window. I frowned at the figure I saw. It was Lucas; the stranger I had met yesterday, just casually standing out in the rain. A cold chill ran up my spine as I quickly spun to look behind me, I could have sworn I had seen someone run by.

Looking around the classroom, it was obvious there was no one there. Unsteadily, I looked back through the window glancing at Lucas behind me, paranoid with the feeling of being watched.

Lucas wore dark grey jeans and a black trench coat, holding up an umbrella. I could clearly see his expression and he seemed to be in an argument with whoever he was on the phone with. He had done the very same to Paul last night. I wonder if that was something he did all the time, provoking people and causing conflict.

Another black flash crossed behind me. I spun once again in a panic, fearful that I was not alone. I froze, shivering at the coldness that now swept through the room. I looked from Miss Simon's desk to the other side of the room, searching through the windows that fogged slightly from the heavy rain.

Again, the black flash caught the corner of my eyes as I stared back out the window. My eyes moved to Lucas, who waved his arm around in the air yelling into the phone. He put the phone into his pocket and stared out into the rain. His eyebrows were narrowed and his jaw was tight, making his face look fierce. This was the second time I'd seen him and both times he was angry. As another cold shiver ran up my spine, I saw the same black car I had seen yesterday in the same spot. Was there a new teacher employed? The weather made me feel queasy as for some reason I began to be paranoid that someone was following me or people were closing in around me.

I closed my eyes for a breather and imagined the rain wash over me as I focused on its calming sound. *The rain is soothing; there is nothing to be scared of.* I sniffled and reopened my eyes, finding his gaze staring in my direction. I flinched under his direct gaze.

Can he see me? I raised my hand to the chilled window and forced my eyes upon him, trying to figure out whether he could. The water bounced off his umbrella and I could see the particles of air that froze from his mouth and huffed out into mist when he breathed. It would be so much colder outside, and I forced my body to hug itself, thinking of that frosty pinch on my bare skin.

My breathing fogged up a patch of the window and I looked away from his gaze and stared at that instead. I placed my finger on it, drawing a smiley face. I knew he couldn't see it, but I amused myself. I then looked up again, expecting to see him. But what I saw instead was an outline of something behind me through the reflection of the window and I tried to turn around with a silent gasp.

My body got interrupted in its twisting, and a hand was wrapped instantly around my waist, pinning my elbows to the person's stomach. One hand was covering my mouth, pinning me to the intruder's body. I could feel their chest up against my back and their legs pinned to the back of mine. Their chest wasn't very soft and was muscular, so I assumed it was a male. I tried elbowing him, but he held my waist tighter forcing me to gasp for some air. I used his plan against him and lifted my legs up near my chest and slammed my feet down onto his, with little success.

I could feel his breath against my ears as his grip tightened. His cool harsh breaths made me shiver, and I forced out a tear of fear. I tried to remember to take shallow breaths and kept tugging my weight against his. It was getting me nowhere. He slowly moved his mouth closer to my ear and my body froze instantly. My feet were left frozen near my waist as I had them lifted, relying on my weight to be too heavy for him, hoping it would force him to drop me. But it wasn't, and I couldn't move. I felt a rush of his cool breath as he opened his mouth to speak.

"Boo!" a familiar voice spoke, but my fear kept me from recognizing who it was for a moment. I refocused on the reflection in the window and dropped my feet even harder in anger. Paul loosened his grip around my waist and arms as I tugged them free and slammed my elbow into his stomach. He was surprised when he felt the jab and let out a huge gasp of air.

"Paul, you jerk!" I coughed out through my tears. "You had me scared to death!"

The adrenaline was still pumping through my veins and I was shaking and gasping for air. I held on to my waist and concentrated on my breathing, blinking back tears of relief.

"Aw, Karla. I'm so sorry!" His voice was pleading in apology. "I thought you saw me, so I didn't think you'd freak out so much."

I snorted and wiped away the water that was flowing from my eyes.

"Come here." He held me again tightly and patted me gently on the back. I let the rest of my frightened tears wash over his jacket and sobbed quietly.

I realized the only thing that was between him and me at that moment were my hands, which were clutched up into balls against his chest. I tried slowly wriggling them free, but his huge bear hug was too firm. He rocked me from side to side, hushing me until my breaths were at a normal pace.

"I'm so sorry, Karla." He shifted his weight away from mine and raised his finger to my face. He gently wiped away the remaining tears that had flowed down my face. My skin reacted to his cold fingers and my entire body tensed. It was really cold now. His body was warm against mine, as well as comforting. I got a little flustered as he smiled grimly, still not taking his hand off my cheek. "I'm sorry. I didn't mean to frighten you so badly. It was meant to be for a good laugh," he said innocently.

"Well... I...um..."

I was speechless. I was stuttering. *Oh no!* I put my head down. "Well, ah... Maybe I have a different sense of humour," I whispered.

He let out a sad little laugh and hugged me again. This time, nothing was between us. I returned the gesture slightly, placing my hands along his broad back. My heart sped up and my body acknowledged the body warmth of his again.

"Maybe," he sighed in relief.

My mind was racing. Ticking. Trying to grasp something smart to say, but I was unused to this kind of contact and I was overwhelmed. After a minute or so, my brain finally managed to throw something at me. I leaned my head back, so I could see his face as he studied my eyes calmly.

"What are you doing here?" I asked.

He raised his head to the ceiling and I could feel his body jolt in laughter. He looked back down at me, amused. "We both have detention. Remember? And besides, I was wondering if you wanted to hang out afterwards..."

I let a little puff of air shoot out of my mouth, frowning. I released my grip around him and refocused on his earnest eyes. "Hang out?" I gave him a crooked smile and looked down at my bucket of water.

"Yeah. Why not? Let's go to the shops or something." Paul said, with an enticing smile.

I looked at him dumbfounded, and considered what he was saying. Embarrassed, I dipped my head away shyly. Another cold shudder ran down my spine as once again I had the horrific feeling of being watched. I looked behind Paul, imagining I saw a figure race past the window as a flash of lightning struck close by. I froze for a moment, remembering my frightened state before Paul had gotten here. *Why was I so scared?*

Remembering Lucas's presence, I threw myself up against the window, pressing my hands against the cold glass. I searched for where I had last seen him, and then looked from side to side across the road. *Where is he?*

I sighed at the thoughts that sprung through my head: *Is he following me? Wait, no, that's just me getting paranoid. I don't want to know him. So far he has managed to be rude, arrogant, obnoxious, smooth, handsome and mysterious, all at once. Argh.*

I felt frustrated by my conflicting inner thoughts. *I do not know this stranger—Lucas—and he is gone. He is not following me and I am simply being paranoid.* I slid my hands down to my side, watching my fingers wipe away the cold fog from the window. My fingers left a clear streak on the glass, but slowly it fogged up again.

Paul was waving his hand up and down in front of my face and my thoughts abandoned me. "Karla?" My eyes trailed up Paul's big arms, finding his beautiful green eyes and then they moved to his small smile. "Were you even listening?" he questioned.

I shook my head. "I'm sorry. I must have let my mind wander. So, why are we going to hang out?"

"I want to take you out to dinner or something," he said, placing his hands in his pockets and leaning back.

I smiled as I was both confused and flattered, while I toyed with my lips and gave an uneven smile as I thought of what to say. "That's generous, Paul. But you don't have to."

Is Paul Stuart asking me on a date? I wondered.

He picked up my hand and gently placed a cloth in it and curled my fingers over it. With his other hand he picked up the mop, still not letting his hand leave mine. "You wash the board down and I'll do the rest."

I opened my mouth to argue with his delegation of chores, but once again I was speechless. He then squeezed my hand gently, giving my body a jolt of unknown warmth. My hand rested in his. "Come on let's get this over and done with so we can get something to eat." He gave me a wink and let my hand fall to my side. He started dipping the mop into the bucket of water. The cloth nearly slipped through my numb fingers.

Is he taking me on a date? I didn't want to look at him just in case curiosity got the better of me and my mouth said something I didn't want it to say. I rinsed out the cloth before starting to scrub the board thoroughly. I wondered whether I should count this offer as a date. If so, it was my first. I scrubbed over the same patch again and again, making sure there wasn't a speck of dirt that Miss Simons could complain about.

When I reached the end, I peered over my shoulder, trying to glance what Paul was up to. His arms tensed at every forceful stroke into the floor, his bulky arms visible through the jacket that he wore over the dull, grey school uniform. Even the tight black jeans he wore showed how perfectly proportional his lower half was to his upper half. My scrubbing slowed into small circles in the one spot while I let my eyes wander over Paul. *I still can't believe he's here for me.*

His hair shook from side to side against his face, and his eyes strained at the mark he was trying to scrub out. He finally got the blemish out and looked up at me. My head was cocked to the side, my arm not even bothering to draw little circles anymore with the cloth. I jerked back; embarrassed at being busted watching him, and my hand let go of the cloth leaving it to slip through my fingers. I dove for the cloth, jumping up as soon as I had caught it.

Stupid. Stupid. Now he probably thinks I'm a creepy weirdo. I peered up at his smiling face and lost all the words I was going to defend myself with. I was getting really annoyed with my mind for its recent inability to multitask.

"I'm... I'm..." *Stop stuttering, Karla! Come on.* "...Done!" I said, a lot louder than I intended. *Why am I so weird all the time? Then again, having conversations with myself in my head doesn't help.*

"Ok." He crinkled his nose up in amusement, giving his face more room to spread his smile. "I'll be done in a sec."

"Ok," I said, nodding my head vigorously. He stopped his mopping and let his elbow lean on the top of the handle, trying to squish his lips together so that his laughing couldn't be heard. My face burned with shame and my body froze with what little dignity was keeping it upright.

"I'll bring the tables and chairs in," I said, sprinting down the few stairs to avoid making eye contact with him again. *Oh yeah, Karla! Real smooth.*

I faced the thundery clouds and let the rain wash over my face and down my neck. I inhaled deeply, trying to get the smell of fresh air through my lungs. I poked my tongue out, enjoying the few drops of rain that ran down my throat. I closed my eyes and just listened to what was happening around me; relaxing and calmly visualising what it would look like in my sketchbook.

When I opened my eyes, already half of the tables were inside as Paul dashed into the rain, carrying the heavy desks with no sign of strain. He jumped over the three steps and came to me, taking his jacket off and wrapping it around my shoulders. I looked down at my clothes, embarrassed, as they were now damp. When I looked back toward the stairs, he had already walked back into the classroom with another desk.

I followed him, taking the chairs in two at a time, and enjoying how Paul's leathered jacket fit my body. Obviously too big but it had an amazing smell to it and it was extremely warm.

"Detention's over, Karlz. You're all mine now," he said, looking around the classroom happily. He grabbed the keys from Miss Simon's bench and took my hand. I looked at his hand over mine and smiled as red stained my cheeks.

What am I going to do? Do I even want to go on a date with Paul? When Sarah finds out about this will she be angry with me?

I trailed behind him while he locked up the classroom door. He still didn't bother using his other hand, which only made the process longer. I peered out over the school gates and saw the same black car I had seen only moments before and yesterday. Instantly I felt fearful again and wrapped my fingers tightly over Paul's hand.

Why do I have such a bad feeling that someone is watching me? Curiosity and fear got the better of me and I had to question who would be parking their car near the school grounds so late after school hours.

"Do you know whose car that is?" I asked. Paul swept his gaze over the car I gestured to.

"The Porsche? Nah. But it looks like a sweet car. But not as sweet as my baby." His face beamed with pride and finally the key clicked in and locked the door.

We walked up to Paul's green Ute and he unlocked it. I really knew nothing of cars but it looked nice, new, and expensive. "Where are we going?" I held my bag to my chest self-consciously and looked back over to the black Porsche that was still parked in the same spot.

"That's a secret," he murmured cheekily.

Chapter Five - Suspended Life

"*G*rab something to wear," Paul insisted shyly.

"I'm not spending your money." I was surprised that he wanted to buy me something.

"What about this one?" Paul raised a green dress to his body. The green, mid-length dress was almost the same shade of green as Paul's eyes, with a black ribbon that tied around the waist. "I think it'd look stunning on you."

I stood with my arms strapped to my chest in reply. There is only one small shopping complex in my hometown, so I felt self-conscious. I dipped my head when people from our school looked over at us oddly. The store we stood in now had a mixture of many different designs for both men and women, with prices that ranged from as little as ten dollars, to the more expensive price range. I would never usually consider looking at clothes so expensive, but that was the section Paul had taken me to. As pretty as the materials were, the price tag always seemed to be twice as breathtaking. Paul seemed unfazed by the price—even though it wasn't himself he was spending money on.

"Try it on. Your clothes are soaked." Paul held the dress up to me, smiling as he swept his eyes over my damp school uniform.

"I'm not wasting your money," I replied shyly. I never really went on shopping sprees, nor had anyone ever offered to buy things for me. Paul lightly pushed me into the changing rooms, holding the door closed when I tried to open the door. I banged at the door, already feeling defeated. The dress was thrown over the small opening between the door and the ceiling, covering my sight when it slipped over my head. The silky material swept its cold material over my skin, making me shiver, before falling to the floor.

"Let me out!" I groaned, though only loud enough for Paul to hear. He still held the door shut, leaving me no other option but to contemplate the dress. A small smile spread on my face as I played with the tips of my light brown hair. *No one has ever done this for me.*

Examining the dress, I allowed myself a small smile. It *was* a beautiful dress.

I tried it on, defeated, and tapped the door lightly when I had it on. I couldn't zip the full length of the dress but I could see that surprisingly Paul had accurately guessed my size. He opened the door, smiling at the sight. I shyly fidgeted with my hands, embarrassed to have Paul look at me like this—all of me.

I turned around, facing away from him so I could look at myself in the mirror. I was surprised at the transformation; I hardly wore clothing like this. It was very beautiful. Paul took a step behind me so that his cool breath was now shivering down my back. He fiddled with the back as he slowly closed the zipper. I looked at him through the mirror, stunned. His piercing green eyes stared back at me.

I looked so small in comparison to his large frame behind me. His tanned skin and dark brown hair—all of him, in fact—now appeared to me so perfect. I looked away, flushing red in embarrassment. I was looking at him like it was the first time I had ever seen him. He was amazingly sexy.

Paul stepped back with a smile. "I love it," he said, complimenting me. "I want to buy this for you." Before I could argue he had already left for the cashier. I smiled back at the mirror. I couldn't have wiped my smile away even if I had wanted too. For some reason Paul was making me exceptionally happy.

I examined myself further in the mirror. The black ribbon complemented my small waist. The dark material somehow made my eyes look like the most beautiful moss green. It actually looked like I had a chest in this dress. I tucked the fringe of my long light brown hair behind my ears, still smiling as I bit down on my now red lips. The cold rain earlier had brought out the color in my lips and cheeks.

"Here, I think they are your size, but if not, the lady said we could change them." Paul had come over holding a pair of black shoes in his hand. Before I could begin to argue he cocked one of his eyebrows at me. I bit down on my lip in silence as he smiled and brought them down to my feet. Surprisingly, he had also correctly guessed my shoe size.

After leaving the shop, I decided the least I could do was buy us both a drink. As Paul went to another store I walked towards the drink machine, lost in thought. Someone barged into me, throwing my shoulder back as they pushed me roughly aside. It was Lucas. My whole body shuddered as I felt my stomach sink. I pushed away my paranoid thoughts of him following me as my gaze met his. His deep, brown eyes sent a jolt of electricity through my body, which made me gasp.

"Watch where you're going!" Lucas said rudely. He no longer wore the long coat he was wearing only hours ago and now walked around in a firm fitting black sleeveless shirt and black jeans with leather gloves.

"Excuse you? Well, if you saw me, then why didn't you move around me?" I hissed angrily as I rubbed my irritated shoulder.

"Karla, why should I look out for you? Look after yourself and you won't get hurt," Lucas scolded.

"What are you on about?" I asked, outraged. "I still have to talk to you about the other night." I threw my hands up in fury.

"I don't like green," Lucas said critically, as he looked over me. I'd never been on the receiving end of his provoking tone, but now I knew how easily it was to want to hit him. "Whatever," Lucas said when I didn't answer. He shrugged off my anger and continued walking. I clutched my shoulder and rubbed it vigorously. It felt almost itchy like something had bit me. I watched him leave, angered by his very presence. *How rude.*

Grabbing the two cans of coke out of the drink machine, I held one against my forehead. All of a sudden I felt extremely feverish—I was terribly hot. *How did I get so sick so fast from the rain?* I rubbed vigorously at my arm where Lucas had bumped into me, noticing the heat of my skin.

As I walked over to Paul I became even more aware of how my body was reacting: goose bumps, shivers and I could feel myself getting extremely sweaty. I wiped the moisture away from my forehead and stared at the blotch of liquid on my shaking hand. I felt awfully sick all of sudden, like I might vomit. *Something is very wrong*, I thought.

"Paul. I have to go. Something's wrong." I didn't even wait until I reached Paul, instead yelling it across the open space. I could see the concern on his face as I stumbled towards him.

"Karla? What's wrong?" He stared into my disoriented face, looking for an answer. My hands were shaking and my forehead felt like it had been dipped in hot water.

"I…. I…." I had no answer for him. "Please can we just go?" My eyelids became sticky and blinking became a chore. *This isn't right.* I slid my shaking hand through my fringe and weaved my fingers through to the back of my hair. Paul grabbed my shaking hand and focused on it, trying to keep it still.

"Oh my gosh," he muttered. He held my face with both hands, cupping my face. My disoriented eyes searched around me for anything but his intense gaze. "Karla, why didn't you say you weren't feeling well?"

I wrapped my trembling hands around his, trying to get a firm grip for support. "Paul, take me home," I whispered. "Please."

Paul walked me out of the shopping centre at a quick pace. The drizzling rain had never felt more alive on my tingling face. Every drop made the pores in my skin feel like it was combusting with heat; the feeling became more intense until I felt as though poisonous ants were biting my face. I dealt with the pain until Paul got me into the car. *What's happening to me? These symptoms can't be from the flu. It's affecting my whole body.* While in the car, my breaths were heavy and cold. My lungs didn't accept the air I inhaled, leading me to clutch my ribs in pain.

"What doctor do you normally see?" Paul asked, panicking. His speed limit was way over what it should be as he hurried me through the streets.

"Paul, you're going too fast," I croaked. My voice was edgy and pleading and I felt like a sword had been forced down my throat. I clutched it and noticed that the heat had spread from my cheeks to my neck.

"Karla. I'm taking you to the hospital," Paul said in a panicked manner.

Did I really look that horrific? I leaned my face away from his, not wanting him to see me like this. I looked at the side mirror in shock—seeing why he was so panicked. My hair was plastered to my face from sweat and my eyes looked like they were welt marks. Sweat covered every part of my face. *Something is wrong,* I repeated to myself. My lungs still begged for air and my heart pumped quickly.

Despite my pain I noticed the black Porsche from earlier was now following us. Fear strangled my mind and pain engulfed my body. *Am I being followed?*

Paul looked away from the road at his review mirror, staring at the black car. His grip tightened on the steering wheel as the Ute now swung from side to side on the slippery road. Flashes of light and rain splattered against the window.

Suddenly, I was thrown forward in my seat. The rain pattered on the windshield as I took a sharp intake of air, realizing the car had come to a stop. I looked out the window in confusion. We must have hit the large tree that jutted out over the pavement, knocked over into the road by the storm. I slid my shaking hand through my hair and clutched the back of my head. I brought it back to eyelevel; there was no blood on my hands, a good sign.

"Paul?" I said in a husky voice, clutching at my raw throat. I looked over at Paul's slumped figure beside me, horrified to find his eyes were closed. "Paul?" I asked again, clutching harder at my throat as I raised my voice over the rain. Small puffs of white air were leaving Paul's lips. *Is he unconscious, or...?* I could only see a small cut on his chin.

I ripped at my seatbelt, my eyes going in and out of focus. *I must walk around the car to see if he is okay,* I ordered myself. I stumbled out of the car, my body feeling extremely heavy. My legs shook from pain, fear and shock. *What's wrong with me?* My legs buckled beneath my weight; the blistering fever made them feel like they were going to melt.

I placed my hand on the roof of the car for support. Pins and needles shot up my legs. My pocket started to vibrate: *of course, my phone! I should call someone for help.* My hand wasn't steady enough to grip the phone so I had to use both, holding the phone awkwardly.

"Hello?" I croaked. My kidney had felt like it had frozen; shards of ice stabbed me from inside. My knees buckled and I fell, tumbling to the pavement. I managed to keep a firm grip on the phone that was now clutched to my stomach. I opened my lips to release a scream—the pain was horrific—but no noise left my mouth, leaving the tension locked inside my body.

"Karla, where are you?" Mum's voice was panicked and teary; my dear mother that had always taken care of me. My body felt like it was decomposing under the force of a hundred spears. My wrist shook with the intensity of supporting my weight against the pavement. It felt like a good time to tell Mum that I loved her and that this may be goodbye—because that's what my body was telling me.

"Karla?" I could hear the pain in her voice. "Karla, you need to get home. Now." I heard my dad in the background telling Mum to ask where I was and where he could pick me up. It ripped me to shreds to imagine how heartbroken they would be to know how much pain I was in. I braced myself and yelped as I raised my body, only for my feet to sink once again beneath my weight.

"Karla, I'm so sorry, baby!" Mum started crying and I heard the shifting of the phone. My body felt like it was drifting—panic swept over me making the pain unbearable.

"Karla? Karla?" Dad's voice was as frantic as Mum's. "Karla, get home now. We have things to discuss." He sounded jumpy and tearful. I took one step back, and my leg buckled again. I tried dragging the other leg under my body but they could no longer move. *My body is shutting down on me.*

My eyesight was blurring into blotches of black, and then blotches of green. The pain was like venom triggering every nerve of my body to shut down. *I can't handle it anymore.* "I love you," I gasped into the phone, while tears replaced the stream of rain drenching my face.

"What? Are they there? Don't become what they want you to, sweetie. Please!" my dad shouted. I heard Mum scream in the background and I felt her pain layer on top of mine. *I can't breathe. Don't become what they want me to? What is Dad talking about?*

"What who wants me to be?" I whispered, wincing as I felt myself slipping in and out of consciousness. A loud ring echoed through my head blocking out the noise of my father and the rain. Then silence. All noise was lost. My knees collapsed at the same time as the world around me. *I can't breathe. I can't breathe.* I thudded to the ground again, barely able to see my hands in front of my face. My lungs wouldn't accept any air now.

My body had completely stopped. My mouth filled with blood, and I could feel it trickle onto the road below my face. Relief and fear was all that functioned in my mind. *Relief to know that the pain will go away; fear to know that I'm dying.*

I felt ice-cold hands lifting me off the ground from the waist, while another hand cradled my head. My eyesight could only determine the outline of his shadowy face. The sadness it contained reflected my own. Rain washed over his face and dripped off onto mine. His lips moved as if he were shouting, but I heard none of his rage or fury. *Only bliss.* My face was cradled in his chest; he was embracing me in his arms. My eyesight slowly was taken away from me, leaving me in the dark. *I can't breathe.*

Chapter Six - A Second Chance

*M*y eyes squinted into the dark room I woke up in. It was darker than my room usually was. I raised my hand to the thumping headache I endured. I waved my hand across the bedside table, looking for the lamp. *Success.* The room shot up with very little light, but enough so that I could adjust my eyes to see something other than just the outlines of the objects that surrounded me. I pushed the blanket down to my feet for a brush of cool air and to assess the foreign room I was in. The stretch had only made me wince in pain and I clutched at my stomach where I was hurting. I lifted my shirt only to find bruise marks were visible all over my stomach. I looked at the marks, remembering the pain that put them there. *There's no way I'm alive,* I thought. I felt the agony of my body shutting down on me. I felt pain in every sense I had. I thought I was dying.

I looked around the unfamiliar room before panicking; unsure as to why and how I got here. *Am I dead?* I fumbled my feet onto the ground, wincing at the pain of my stomach and leaving my legs to rest where they were laying previously, in defeat. *Surely if I am dead and in an afterlife I wouldn't feel such hideous pain...*

My mind recalled that the night before was a surprisingly hot one, especially for winter, and I had slept a long time. I heard a click of the door and I braced myself. I defensively shot up straight with my back up against the single bed frame.

"Ah, I'm sorry. I didn't mean to scare you," Lucas said, closing the door behind him. My heart pounded as fast as my head was throbbing—I was scared of this man who had just walked in. *Why was my body reacting to Lucas like this? I can remember his face hazily in my thoughts when I think of what happened.* I had nothing to say to him other than to address the questions that needed answers. *Every time I think of the pain I went through; every time I think of that degrading and painful memory... I remember his face.* I remembered Lucas's face when I recalled my body being awakened by pain, as I cried out for help on the sidewalk. I had died.

"Good Morning," he mused. Lucas walked slowly across the room, seating himself at the end of the bed, well prepared with some food. "I brought you some cornflakes and some juice. It might not be as good as the breakfast you make at the café, but it'll suffice, I guess." He stared at me, waiting for a response. I stared into his dark brown eyes warily, recalling the image of him shouting out to me when he collected me in his arms. He was yelling my name at me: a word that rang in my ears as I struggled to take a breath. It was Lucas.

"Where am I?" I asked, trying to push away such painful memories. A flash of Paul's unconscious figure came to mind, sickening me with panic. "Where is Paul, is he safe?" I asked, feeling my heart stop.

"You're safe here. And yes, Paul is safe at his home," Lucas answered. "Karla?" His eyebrows burrowed, not in anger, but as if he were trying to find the right words to approach me with something important. "Have you ever had anything like that happen to you before?" His voice was serious, as well as interested.

"I... What do you mean? Have I had a near death experience before? No." I shook my head slowly, recalling the horrific memory. His face was trying to understand my answer and I found it hard to break the silence. "I don't know what happened but it started soon after you bumped into me near the vending machine. What exactly happened after you found me?" I held myself tightly, trying to comfort myself as I waited for an answer.

"Your whole body shut down on you." He searched over me before dropping his gaze to the breakfast tray: "Your body just stopped."

"What do you mean by 'stopped'?"

The fear I held close to me on the pavement was the fear that pinched at my skin now. I feared for my life and yet, I was relieved when it was over. When I couldn't breathe, when my final breaths were the final thrashes of unbearable pain, I had welcomed death in that moment.

"You died," he hesitated to say.

My jaw dropped. I died? My eyes studied his face, hoping for a twitch, for some sign that he was lying. His face was motionless. *I died.* I didn't want to believe him. I raised my hand to my head again as the thumping increased in a confused rage at what I was being told.

"We were able to help you. By some kind of miracle you regained consciousness. It was a panic and a rush but we brought you

40

back to life through different ways. You died and we don't know why. But we want to prevent it from ever happening again."

I simply stared silently at the wall across the bed I was in. *I died? And now I am alive. How did I die? How did something like that come to be?* I remembered my parents' scared voices as they pleaded with me to come home and to not become what 'they' wanted me to. I looked at Lucas with convicting eyes. *Is he who I must stay away from?* Instead of being overwhelmed by the news that I had died only days before I felt my body pump with some kind of energy. It felt fierce and fiery. It felt like I was thriving for survival on instinct.

"So where am I now?" I asked again, searching over the dull room and trying to find a way to convey my mixed emotions of shock, fear and determination. It was the only thing I could say while trying to absorb the realisation of what happened: *I had died.*

"I have brought you back to where we stay so Helena can help you. You haven't been here for that long, but your recovery…" He trailed off. "Your recovery is taking its time. You kept having fits and reactions to something. We can't figure out what it is though." Lucas's eyes trailed off towards the door.

My recovery? Fits? I have never had a fit before and my family record was more than healthy. I felt my chest constrict in panic as the word 'dead' played around in my thoughts over and over again. *Dead. I wonder how Mum and Dad feel about that? They would be so upset and angry with me for not coming home when they said to. How did they know I was in danger? Do they know that I died?* The panic absorbed my being completely as I jumped out of the bed, flicking the sheets and blanket through the air. I ran to the door, almost crying.

I scampered to the door, leaping across the room in one clear sweep. I was so tightly wrapped up in my own fluster of grief that I was now completely oblivious to Lucas's presence. His arms wrapped tightly around my waist so I couldn't squirm any more. I felt his breaths shivering down my neck. It stunned me. Like a snake biting a mouse. The sheets and blanket slipped to the ground behind us.

Within seconds I found myself grasping for the knob of the door, not even realising what I was doing. *What is going on?* My breaths slowed from their frantic state until they were in time with Lucas's. Mine were harsh and deep. His were coarse and strong. But, together, we inhaled as one, calming me down. I looked at the doorknob trying to figure out what was happening. I needed my family, not Lucas.

"Let me go!" I shoved and pushed his face away from mine trying to break his grip, but his arms were still tightly wrapped around me. "Lucas, please. Please, I need my mum."

The word 'mum' put tears in my eyes. They welled up inside me, and I allowed myself to physically and mentally crumble. My legs buckled in defeat and I collapsed in his arms. Luckily, his muscular frame still had a hold of me. He slowly placed my knees to the floor, but didn't release his grip.

"They're not there, are they?" I held my breath, waiting for a reply. My tears stopped, as well as my heart as I waited for his reply.

"No," Lucas answered hesitantly.

"Why not, Lucas? Why not? They should be in the next room!" I cried out for help, but nobody heard except for Lucas—and he couldn't do or say anything that would help. I knew in my heart my family was gone. The only part left of me that made any sense up to this point was my family. The only people that would've made me understand what was going on. The only words I could murmur were: "why?" Lucas had embraced me as if he were my own mother stroking my hair, swaying me back and forth.

"Get away from me!" I pushed him away, firmly forcing his palms behind him for balance.

"Please Karla, understand. It's my duty—..." Lucas said.

"Your duty? You have no right to talk about duty to me. You come in and offer me juice! No answers and take my family away from me," I said, almost crying. The door opened, revealing a tall African-American man in a tight grey sleeveless shirt. He looked like he was in his fifties. He had greyish eyes and his head was bald. He had many scars over his arms and head; some had almost dissolved into his skin from age. He walked through the door while looking at me.

"Don't be alarmed, Miss Grey. Your family's fine. We welcome you into your new home: our home. I'm Mr Schmidt. Kurt Schmidt," the man said with a small smile, gesturing his hand in politeness to his chest.

He had two other people beside him. A small Japanese woman, whose hair was spiked out to the side, dyed all the colors of the rainbow —red being the main color, as it took up her fringe and most of the spikes. She looked like she was only a few years older than the Jamaican man who stood next to Kurt. He seemed to be in his twenties, with dreadlocks to his shoulder, green piercing eyes, and very bushy and distinguished eyebrows.

Kurt raised his hand out to me. He held my gaze for moments before exchanging an annoyed look into Lucas's direction: "Lucas, it seems you've startled the girl. What did you do to the poor thing?"

I stared between them all, unsettled to be in a room full of strangers that still weren't explaining anything.

"Follow me, Karla," Kurt gestured towards the door. "I'm sure you're hungry. You obviously don't like the meal that Lucas proposed..." Kurt raised his hand to the spilt bowl of cereal on the ground where, the glass had shattered across the floor.

I didn't even notice I had my own palm in a small pile of the broken glass. My hand had already started bleeding—staining the lush, white carpet with a deep red. I grabbed my wrist and embraced it with my other hand. It still had a tiny fragment of glass through the slash that shone a lighter red. I looked up at Kurt who had also just realized I had hurt myself.

"Take me back to my parents!" I shouted towards all three of them, before placing my injured hand in my lap to hide my vulnerability. My demand was aimed at Kurt. I didn't know who he was, but he seemed to smile calmly at my anger, agitating me more. I heard the Jamaican beside him snort, amusing himself.

The Japanese woman spoke clear English and stood in front of Kurt in an almost protective stance. "How dare you speak to Kurt like that? He's the reason why you're not dead, in fact all of us are. You should be thanking us!" she exclaimed, flustered.

"Suz, drop it. She's just scared. Lay off a bit." Lucas's voice was harsh. He was now standing behind me, leaning against the wall.

The Japanese woman whose name was apparently Suz flustered red once again. "Don't you defend her. Kurt was the one who gave us the order to protect and save her. And you think now you're going to stand against Kurt in disrespect and defend that girl? She can't even defend herself. She's not leaving. She's needed. If Kurt says she stays, then she stays. If you have a problem with that you'll be dealing with me!" she spat out angrily.

"Suz," the Jamaican pleaded while rubbing his temples. It seemed he was used to the bickering because he and Kurt seemed exhausted from the argument, yet neither of them tried particularly hard to intervene. My thoughts thrived in frustration. *How am I a little girl? Who are these people?* I flared my nostrils at her and dug my nails into the wrist I was clutching, trying to contain some of the anger I suddenly felt.

"If you haven't noticed, I'm still here. Who the hell are you calling a kid? I can defend myself just fine, thanks. Take me home now!" My voice quivered as I held in the tears of fear and frustration.

She raised her hand, directing it towards my injured hand in support of her argument: "You're obviously incapable of even looking after yourself when there's some broken glass around. You have—..."

"Touch her and you're mine, Suzumiya," Lucas hissed. I looked at Lucas, surprised by his raised and dominant tone. He was scary when his voice was deep and projected. He was intimidating and it was obvious his words were a threat. He stood up tall, no longer leaning against the wall. Lucas shifted his eyes off Suzumiya and glanced at my startled face. His eyes softened, ashamed, and trailed back to Suzumiya.

She coughed over her words, just as caught off guard as I was: "You honestly think you can speak to me like that? What's come over you? You're lucky I don't beat the crap out of you right now, you ungrateful boy..."

Lucas opened his arms widely. "Like I said, my offer still stands." He made his voice sound like a gentleman's, obviously mocking her. She blew red and took a huge aggressive step forward. She crouched down to the ground, well balanced. She looked as if she were a cat, ready to pounce on her prey.

"When will you learn?" Lucas's voice was serious. He placed one foot in front of my view, and put his hands casually in his dark blue jeans.

Kurt put his hand in front of Suzumiya as he spoke: "That's enough, Suzumiya. You know you can't penetrate Lucas's Shield. This is a pointless fight for you to get flustered over."

What is a Shield? What is he talking about?

I followed my gaze up Kurt's arm and to my surprise his other hand was raised towards me. "We don't want to scare her off, Suzumiya. And Lucas, I'll be discussing this with you some other time. Suzumiya leave. Chris, go patch up Karla's hand, before she bleeds anymore over the carpet."

That's right, my hand. I had briefly forgotten all about it. I looked back down at the bleeding wound, and my body went rigid with alarm as the Jamaican begun walking over to me. I assumed he was Chris. Kurt was almost out the door and Suzumiya had already left in a huff over the argument.

44

"Wait..." I stumbled, caught off guard. "No. What? I don't know what the hell just happened, but nobody's touching me." I waved my hands around frantically as I cornered myself against the bed in dread.

Kurt didn't bother turning to face me and kept his face to the door. "Miss Grey, please be reasonable. I know this is a lot to adjust to, but you must understand, we don't want to hurt you. We are here to help you, hoping you can do the same in return," he said calmly.

"No! Take me home!" My voice jumped. *I am so scared.*

"Perhaps it would be easier if I took her, Kurt," Lucas interjected. "I'm the only one she's formally met. It might not be as difficult or hard for her to understand a voice she knows," Lucas said in a respectful tone. They all seemed to highly respect Kurt. He was obviously in charge around here. Lucas's words seemed to have caught Kurt's attention as he finally came to a stop and stood by the door. He glanced back towards Lucas.

"Lucas, I find it quite interesting how you are so concerned for her slightly grazed hand, and yet, you don't seem to care for those who are dying around you," Kurt stated bluntly. "Chris. Patch her up."

"Hey, I don't care..." Chris raised his palms in a carefree manner. "I better go to Suz, anyway. She seems pretty upset over the whole thing. It's only a simple cut. Lukeyboy can fix it."

"Very well." Kurt left the way he had entered and Chris followed behind him. Not as gracefully—he walked with a bouncy beat, as if he were ready to dance. Lucas knelt down beside me, looking at me with even eyes.

"You okay?" His dark brown eyes were concerned, but wary at the same time. I didn't know what to say. I was so confused and scared. They didn't seem like the usual bunch of kidnappers, but it was hard to grasp the fact that I had died and had been brought back to life—only to be kidnapped. *Nothing makes sense and I can't imagine where I will find the answers.*

"Where am I?" My whisper was barely audible and the fear that cloaked my words made it come out in a screech. The hair in my eye was making my eyes water. I kept tracing my eyes frantically over the carpet that was now savouring my blood.

"Come on. You'll be fine." Lucas swept his hand over my cheek, drying up the tears, and then he swept my hair out of my eyes. His touch made me feel drowsy, but my eyes still managed to react to the coldness of his leather glove. His lips, nose, prominent cheekbones, and the sharply squared jaw somehow looked so gentle. Then, I reached his eyes: his deep brown eyes. He was concerned and I was scared.

Lucas's face vanished into my blurred vision. *Why was this happening?* I was a mess. I was so tired, confused and pained. He gestured for me to rise, directing me towards the door.

Chapter Seven - Wind's Passage

$\mathcal{W}$e left the room and walked through a small hallway with unpainted walls. I noticed small windows high in the wall letting in streaks of light as I followed Lucas cautiously. On the other side of the wall, candles stood in tall metal frames casting shadows across the cement floor. We walked past two doors on my left before reaching a small room.

I leaned against a shiny silver bench to compose myself before approaching Lucas. "Lucas. I don't know you and I don't want to be here. You told me I died. Do you have any idea how terrifying that is? Yet you've told me nothing else."

A man walked through the doorway as Lucas went to say something. The large man startled me, forcing me to quickly leap back in fear with a gasp. He was a tall Englishman. He stood between the doorframe, blocking my view of the hall. "Sorry, darling. I didn't mean to startle you." He was very tall and it strained the muscles in my neck to peer up at his face. He had bleached hair, hazel eyes, and he seemed to be nearing his forties. He had a distinguished nose that looked like it had been broken a few times. He was very formal-looking: wearing dark blue designer jeans, and an even darker blue turtleneck shirt with a black coat that reached down to his knees.

"Karly, isn't it?" The foreign man offered his hand out in a gesture of peace.

"Um… Karla, actually." I was still a little unbalanced, but caught my breath soon enough. All these strangers keep introducing themselves and gesturing to me, which made me feel even more unsettled.

"Oh sorry, hun. Are you hungry? Do you want me to cook you something? I can still fix you something now." He gave Lucas a suspicious looking black bag. Clinking noises came from within—it sounded like small glass bottles rattling against each other. "Oh I'm sorry, I forgot to introduce myself! My name is Seth."

Lucas quickly walked out of the room with the black bag, leaving me with this man named Seth. He opened a few of the drawers and removed a pair of tweezers before continuing his search. I looked warily between Seth and the tweezers he had just put onto the bench, saying nothing.

"He's made an impression on you too, huh?" Seth said, laughing a little under his breath. His mirth didn't last very long. Whatever had amused him seemed to bore him instantly after he had said it.

"I do apologise, I'm not trying to be insulting." He looked back at me, throwing me a reassuring look before continuing to scurry through the drawers. "It's just...we all have to put up with Lucas as well. He's not a very people-friendly person, as you can see." His voice was concerned and he seemed like he was ready to listen, but I wasn't feeling up to confiding in a companion of my kidnapper.

I simply nodded in agreement, focusing my full attention on the tweezers that still lay on the bench—not too far out of my reach. If I could just quickly reach them and use them against Seth, I could hopefully make my escape. I didn't even know if something like that could work. Would such a small, innocuous weapon puncture his leg if used forcefully? I squirmed at the violent thoughts that danced vividly in my mind, but before I could think the plan, any further Seth picked up the tweezers and the bandage.

Seth held out both items cautiously as he approached me with warm eyes. "I am here to help," he said calmly. I panicked at the sight, feeling like a caged animal.

When he reached out for my hand something in me snapped. Perhaps I acted on instinct. I grabbed his wrist towards me, pulling him with all my might and wrapping my arms around his neck. I burrowed my knee as deeply as I could into his groin, throwing him to the side with all my force and I quickly run for the door as he dropped in pain to the floor. I felt the ache of my stomach as I reached the door. Wincing in pain, I held my hand to my stomach; somehow feeling that if I didn't, my stomach might fall out.

Forcing myself to carry on despite the pain, I quickly scanned the rooms in the hallway searching for an exit. I sprinted forward into the narrow hall, painfully aware of the growing ache in my stomach. My long hair kept bouncing heavily into my eyes as I ran. *I must get out.*

I came to a stop at what looked like a reading-room with maroon carpet, bookshelves, cushioned seats, and a fireplace. I heard a noise and wrapped myself around the wall to my right where the hallway ended. My breath was heavy as I searched towards my right, finding what seemed like a poor excuse for a dining room. A table with a few chairs huddled around it stood in the centre of the room. I could see the kitchen through the half-demolished wall. It was no better than the dining room, with just a fridge, a stove, a kettle, and a microwave to fill it.

There were no windows, so I was relying on the light from down the hall. I tried to focus on the noises I could hear: grunting noises echoed from the roof. I noticed a bright light directly in front of me, underneath a metal door. Instinctively I ran for it—*this is the exit, this is my escape.*

I pushed into the room. It seemed like an extension of the house, with shed-like walls and a rough cement floor. The room had ropes hanging down from the roof, exercise equipment, obstacle courses, a huge open area of padded floor, punching bags, and kicking bags. It had everything. Suzumiya looked up at me from the punching bag where she was doing sets of four. She stopped and narrowed her eyes on me as I stared back at her in surprise. Chris was sitting not too far away from Suzumiya on a beanbag, raising himself to his feet with his eyes focused on me. *Run—I must run.*

My eyes fell on a doorway that looked like an exit. A huge ray of sunlight hit my face as I opened the door, flinging myself into the outside world. I tried blocking the sun, covering my face with my hand so that I could look over the landscape before me.

I must escape. I didn't see much besides the open field that was directly ahead of me and I ran to the edge of the field as fast I could. I didn't dare look behind me to see how close my kidnappers were. I finally got to the edge, and paused for a few seconds to catch my breath.

The wind blew through my long hair, allowing it to flow off my shoulders and down my back. All I could hear was the breeze rustling through the trees. In front of the open space was an amazing view: an entry to a forest.

Something pulled me forward, forcing me to take one unstable step. *I am being drawn into this place and it is the wind that is pushing me forward. The wind whispers that I must follow; it will guide me into the dark unknown.* I found my legs again and began to run towards the woods, listening to the awful noise of my feet crunching the lush grass underfoot as I ran. Fear rippled through me, making me doubt that it was even my feet making such a terrible noise. These thoughts only forced me to run faster. *I must escape.*

I would trust fate with my life in the unknown woods; hopefully I would find my way back to my family and be safe. I would seek protection from this place, even if I were unsure of what it contained. The forest certainly *looked* beautiful, but I could feel something inside it was disturbed and unwelcoming. However, I was well aware that this might have been my only chance. Why did it even matter now? My parents believed that I was either dead, or perhaps even worse, that I abandoned them. As scared as I was, I also couldn't help feeling that I was dead if I stayed. This was the only way to be free of those who claimed I owed them my life in exchange for 'saving' me.

Chapter Eight - Dark Forest

The trees' branches tugged at my hair as I ran hysterically through the woods. The wind blew leaves into my face as the forest floor crunched under my feet. I felt as though the dark forest watched my every movement and traced my every step. Fear haunted me every time I heard a noise that did not come from my own feet. The woods were an eerie place. In my panic, my eyes flickered through the trees that now looked like they had ghostly faces on them.

I had lost what little bearings I initially had and I was running endlessly, scared of what was occupying the woods. The thought of the place I came from pushed me harder, and rage pumped like fuel to my legs. *I cannot stop.*

The wind was fierce and blew my hair wildly around my face and shoulders. I had been running nonstop for a long time, maybe over an hour, while I searched for help. I had taken the chance that I would be able to find a road on the other side of these woods but so far I had not yet been rewarded.

My legs got caught in one of the tree limbs and I tripped over its roots. My body slumped onto the forest floor. Instinctively I tried to save my face from any damage and I raised my hands. My hand got caught on a rock, causing a deep gash. I winced at the sudden pain in my already injured hand.

I scowled in annoyance at the tree trunk that had tripped me. I felt an itch that pinched at my face and I softly let my fingertips brush over the place it pinched the most. I placed my hand in front of me, viewing the blood that was slightly smudged across my fingers. *Great.* I had scrapped my face too. I groaned at the distinct color on my fingers and slowly pressed my hand up against the tree and pulled on it to get back onto my feet.

The fall had given me time to stop and think rationally about what I was doing. I hadn't realized how little breath I was taking into my lungs and how much exertion I had placed upon my body. My breath finally caught up with me and I was gasping for the air that surrounded me. The wind still blew at my face and pushed the sweat away. My head pounded from the heat and I felt as though my blood boiled under my skin. I finally had time to embrace what my body was feeling, leaning against the tree to catch my breath. I could rest and for the first time and think about my escape plan.

I had already run into the woods without any bearings. The sun was no longer visible above me, and it now glistened through the trees. My stomach ached from exertion and my mouth thirsted for water. I was unprepared and had no supplies for my escape.

What do I do now? I have to think quickly. They could be so close, Lucas and the others. I must prepare. I can either find a place to rest and hide, or, continue my search for a nearby road that will lead me back home.

I felt a thick paste on my hand from the tree. Examining the substance, I found it to be sap. The tree bled from where it had been sliced through: a freshly inflicted cut. The cut was deep and clean, leading me to believe it was sliced by a sharp blade.

Someone's foot snapped a branch as they approached, forcing me to hold my hands up in defense. A small child that looked no older than twelve slowly walked out from amongst the trees. Dimples appeared in her cheeks as she smiled: "Hello."

The child's hair was black and her skin was porcelain. Her eyes were as blue as the sky that had surrounded me brightly only an hour ago. The girl's eyes did not leave mine nor did her smile falter. I stared at the strange girl with the elusive gaze; her head was cocked to the side with a wide grin. I now noticed how oddly the child dressed: she wore a black leather jacket that covered her to her knees and a short black dress that puffed out like that of a princess'.

Her eyes flashed briefly with anger and her expression became more alert. "Are you alone?" the girl questioned, flashing a set of pointed pearly whites, cannibal-like and sharp.

When I stared at the girl and said nothing she flustered red across her face and pouted her lips. Her face lit up and she reached for her large leather bag. The straps stretched across her chest and the bag sat on her little hip. She dug around the bag and finally found what she was after. She offered the water bottle to me, and without hesitation, I grabbed the bottle and let it stream down my throat. My stomach stung at the refreshment and my face searched hers to see if she had any more. The girl's face was no longer smiling and was once again wary. I was startled to see such an expression on such a young child. I forgot that she must be more frightened of me. After all she looked no older than twelve. *The right thing to do would be to reassure her I won't bring any harm to her,* I reminded myself, instead of being fearful and judgement of a small child's odd appearance.

"I'm sorry if I startled you. I won't hurt you," I cautiously said. Her face studied mine for more than a minute before she finally spoke.

"Are you alone?" she repeated. Her voice was stern, sounding more like that of an older woman than of a child's.

I narrowed my eyes at her question. *Why does she want to know so desperately if I am on my own?*

"Why are you here?" I asked. It was strange for a twelve year old to be out in these woods. She smiled at me once again, showing off the dimples in her cheeks.

"I was chopping wood for my daddy. I left my axe over there." She pointed to the direction she came from. "And then I heard some noise come from over here so I came to see."

"Oh," I said, unsure what to say next.

The little girl pulled part of her long fringe back. "Your hand is hurt. Won't you come back to our cottage so we can fix it?"

"It's okay. I have somewhere to be," I stayed weary of the girl, following her gaze as she looked into the direction I had come from as if she was expecting something.

She then looked back at my startled face once again with a huge cheesy grin. "Well you can use my phone. So you can get someone to drive you to town."

"You have a phone?!" I tried to regain my composure before saying anything more in such a desperate tone: "I would very much like that."

If I could call Mum and Dad they will find me. I will be safe.

Her eyes stared over my head and I looked behind to see what she was looking at, though I saw nothing. I looked back at her and she was still smiling. "Let's go then." She said. I nodded in agreement. She started walking into the direction of where she had pointed to previously.

"Don't you need to get your axe?" I strained to make myself heard over the wind.

"No," she simply said. "I can get it later." Her blue eyes reached my astonished face. The distance between us was enormous, yet the color of her eyes still struck me.

"We must run though," I quickly said, pacing to her side. "I have people chasing me." My throat choked on the words as I found myself quivering in fear again. *I must run*.

The girl effortlessly ran much faster than I could while asking many questions about who I was running from, what route I took and where I had been before entering the woods. I told her I had no idea where I came from, but didn't want to tell her any more than that.

We ran for ten minutes before I was able to catch up with the girl. Her smile was bright. We broke out of the cluttered trees into a somewhat small, open clearing.

"We are here," she stated. I looked behind the child at the worn-down, small cabin. It was the size of a shed and pieces of wood hung from single nails. The cabin was very old and it was hard to imagine how it was still standing. My eyes searched long and hard at the cabin to see how such a place was liveable. I then refocused on the girl.

Her gaze was once again behind me, and her forehead creased as her lips ripped into a snarl. I jumped a little at the reaction of the girl. I couldn't believe I was seeing such fierceness in the child's face. She focused her eyes on me, not changing her expression. My breathing stopped, as I did not know how to escape her the fierce look on her face looking up at me. Her nose scrunched up, showing her teeth, and she let out an angered growl. I followed her gaze in search of whatever it was she was looking at.

I slowly started walking away from her towards the cabin, as I felt so unsettled by her angered face. *Something is not right*. My body told me to walk away. *Get away from this girl*.

My steps were slow as I walked towards the cabin; her eyes never leaving mine. My feet caught on something, almost tripping me over until I regained my balance. A loud scream left my mouth as I looked over the dead man that was at my feet. The man was a dark shade of blue with a scorched mark wrapped around his wrist where it bled in blotches. The scorch mark was blistered into the shape of a hand.

Without having the chance to blink or interpret what I saw, I was pushed to the ground. I let out another scream of horror. The little girl clutched at my throat. I screamed at the pain she inflicted on me as I scratched at her hands. Her hands burned at my throat with a heat that I could feel melting into my skin. Her eyes were large and crazed as she smiled brightly on top of me.

The girl jumped off me as a dagger flew past her head, narrowly missing her. I felt a frosty burn crisp at my throat as I clutched at it, gasping for air. I heard footsteps surrounding me. I tried to steady my pain but I was incapable of even silencing my bellowing cries. I managed to slightly lift one of my heavy eyelids and search for the dagger that was thrown towards the girl. I found the piece of metal and placed it to my chest while I rocked myself.

"Please, someone." I croaked out a sad cry. The burn felt as if it was spreading through my jaw. "I can't take it!" I bellowed. I raised the dagger to my face ready to cut the venom out. A hand caught mine before the dagger reached any closer to my face and I screamed for help.

I dropped the dagger out of my hand and caught it with my other one, stabbing it into the person who I thought to be the girl. The grip around my hand had loosened, and there was a deep groan. I flung my eyes open, only able to make out his deep brown eyes with my poor eyesight. His hand clutched onto mine harder.

"Lucas," I whispered. Lucas let go off my wrist with a loud gasp. He coughed and sputtered onto the dirt. My vision was still uneasy but I could focus on his figure. I held my hand out to him but he shrivelled away from it.

A loud scream pierced the air as a filthy man came running towards us. He had only one arm with discolored skin. As I screamed, the tall Englishman I had escaped from came running out of the trees from behind the cottage, pinning the deformed man to the ground with his sheer size. The disfigured man growled with wildness, trying to scratch at Seth's face. Seth wrapped his hands around the man's neck and a loud crack was heard, stopping the man's movement. A heavy breeze swept through the lush green grass as Seth slowly raised himself off the man's figure. I raised my hand to my mouth, gasping in shock as I had just watched him kill someone.

"Are you okay Karla?" Seth asked as he came to my side with a cut above his eyebrow. I stared at him in horror.

"Come on. I'm sorry love, but we don't have time for this," Seth exclaimed as he held his hand out to me.

Another large male broke out from the same line of trees that Seth had come from. The trees he ran out from seemed black in the fading sun; the moon was now shining dimly as the night began to claim the forest. The man that ran towards us from the trees had a solid build, with a rounded face. He had blue eyes with a piercing above his right eyebrow. He quickly came to Lucas's side, helping him to his feet.

"I'm okay, Ashley." Lucas ushered him away, raising himself to his feet as he clutched at where I had stabbed him. Tears spilled over my cheeks as I realized I had just stabbed someone. I had just hurt Lucas.

Suzumiya and Chris ran towards us shouting something I couldn't understand. "Stay here," Lucas said, leaving my side and sprinting over to Chris and Suzumiya. Another deformed man blocked Lucas's path as a disfigured woman tried to attack Chris from behind. My eyes felt like they were splitting over the open field as I searched back and forth from the fight that had just broken out in front of me so suddenly. All those I had met in the place I had just run away from had arranged themselves into strategic fighting positions. They fought with a strength and elegance I had never seen before—their movement and balance perfectly executed. The group complemented each other; they seemed to know instinctively if help was required. They just knew how to fight, slicing their weapons expertly against the limbs of their enemies. Many mutated beings flooded in over the small open field in front of the cabin where I still sat, slumped in disbelief.

Suzumiya jumped into the air, poised like a cat, while slashing at a woman's face with a large sword. She then wrapped her chain around another's ankle that tried to attack Chris, yanking the attacker to the ground. Her top lip pulled back angrily as she groaned at the force she exerted, before plunging a large knife into her victim.

I choked at disbelief in what I was watching. Seth and the young, bulky man named Ashley hovered near me with weapons of their own. I had hardly noticed them standing there as I looked on at Suzumiya and Chris fighting. No not fighting, *killing*.

Seth and Ashley are here to protect me? From what? And why are they killing? They are murderers. How is this happening before my very eyes?

Lucas elbowed a woman in the stomach that had run towards him snarling and screeching with long claw-like nails extended. At the sudden force on her stomach, she dropped, gasping for air. Another man came running towards him before Lucas easily jumped over him, kicking him in the side of his knee and dislocating it.

A man tried forcing an axe down on Lucas as he simply dodged it, spinning in a small circle elegantly, before forcing his hand into the back of the man's neck, leaving him unconscious. Lucas had not yet killed one. *Is he not the same as Suzumiya and Chris? Maybe they are not all murderers.* I still sat there on the ground, staring in horror. Lucas,

Suzumiya, and Chris danced among their attackers, cutting them down with their weapons.

The young child who had dragged me to this place became visible from the trees. I almost cried at the thought of her holding me down firmly, clutching and melting away my throat with her hands. It was because of her attack on me that I accidently stabbed Lucas, thinking it was she. I was acting in self-defense. I looked back at Suzumiya as she hauled her long sword out of someone's stomach. *Is that what they are doing, killing things that are like the young child who attacked me? Is it really murder?*

The young child ran towards Chris from behind with a large sword. Suzumiya noticed her creep from the dark shadows of the trees before Chris had. Suzumiya ran towards her, charging at the young child with her sword aimed at her chest. Suzumiya's sword shattered instead of slicing into her target, and she was thrown back onto a jagged-edged rock. She screamed out briefly in pain. *What just happened? How did her sword shatter and what was Suzumiya thrown back from?*

"SUZ!" Chris bellowed, as someone wrestled him to the ground. Lucas hadn't noticed the harm Suzumiya was in as he wrestled amongst those that attacked him. Seth sprinted to where Suzumiya had scampered, clutching at her back in pain. She tore a small dagger from her waist, pegging it at the child swiftly. The dagger briefly stopped a meter away from the girl's face—just stopped in midair, until it was thrown back by something towards Suzumiya. Seth quickly stepped in front of Suzumiya, deflecting the dagger with a wave of his blade. He then placed his foot back with his blade in front of him in a defensive stance, ready for the girl's next attack. The girl toyed with the large sword in her hand as she slowly walked over to Suzumiya, ignoring the others around her.

"We need to run," Ashley said, grabbing my arm and lifting me. My legs found a balance while he supported me. Lucas now ran towards Suzumiya and Seth, blocking the small child with the knife he held in his hand. I looked back at where he once was, finding all those people who attacked him to be on the ground to be either groaning or unconscious. But from what I could see, none of them were dead. The colors around us swirled as I found myself almost incapable of breathing. *What is this? What is happening around me?* Seth lifted Suzumiya, placing her weight on him for support before running back into the trees.

A hideous woman with no eyes and wired hair came screeching out of the woods and jumped onto Ashley. He struggled beneath her for a while, balanced on his back, as she scratched at his face with her legs firmly wrapped around his stomach. Ashley gathered his fists beneath her, grabbing her shoulders tightly and somehow managing to flip her off onto the ground in front of him. He plunged his knife into her as she let out a coarse breath that stuttered and then stopped. He pulled his knife out of her stomach, looking up at me in discomfort. His face had a few light cuts to it as his blue eyes looked over me calculatingly.

I reached my hand out to him in shock, but also concerned as his face now bled. He was trying to protect me.

"Can you mo—…" Before I could finish I was thrown into one of the trees behind me, slumping to the ground. I rose to my feet using a branch from a tree next to me for support. The young child instantly closed the space between us, while wearing a perverted smile of excitement.

Lucas ran at her, tackling her to the ground and holding her down where she twisted underneath his weight, screaming in anger.

"Go!" Lucas yelled out to Ashley, who had already grabbed my arm and was leading me in the direction of where the others had already retreated. We ran for a few minutes before I had the courage to speak.

"Will Lucas be alright?" I whimpered. Chris ran by our side, his long dreadlocks bouncing as we caught up to Suzumiya and Seth who were hidden amongst the trees.

"I'm fine." Lucas had already caught up to the five of us as we continued running. "They're all dead," Lucas said to him simply. Everyone slowed their pace and stopped to catch their breath. *They are all dead? Did Lucas kill them?* But I watched him and I thought he hadn't killed any of them. *Is he like all of the others here as well?*

Suzumiya rested herself against a tree, holding her ribs while breathing heavily. Chris went to her side to examine where she clutched her body in pain, making sure she was okay. Hunched over her, his concern was obvious. She nodded to him in reassurance and he nodded back with heavy eyes.

"Are you okay, love?" Seth came over to me, his eyes searching me for signs of injury. I flinched as his hand pushed away the fringe that was in my eyes. *I have no words.* Seth nodded to Ashley and Lucas as they began walking forward. "Let's go back and give her some actual answers this time, yea?"

Lucas held onto his chest with the dagger still protruding from it. *I did that to him. I put that dagger there.* He only gave me a brief, unreadable look before nodding at Ashley and walking alongside him.

We all continued walking silently as I held my arm in discomfort, forcing myself to concentrate on placing one foot in front of the other. I looked up to the backs of those who walked in front of me, remembering vividly what it was I had just seen. Right now I didn't want to be told what had happened because I was too scared to hear the answer. My kidnappers had just saved me from some kind of creatures who desperately wanted to kill me.

I let my mind go blank over the duration it took us to walk back through the forest. By the time we got there only a dull light from the moon guided us up to the metal door. *Am I ready for these answers?*

Chapter Nine - Shielder

$\mathcal{T}$he others walked ahead, while Seth dropped his pace staying close to my side. I stopped and began staring back into the woods for a dreary moment. The sun had completely dropped and only the moon shone over the woods we had come from. They looked so much more eerie than they did when I had first ventured into them.

Seth patiently waited by my side as I closed my eyes, thinking of nothing. I was still shocked. *What has happened*? After what felt like hours Seth finally broke the silence, quietly grunting. I looked at him, focusing on the dry blood on his face.

"Come on, love." Seth slowly walked beside me, ushering me towards the door. He moved ahead to open it, and patiently waited while holding it open for me to enter. "Let's get Helena have a look at that hand." He welcomingly held out his hand, the exact same one I had run from. I blankly walked in and looked down at my hand. I have forgotten I'd injured it. After inspecting it, I thought it seemed fine.

Lucas came in from the hallway adjusting and buttoning his black shirt. A thick bandage wrapped around his chest caught my eye, which he noticed and quickly fumbled to hide. "I'll look over her Seth. Helena wants to look at your eye."

Seth looked back at me questioningly; I nodded at him agreeing it was okay.

"Very well, then. I'll be off." Seth turned left into the hall, vanishing from sight. I searched over the large room down a few stairs with the exercise equipment that Suzumiya and Chris were using that morning.

"Come on," Lucas said. We walked past the dining room on our left. To our right was the room that appeared to be the lounge-room with bookshelves, cushioned chairs, and a fireplace. Kurt sat in the big maroon single couch with glasses on, reading a book. Suzumiya held an icebag to her back, and was lying across the long blue couch talking to Chris as he sat on a blue beanbag next to her.

The two of them stopped and simply stared at me before Suzumiya looked away in disgust. Chris gave me a small smile and then looked into the direction of the fireplace, fiddling with his long dark dreadlocks. Kurt too continued reading his book as if there was nothing to see.

"Come on." Lucas lightly nodded his head to the direction he wanted us to go. Just after the lounge-room was a small bathroom. I leaned against the small basin as Lucas searched through the drawer beside me. I caught another glimpse of his bandaged chest and winced at the mistake I made. I thought he was the girl.

"It'll heal in no time," Lucas said, catching my gaze through his sandy blonde fringe. "Let's have a look at your hand."

I offered my hand out to him, trying to push the guilt away. He wrapped his fingers around my wrist gently and began wiping around the cut with a small cloth. I stared into the top of Lucas's sandy blonde hair as he concentrated on cleaning my hand. Lucas was gentle as he examined, cleaned, and bandaged my wound.

"How's that?" Lucas asked, adding a few finishing touches to the bandage. I leaned over to look at my hand at the same time that Lucas's head flung up and smacked me in the face. A huge gush of air blew out my mouth and my hand automatically clutched at my nose. Water filled up my eyes, just as quickly as it did my nose.

"I'm so sorry," he blurted out. He scrambled around on the bench, searching for something. He kept apologizing over and over again until he finally found what he was after: a tissue. I raised the tissue to my nose, determined not to show him any blood.

I let the welled up tears I had from the blow build until one by one they came rushing out— releasing everything I had kept inside so tightly. Lucas had tilted my head upwards trying to assess my nose, but he slowly released his grip on me as I began to cry. *What is going on?* I cried not only from the pain of my nose, but from the feelings I had buried deep inside after everything that had happened.

"I don't understand," I whispered, as I raked my hands through my long hair in stress. Lucas leaned against the basin patting my back as I cried, until I could cry no more.

"It will all be okay," Lucas said quietly, still rubbing my back slowly.

"What was that?" I asked, looking in the direction of the woods through blurred eyes. His face tightened as he understood what I meant: the fight I had seen, the child that attacked me, the kidnapping—everything. Tired from crying, I finally found myself thinking somewhat clearly. I have released all the emotion that had built up. After several minutes of calming myself and pushing away my thoughts, I cleared my mind enough to know I had to be the strong young woman I was raised to be.

"What am I doing here?" I asked, coolly wiping away the tears that had pooled beneath my eyes. His eyebrows lowered, as if he were trying to understand what I was saying. He looked deep in thought.

"We are protecting you," he said with earnest eyes. "Those things out there are called Starkorfs, and for some reason, they are after you. I brought you back here to keep you safe from them, but before I could approach you about it properly in your hometown, your body... well, you died. I have no other answer for you. I don't know how or why you died. We couldn't take you to the hospital because it wasn't a normal human death. We did everything we could to bring you back alive and we were successful in doing so. I don't know how you came back to life, but luckily through all the attempts you were revived. Those creatures out there that you saw, they will still look for you, so we are keeping you safe here."

I slowly took a deep breath trying to accept and absorb the words he spoke. After the strangeness of the girl attacking me, anything was possible. *What does he mean by a normal human death? And why are they following me?* I thought, trying to find the courage to voice my concerns.

"What do they want with me? And why—..." I hesitated to say it, recalling the memory of the girl and the demented humans that had attacked us. "Why did you kill them?"

"Because if we didn't they would have killed all of us and taken you."

He looked at me as I stared back at him blankly. "You are like us. We have the ability to project Shields for protection. Nobody can break through them with anything, except someone who is equally matched in strength and ability; and Starkorfs have that ability. Not all of them, in truth it is quite rare to meet another who has the same ability. Their whole being is sickening.

The Starkorfs were once Shielders but a few strayed from protecting humans a long time ago. They found that through our ability to project their energy into a Shield, they could also use such a force to drain and absorb. Through this they can pause physical aging. And now they live for only that—draining humans of their life, trying to gain a near immortality. We have been fighting them for a long time now and to our understanding they are after you because you are a Shielder—but they've taken a particular interest in you, which seems peculiar."

"I don't understand. I don't have this ability you speak of," I said forcefully, trying not to stumble over my words. I can't be anything other than human.

Lucas continued his explanation, unfazed by my tone: "If a parent of an unborn child has the ability, it creates a kind of virus in the womb. The child then fights the virus during its developmental stage. If it can fend the virus off, then the child will become normal. However, if the unborn babe accepts the virus, it will be born with the Shielding ability.

You can only receive it through blood, but in your case, it's different. It's not contagious which means you would've been a Shielder from the first day you opened your eyes. Neither of your biological parents have the gift. So we're wondering if that unknown reason is in any way affiliated with your body shutting down on you. You can never be treated at a hospital for this, Karla. There is nothing they can possibly do for you," Lucas said seriously.

I gasped in shock, trying to swallow what Lucas was telling me. Two days ago I would have called him a liar. But after what I saw today—and what I felt when that little girl attacked me, squeezing my throat—I couldn't help but believe him entirely.

"What we are, Karla—what we are capable of —is so much more than you could ever imagine. It is a gift, and, over time, it will turn into a powerful talent," Lucas said.

I stared at my bandaged hand, feeling his eyes on me. I swallowed harshly as if I were trying to push down everything Lucas told me. How does such a being manifest into reality? Like a journal I flicked through the vivid images from the day. Overwhelmed by them, I stopped thinking, calming myself, and breathing slowly.

"How did you find me?" I asked absentmindedly, still trying to calm myself.

"We watched the Starkorfs closely and noticed they were hovering around your town but not feasting. Very rare for them, so we watched them a bit more, realising they were following you. So we did the same."

I thought about this, remembering the paranoid feeling I had of being watched; the flickering shadows before Paul had come to the classroom and scared me during my detention. *Was that them? Was*

Paul in danger as well? Had I put him in danger without realising it,? So the feeling of being watched wasn't just my imagination, I had been followed.

"You were in the black Porsche?" I asked harshly, trying to keep my composure. *He was following me. They all were. How was I not fully aware of being followed?* Panic rose in me again as I held my hands together tightly, desperately trying to supress my anger and panic.

"Yes, that was us," Lucas said slowly, watching my fidgeting hands. "Kurt's getting older and isn't as powerful as he used to be. He'd be an easy target so he no longer fights. We are all too reliant on his knowledge, and for keeping us together as a whole. We still live the normal lifespan of a human, and like them, our ability and strength weakens in age." Lucas continued dumping all this information on me, ignoring my discomfort after the simple 'yes that was us', said in answer to the question of stalking.

"The rest of us fight. We hunt the Starkorfs so they stop killing humans, all of us except Helena. She doesn't fight anymore."

I had heard the name 'Helena' many times but have not yet seen who she was. Lucas continued explaining all these foreign concepts to me. My head ached at the rate it was trying to absorb everything.

"Although we are all Shielders only Kurt and I have the ability, however Suzumiya and Chris are skilled fighters," Lucas continued. "You'll be training with them for physical strength. Kurt will teach you Shielding."

"But —..." I intervened. "...I don't want to do any of that. I just want to go home." The thought of tasting Mum's pancakes right now made me even more home sick as I remembered her and Dad's warm smiles at the breakfast table. "It's a lie. I am not this thing you call a Shielder, with this ability you're talking about. I am just a normal girl who goes to school and has a part time job."

"Karla this is the safest place for you. If you go home, the Starkorfs would come after you again. It will put your family in danger," Lucas said urgently.

"But my parents knew you were coming for me. They are probably looking for me right now," I shakily said. The thought of Mum and Dad pierced my chest with a longing to see them.

"What do you mean they knew we were coming for you?" He was serious now; his dark brown eyes were deeply intense.

"Just after I was in that car accident and my body began..." I felt it all vividly, quickly shutting down the memory of that pain I once felt,

"…dying—they called me, crying. Mum and Dad said they had to talk to me about something. Well that's what I made of it all… and then, when I could barely breathe and I was on my knees gasping…" The reminder of the experience made my hands shaky and I rubbed my arms for warmth. My eyes began to water at the memory. I collected myself, reminding myself not to fall apart again.

"When I was going through that unbearable pain…" I said, eventually able to continue. Tears welled in my eyes and my voice became croaky. The breath had turned stale and the taste in my mouth left my lips tasting bitter. "…I told them I loved them."

I wiped the unwelcome tears away and Lucas put his leathered hand on my shoulder, trying to comfort me. I shuddered under his hand and moved away from his touch, thinking of him once again as the enemy that stole me from my parents.

"They screamed through the phone, asking me if they were there," I said, wiping another stream of tears away. "They knew you were coming. Telling me not to become what you wanted me to be." I wiped the stale, burning tears away from my eyes. He considered my words and let me compose myself for a few minutes.

"I see," Lucas hesitantly said. "I will have to tell Kurt. Maybe he will have an answer." He combed one of his hands through his hair, concentrating on nothing in particular. Lucas stood up, no longer leaning against the basin next to me. "We aren't here to hurt you Karla." He looked at me with soft eyes. "I promise I will look after you. So please don't be scared. I know it's a lot to take in right now, but I am telling you the truth."

Seth walked in the bathroom, flashing me a small polite smile. "Here, love," Seth said, handing me a bottle of water. "Helena is about to start cooking dinner for us. I hope there is nothing you dislike to eat?"

I accepted the water with my bandaged hand, looking up at the small white patch of cloth that was stuck above his eyebrow. His light blonde hair had been washed and combed back making me realize how long Lucas and I had been in here for Seth to have already showered.

"I'm not really hungry," I said quietly, as I stopped leaning against the basin. "I think I would just like to be alone and sleep," I sighed in exhaustion. I didn't want to think nor accept what was happening. I wanted to wake up and find that this was all a nightmare.

Seth looked at me with sad eyes before giving me a tight smile, as Lucas squeezed past him and left the room. "Very well, love," Seth said, placing his hand on my head like a father would to his child. "I'll walk you to your room."

He walked me down the hallway quietly, ignoring the others who were in the lounge-room. This was the same hallway I had run from when I had hurt Seth, making my escape. I tilted my head up, examining his face once more. He was so tall and when I looked over his features, I saw a very kind-looking man. Not a kidnapper, but a gentle giant. Seth opened the door to the room I had woken in this morning, turning on the light for me as I walked in and looked around the dull room.

"If you need anything come and find me, love." He nodded with a small smile before closing the door and leaving me to be surrounded by blank walls. I walked over to the small mirror, staring at myself in confusion. Somehow I appeared different. My green eyes looked back at me, lost and bewildered. My light brown hair had turned into a dirty, dark brown from the filth in the woods. I stroked my hair, trying to comb it as if it were my only care in the world.

Walking over to the bed I stared at the bandaged hand. *Am I safe here*? I curled myself into a foetal position on the bed, trying to squeeze out any thoughts that came to me. I was scared to think about any of it. *What am I going to do? Can I really be something other than human? I mean how do I even begin to believe that?* Every time I tried to engulf that thought, a block was put up and my mind goes blank. I couldn't accept this, but was that because I was just too shocked and overwhelmed by the day? I held myself tightly, thinking of my mum cooking me pancakes, wearing the smile she always had for me when I woke... my dad making some lame dad joke at the table while chowing down his breakfast.

I thought of Sarah and I walking to school every day; our only concern: her love life, and how she compared to Courtney. To us, that was the extent of our problems—*and now all of this? This is what I now have to contend with?* Paul's beautiful green eyes came to mind and I felt instantly sad, tightening my arms even harder around my stomach for comfort. *Is Paul okay after the car accident, as Lucas said he was? Is Paul angry with me?* I closed my eyes at the thought of him angry with me and remembered his cheeky smile. *Will I ever see Paul again?* I tried to will all these feelings away as they crashed over me—wave after wave of hurtful images—reminding me of my ordinary life that now seemed so distant. I wanted to fall asleep and forget all of this, and wake up to find it all a terrible nightmare. Instead my eyes flooded once again as I cried, rocking myself back and forth. *Tonight there will be no sleep.*

Chapter Ten - The Three Elders

My eyelids fluttered and I awoke to the sound of snickering and smothered laughter.

"Should I do all of it or just make some tacky pattern?" Ashley said, trying not to laugh.

"Do it all. He'll hate it. You know what the pretty boy is like," the familiar hippy, bouncy voice said, laughing as well. It was Chris.

"Oi. She moved," Chris's voice was a low whisper but I could feel his presence by my side now. I heard a shuffle of feet and then a gasp from Ashley. He gave Chris a faint smack on the arm and Chris let out an exaggerated sigh of pain while rubbing it.

"Go get Mum," Ashley instructed, and with that Chris's bouncy steps left the room. I opened my eyes, rubbing them and trying to wipe away the sleep. They felt swollen with little pillows under both eyes from my crying. At some point I must have fallen asleep last night. My eyes squinted at a reflection of light that shone in my eyes.

"You okay?" Ashley asked patiently as I properly awoke. I measured the object that shone in my eyes, letting a little shriek rip through my mouth when I saw the razor in his hand. I quickly backed further into the bedframe, scared that he was going to use it on me.

"Oh no, no, no, no..." Ashley said, shaking his finger side to side quickly and hiding the razor behind his back. "Not what you think."

Chris waltzed in with a tiny woman behind him. She was a very pretty lady who seemed to be in her forties with beautiful bronze skin and deep black hair that met her shoulders neatly. She wore red glasses that rested on her little squashed nose. For an older woman she was stunning. She read my face like a book and then gave Ashley a disapproving look with pouted lips.

"What? I didn't do anything," Ashley said, shrugging his shoulders. "She saw the razor in my hand and freaked." He innocently lifted the blade up for all of us to see.

"You honestly think that her waking up to see an unfamiliar boy with a razor blade in his hand is comforting for her?" She started walking over to me with her hands on her hips. She glanced over her shoulder at the small couch that was placed near my door, blocking my view of what she stared at. "Ashley I wish you didn't, he'll be furious," she said with thin lips.

"I'm sorry Mum but I couldn't let the chance slip," Ashley said proudly. He shrugged her anger off with a sly smirk across his face, turning to Chris who was also trying to keep his amusement to himself. Together they burst into a short laugh.

"Chris, don't encourage him," she said. The little woman was by my side, sighing.

"Hello Karla. I'm Helena. How are you feeling, sweetie?" she asked kindly.

My scared expression changed as I let the tension slip and I sat up into a normal position. I looked between Helena and Ashley briefly, trying to see the resemblance of mother and son. I stuttered a little and then finally produced all the words that would come out of my mouth.

"Ok," I said, frowning at my empty words and croaked voice.

"You scared us all yesterday. You must be pretty hungry and thirsty. Seth's making you something now," Helena said smiling. "Hope you like scrambled eggs?"

I rubbed my head with one hand while my other clutched at my stomach, realising how hungry and sore I really was. "Thank you," I accepted quietly. My gratitude shot sparks in her eyes and she looked at me adoringly. "Where is Lucas?" I asked, wanting to talk with him more about his explanation yesterday. Today I felt my mind was clearer and perhaps I could approach and understand this all differently.

"He's been here all night." Helena moved out of my way and pointed into the direction of the small couch. Lucas sat in an awkward position, sleeping contently with a soft snore. The size of the couch was no bigger than that of a school chair. It was an aquatic blue and his hair stood out against the color, making it look like an unnatural gold. My body relaxed just seeing his content face and the feeling made my own eyes go sleepy once again.

"He's normally such a light sleeper and jumps at the noise of even a cat scratching at the front door, but now he's dead to the world," Helena said, sounding like a mother watching her young child sleep. I looked back over at his content face, looking at him differently to how I had before. Maybe Lucas wasn't a bad guy and actually did care for my safety.

"Mum, you should go help Dad," Ashley said, grabbing his mother's arm and slowly prodding her out the door. So Seth was Ashley's father and Helena's partner. I looked between the two, envisioning Seth. Now that I looked at Ashley I could see the resemblance between them both.

"We'll look after her," Chris confirmed before Helena could argue. Chris was standing next to Ashley with his hand on his shoulder as if they had done something heroic. Helena looked over my face, uncertain.

"Okay..." Helena trailed off. "But Ashley Taylor if you—..."

"I know, Mum. Nothing's going to happen," he said, ushering her out the door. When Helena was outside the door, she stopped and reached her hand out to Ashley.

"Give it to me," she ordered with her hands on her hips and her lips in a thin line. Ashley looked at her, innocently fiddling with his pockets. "Now!" Helena demanded. A huge moan tore from Ashley as he gave his mum the razor. When it was in her hand she smiled and gave a quick glance in my direction before she marched off out of view. Ashley grumbled under his breath and Chris seemed just as disappointed. Ashley looked over at Chris as if a light had just been turned on in his thoughts.

"I'll go check my room," Ashley said as he left. I looked over at Chris awkwardly, but he only gave me a playful grin and then continued chewing on his gum. In the corner of the room was a large brown wardrobe and next to it was Lucas's limp body. I sighed, adoring his contentment. Next to him was the door that Ashley had run out of.

The walls were unpainted with gold trimming around the base of the wall. The carpet was a lush white with a small red stain next to the bed from my injured hand yesterday. I looked at my bandaged hand, recalling what had happened. A bang startled me and I was greeted with Chris's cheesy smile that now had bubble gum all around it.

There was a low murmur from Lucas as he began opening and closing his eyes as they got used to the light. When they were awake, he looked up at my bed expectantly. A faint smile pulled at the corner of his lips before breaking into a yawn. He stretched and rolled his shoulder back and forth. "You're awake," Lucas's voice was still drowsy and then a sigh of relief blew from his mouth. Before I could reply, Ashley shot through the door and clipped his shoulder on the doorframe excitedly. Unfazed by the injury he looked down on Lucas, wincing at the sight of him now awake. Disappointment clouded his face in an instant.

"Hey man," Ashley said, hiding the new razor behind his back. Lucas was unperturbed by the greeting and just let another yawn fill the air. Chris tapped Ashley on the shoulder as he walked out the door.

"Better luck next time, buddy," Chris teased. He shot his chin up to Lucas. "Morning, Sleeping Beauty. You were out for a while."

"How long has she been awake for?" Lucas asked, before letting another yawn out.

"Bout fifteen," Chris said casually. "Go tell your mum Lucas is awake and he'll need something to eat too." Chris pushed Ashley out the door playfully. As they were walking Ashley mumbled his disappointment to Chris down the hall.

Lucas picked up the chair as if it had no weight to it and sat it gently next to the bed. He swept his fingers through his hair, forcing his hair to bounce back up ruffled and messy. I tried containing my smile. Lucas only had one eyebrow.

"What are you smiling at?" Lucas frowned slightly, making his one eyebrow look even funnier. I held back my smile, looking down instead at my hands in an effort to contain it. "Not many people wake up to the beauty of an angel in the morning..." He let his hand slide down his face, indicating that he meant himself: "...and find it amusing. Most try to seduce me—but they never *laugh*. Even Ashley's let himself slip once or twice."

"Maybe your modesty overwhelmed him," I said uninterested. "And I can't envision anyone trying to seduce you with your bad attitude anyway. Did you have to make a deal with the devil for charm?"

"You think I'm devilish?" A small smirk crossed his face as he focused on me. His eyes reached mine, waiting for a response. He did have a devilish smile, now that I noticed it. I looked over his messy collar, half unbuttoned shirt and rolled sleeves. He looked at me with sincere, compelling eyes.

"No." I started looking at the walls as if I found something more interesting to stare at. I looked over at Lucas's unbuttoned shirt again. He only had a few undone but it was enough to see the heavy bandage on his chest. His face turned hard as he began buttoning it up so it was no longer in my view.

"I am sorry," I said in a small voice.

"Don't worry about it. I'll heal within the week," he said, stumbling with the last button. I remember mistaking him for the child and stabbing the dagger into his chest. The thought made me shiver all over. "You don't need to apologise..." he continued, finishing with his shirt. "What you did was the right thing. You're lucky that's what you did on instinct. If a Starkorf ever comes near you again, I want you to do exactly the same, but aim for the heart."

"It was like the child was possessed," I said, recalling the clawing girl who held me down by my throat.

"She wasn't possessed. Her name was Raven. We have been fighting her for as long as I can remember and she has always been of that same age. She was easily over one hundred years old. She drains and feasts off humans a lot more than the ordinary Starkorf, so she has retained the body of a child for a very long time now. But I killed her, so you don't have to worry about her anymore," he said coolly.

"I don't know how I feel," I said numbly. So much to take in and yet there was a wall that was blocking me from accepting the words he told me.

"I imagine it would be hard to accept. I was raised knowing what I am, but for you it must feel like you have just stumbled over your feet for the first time." He paused for a moment, thinking. "I will tell you a story that my father told to my older brother and I when we were little."

"Is Ashley your brother?" I asked thinking of the closeness they seemed to share.

"No," he answered sadly. "My family was killed by Starkorfs. Kurt and Seth found me and so they looked after me. My father, brother, and I, were hunted by the Starkorfs because they were Shielders too," he explained with a grimace. There was a heavy silence before he grunted, placing his hand to his shoulder and rolling it. "The war came about because of our Elders. There were three siblings: Misfeata was the eldest, Tyran was the middle child, and Sebastian was the youngest. Misfeata meaning the 'wise one'; Tyran meaning the 'strong one' and Sebastian being the 'compassionate one'.

They all loved one another dearly and it was written in record that there were only another twelve known Shielders that followed them upon their awakening. In the 17th century explorers came across a tomb; they broke the seal that held the three Elders and the twelve followers who slumbered. It was the first time they had ever walked the Earth but it is said they existed far before mankind. No one knows of where this tomb was discovered but Kurt does know it wasn't in this country. Shielders before us simply migrated over here.

All three siblings balanced one another and together they were magnificent leaders. They knew what they were blessed with was for a purpose and they needed no further convincing to protect the species that awoke them from their long slumber: *humans*. They made oaths to protect those who they hid amongst—the ordinary people of the land. Nobody endangered the humans; yet sometimes they bickered and fought over land and religion.

Our Elders still stood by, watching and waiting for the darkness to arrive that they knew would come. They couldn't intervene in the wars because that would mean they would have to endanger humans. They knew there was a greater evil to come: one that only they could evenly match. The Elders are immortal and they never aged. They presented themselves as young adults. It is said their souls are immortalised elsewhere, so unless that object is destroyed they would live forever. Their twelve followers, however, were mortal, like all us Shielders. We die from old age, but we are exceptional in almost everything physical and we are natural born fighters. It is what we are born to do and our ability to Shield aids us in protecting humans.

Their twelve followers lived amongst the kingdom and acted as mere peasants so they could obtain information of the human world. The three Elders stayed away from human civilisation so they could literally watch over the kingdoms from the nearby hills that they resided in.

Tyran, the middle brother, had fallen in love with one of the twelve followers and they had four children, all boys, named: Espon, Hansel, Trey, and Quasha. His sons aged as quickly as their mother. As the years went by everyone around the Elders aged and died. Tyran's wife became disorientated in her old age and when he was not around she showed her ability to the humans and was therefore labelled a witch. They said she conjured the natural disasters, which threatened human life, such as flooding. She could not save herself against the army with her aged and withered Shield. She was too disorientated to project it as they set her alight and she perished in the flames.

Tyran tried to protect his wife from the hill on which the Elders always watched. But the distance was far too great—even for one of the immortals—to project a Shield from. Shielders cannot project their Shield around another being; however they can isolate it around or near themselves. He was forced to watch them poke at his wife, and after watching that, he blamed the humans for his wife's death. Slowly Tyran began to despise the humans, slipping further and further away from the pledge Sebastian and Misfeata had also taken. Although Tyran's siblings loved him, they still believed that they were woken purely to protect the humans and therefore Misfeata had little sympathy for her brother's need for revenge. It was Sebastian who kept his brother aligned with them, mourning with Tyran and his sons at the great loss.

Tyran found it hard to understand how immortality would bring them peace if they could never be at ease. 'If love lasts forever, why doesn't life?' he asked Sebastian constantly. He questioned why they had to protect the humans, and from what. Misfeata and Tyran drifted apart as she saw only their oath and mourned little for her brother's wife. Only Sebastian, the youngest and compassionate one, stood by his brother reminding him gently that they had been gifted so that they could protect the humans, not so they could rise against them.

They had to change homes after the incident, and they left for a faraway kingdom. Sebastian had pleaded with Misfeata to do so as his brother struggled every day to look upon the same people who had killed his beloved wife. Misfeata agreed, for she was not heartless and could never refuse her youngest brother, Sebastian, for he was so pure and good.

Within only a year of moving to this new kingdom, Sebastian became mesmerised and fell in love with a young woman who was said to hold the beauty of an angel. She was also a rich king's daughter: King Pholom. Sebastian dressed as a peasant so he could enter the kingdom and meet her. When word got out that King Pholom's daughter was in love with a mere peasant, the King was furious and commanded many of his men to search for Sebastian. When found, he was of course with the young princess, as they lay in an open space gazing into one another's eyes, hands entwined. The guards had no mercy, not even stopping to hear the princess's screams or cries. The princess never let go of Sebastian's hand, and as the guards tried to force them apart, she commanded them to stand down until she had spoken to her father. She would not let go of Sebastian's hand.

Sebastian looked at her with easy eyes telling her it would be okay. When they finally reached the king, he could not bear to see his daughter's hand entwined with those of a peasant. King Pholom himself tried to rip the young lovers' hands apart but she did not let go, arguing with her father for the sake of her and Sebastian's love."

I slowly let myself rest into the pillow again and turned onto my side to listen to Lucas's story. He continued through my quiet movement, tucking the blanket to my sides absentmindedly.

"Sebastian tried to convince her to let go, but she refused. Sebastian then also held on tightly for if this were his love's wish, then he would never go against it. Her father brought whips out, threatening to lash at her hands until nothing could be seen of the skin. Listening to this, Sebastian was more mortified than the princess. It was forbidden for the Elders to tell humans about their ability but Sebastian—the compassionate one—could not bear to watch his love suffer.

He tried to bargain with King Pholom, telling him of the protection he could provide and that he would stand by him as his second man. King Pholom only saw this offer as an admittance of sorcery and declared Sebastian's death sentence straight away. Still, the princess would not let go of his hand. The man she loved, cried for and would bleed for. Sebastian then tried his hardest to convince her to let go but she would not. Sebastian knew he could easily force her to let go and run, but he would never go against the princess's wishes. He told her he could get her out and they could escape, but he explained that he would have to harm humans in the process, breaking his oath. She did not allow it. She whispered into his ear when the king's men tied them to the wood that she would not allow him to break another oath for her; he was a compassionate man and that it was not in his nature to harm another being. When the men tied them down they still did not let go of one another's hands, and with her last breath she whispered the word 'Mirac' to him."

My eyes peered at Lucas uncomprehendingly. "What does that mean?"

"Mirac was the name of their unborn child: the first of a new kind, a mixed blood of human and Shielder. The child would be killed before it even had time to show its true ability. The whispered name of his unborn child put Sebastian into a rage. He wanted to watch his love live, and watch his unborn son grow. He instinctively attempted the same as Tyran: to project his Shield to protect the one he loved. This did not work because the post they were tied to separated them, and the exertion simply overwhelmed Sebastian, forcing him into an unconscious state. His head dropped at the stake before the fire was even put to the wood. He was burned alive beside his love, yet she still never let go of his hand. An immortal could not be killed so easily, except Sebastian's body perished alongside the blade that held his soul, and therefore his claim to immortality was lost. Tyran was furious and wished death upon all humans in that kingdom. The raw pain of losing his wife, and then his brother, drove him into a frenzy. He gathered his sons and prepared for battle against the humans.

However, Misfeata stood in his way. She was upset about her brother's death but stood by her oath of protecting the humans. She thought that if Sebastian was willing to die at the hands of a human, for a human, then that was a decision he had made quite apart from their sworn oath. She could not talk her brother out of such rage as he had already gathered up so much hatred towards mankind. The path he would now take would be against them. No longer by his sister's side, and no longer abiding by the oath he took; Tyran embarked on his rebel path, with inevitable collisions along the way with Misfeata. It was neither man nor animal that started the war; but the Elders themselves. A war began. It was their fate and somehow they had foretold of its existence when they first awoke. It was the beginning of the war between the immortals.

The rest of the Shielders watched as the blood of both Misfeata and Tyran were shed. At first, it was only words of negotiation, but all discussion was in vain: these interactions only infuriated both sides. Trying to convert each other was futile. These separate paths forced them to hold anger for each other, which eventually turned to hatred for both of them claimed to know exactly what Sebastian would have wanted. And although they could not die by one another's hands, the fighting persisted as they tried to make each other forego their pride and beliefs.

The fight went on for days and nights and no one had fallen. They both fought with their respective blades—slashing at one another's body fiercely. The three Elders when awoken had their own specialised blade and carried it as if it were an extension of their body. Sebastian's Blade perished just as his body did. But Misfeata and Tyran's Blades now lusted for one another's blood. The Blades yearned to absolve the hatred with bloodshed. The siblings were too alike, too powerful for one another to handle. Eventually Tyran slipped away with his sons and two of the Shielders. They left with every intention to hurt the humans, regardless of whether or not they had to cross paths with Misfeata in order to do so. The other Shielders and their children stayed loyal to their oath and stood by Misfeata.

Over centuries Misfeata and Tyran fought against one another fiercely, but neither fell. Tyran renamed his clan of rebel followers 'Starkorfs'. Time moved forward, but Misfeata and Tyran remained locked in battle, and all the other original followers finally died, if not through battle, with one another then through old age. Over time, the impurities of half-bloods came into existence. Half human, half Starkorf; they too were immersed in the war, though only a few inherited the ability to Shield. Despite not all of them being born to be exceptional fighters, they were still raised to fight and kill.

Misfeata did not believe in half bloods; her bloodline was to stay pure. Their people mixed only with their own kind. They were able to continue the pure line for many years. The rules were so strict that even when one of her own daughters was found with a human she was slaughtered instantly. They didn't realize it but the evil they waited for turned out to be amongst their own kind.

They no longer hid amongst the people but tracked the Starkorfs until their blood was shed.

Years after the war broke out, Misfeata and Tyran disappeared, leaving word that someday they would be back to finish the war that they had started. They left the hatred they had bred with the followers and the fighting continued. Now with Misfeata gone, the Shielders had the right to love who they wanted and to give birth freely.

Although they had left, the war raged and a few hundred years ago the Starkorfs formed a new feasting habit. One of the descendants of Tyran hated one of his enemies so much that when they were engaged in battle the Starkorf vowed that he would not leave any traces of the Shielder behind. He promised to eat every part of his flesh so that he became a part of the Starkorf. The Starkorf followed through and his ability became stronger as a result. He also found that his life was prolonged by a short time. Word spread quickly and they learned how to use their Shield—reversing its capabilities of protection and instead using it to drain humans, ultimately killing them. It was named the 'Feast of Immortality', but it would only sustain life for a little time longer. Without feasting, their aging would catch up with them quickly. The stronger the Shielder was that they devoured, the more rewarding the result.

Something happened then. Perhaps Misfeata and Tyran had something to do with the cause. All those with supernatural abilities were locked away from humans into a separate land of sorts. Both Starkorfs and Shielders, and other beings with abilities—they were all trapped. There is much speculation that Misfeata somehow managed to do it to stop Tyran's followers from draining humans. But about a hundred years ago, this haven was infiltrated and all the Starkorfs escaped. They now hunt both humans and Shielders alike.

In recent years, the newborn Starkorfs have become so powerful after generations of consuming Shielders that as soon as they are born they attack their own kind. To avoid this problem, the male Starkorfs mate with human women, and then allow the offspring to drain its human mother, so no harm comes to their women.

Raven was special. In fact, she was the daughter of the second in command. I don't know why she was out on her own with only a few Starkorfs by her side." His eyebrows knitted together, showing that he was deep in thought.

"But it doesn't matter now, because you got rid of her... right?" I asked, remembering the child with porcelain skin that attempted to drain me.

"That's right," Lucas confirmed with hard eyes.

"Thank you for saving me and I'm sorry about your injury," I said, looking at his chest once more. I noticed a necklace dangling over the bandage. Lucas noticed my fixated eyes, and he took the necklace off and put it gently in my hands so I could see it. The pendant was a small silver-plated woman that had a tiny red gem in one of her hands. Her little face looked upset and she was tied up to a piece of wood. She looked no older than me, and her face was carved with the finest detail, showing compassion through her tears. I marvelled at the fine detail in such a small piece of silver. I turned it from side to side in my hand, thinking of the princess in Lucas's story.

"Lucas, is this meant to be the princess?" I asked, realizing that the image was exactly as I had imagined her. I thought of the heroic woman who agreed to her death so she didn't have to watch her beloved betray his beliefs. Gently I put the necklace back in Lucas's hands, knowing how much significance it carried.

"Yes. Beautiful, isn't she?" His eyes gleamed. He looked at the necklace as if it possessed his very soul.

"Yes, she is," I agreed thoughtfully.

"I think that's enough for today," Lucas announced, returning the small couch to where it had once stood beside the door. "Let's go see how breakfast is coming along."

Chapter Eleven - One Big Happy Family

*A*s we left the room and walked down the hallway, I looked back at Lucas with his one remaining eyebrow. The candles that stood tall in the hallway flickered as the wind blew in from the small windows on the wall. Looking through them I could see that outside was overcast.

"Why do you keep staring at me?" Lucas asked, still looking forward.

"You only have one eyebrow. Ashley shaved the other off when you were sleeping," I said, trying to keep my face serious. Realization crossed his face, as he now knew what I was laughing at when he woke. He fumbled at where his eyebrow was meant to be. Lucas's face was sharp and threatening. I could only imagine what he would do to Ashley.

We came to the end of the hallway and entered the lounge-room, where Suzumiya and Chris sat beside a crackling fire. Chris was on his blue beanbag and Suzumiya was flat on her stomach, her hands dangling over the edge of the long couch. "Snap!" Suzumiya yelled, throwing her hands onto the deck of cards. Chris held his hands over Suzumiya's, trying to steal the pile of cards. They stopped fiddling with one another's hands as soon as they saw Lucas and I. They pulled their hands away as if they were little children, busted for doing something wrong.

"Karla," Suzumiya said, startled to see me. Her cheeks blushed red. She looked over my shoulder. I turned to see what it was she stared at; noticing that I now stood alone and that Lucas had gone.

Helena walked from behind me, assumedly from the kitchen as she had a tea towel thrown over her shoulder. "Lucas said you came out," she said with a warm smile. "Let's have a quick look at your hand before breakfast."

"Good Morning, love!" a warm voice called. I looked over to the dining room where Seth sat, waving with a wooden spoon in his hand. I hesitantly waved back at the cheerful Englishman as Helena smiled between both Seth and I.

Helena started unwrapping the bandage around my hand. Finally the cool air swept over it. Suzumiya walked over to Helena's side, looking over her shoulder to examine it too. Her lips parted but nothing was said. My hand had completely healed with not even a scratch or scar to be seen.

"Does this hurt?" Helena moved my hand from left to right, back and forth, and then began wiping over my hand harder and harder, waiting for some reaction. I stared at my hand in disbelief, wondering how it could have possibly healed so quickly.

"No," I said regaining my voice. I looked back over at Chris who was sweeping the pile of cards up. Helena gave Suzumiya a worried look as she stepped closer to examine it, raising the glasses that had slipped to the tip of her nose.

"What do you think it means?" Suzumiya asked, looking at Helena.

"I don't know," Helena answered, as she let go of my hand gently.

"We should tell Kurt—he might know something. Maybe he could look in a few of the old books he's got stashed," Suzumiya suggested, looking over her shoulder at Chris who now came to her side, readjusting his dreadlocks and tying them into a large bundle at the back.

"They're not stashed, they're right there in all those bookshelves," Helena said, pointing at the ones in the lounge-room. "You all just decide not to read them because you think brawn comes before brain. But yes, I will tell Kurt. I'll even talk to Seth; he might know a thing or two about it."

I pulled at the purple long sleeved shirt I had, covering my hand. I was glad they weren't staring at me anymore. "Can I have a shower?" I asked, smelling the stench of my clothes from yesterday's ordeal.

"Of course," Helena said smiling. "I'll get you some clothes. There will be fresh towels in the small cupboard in the bathroom."

Helena gave me some dark blue tights and a purple sleeveless shirt. It almost looked like exercise clothing. She also gave me a bottle of shampoo, conditioner and some soap. I lathered myself four times, trying to scrub off the dirt I felt plastered to my skin. I scrubbed my hair viciously, trying to rid myself of the filth that had been in my hair. The water was unimaginably cold and I quickly washed out my hair, jumped out and looked at myself in the mirror.

It was as if my eyes had changed—they seemed almost unrecognizable. The once plain green eyes I previously had seemed somehow more radiant, with shades of blue touching the edges. Something I had never noticed before. My cheeks had shades of red across them from the cold shower and I had dark pillows under my eyes from too little sleep. *Who am I?* I quickly brushed through my hair, trying to unknot it as much as possible with my fingers, and avoiding the thoughts I would soon have flooding in.

I closed the door quietly, checking that I didn't leave anything in the bathroom behind me. A huge bang from outside made me jump in fear before I remembered the overcast weather that was outside. *Thunder. It's okay*, I told myself. I jumped again as soon as I ran into Lucas who was leaning against the wall. I held the bottles to my chest, feeling a quick flutter of my heart. "Don't scare me like that."

I peered at Lucas who stood in the shadows of the darkened hallway. The sandy blonde color of his hair looked like it had been washed out and his eyes seemed black. "Breakfast," Lucas said simply, before grabbing the bottles and soap from my hands and putting them back into the bathroom.

Lucas escorted me to the dining room as promised. Suzumiya and Chris sat next to one another as Kurt sat at the end of the table. Seth sat at the other end, hand and hand with Helena as they discussed something seriously. Ashley was beside Chris ploughing food into his mouth as he wiped a small squirt of sauce off the edge of his mouth, wiping it and continuing to eat as he put his finger in his mouth.

"Karla. Sit next to me," Kurt said, waving his hand to me. I took the seat he gestured to as Lucas took the one on my right. There was a plate full of food in front of me already. The smell kissed my nose gently, making my mouth water over the food.

Everyone ate breakfast quickly. Helena, Seth, and Kurt quickly washed their plates before leaving, and they began to speak of my healed hand when leaving the room. After only a few moments of Chris and Ashley doing the dishes, Suzumiya joined in on a huge bubble fight from the excessive soapy water the boys had conjured up. I stood against the wall, unsure of whether I could join, and watching Suzumiya, Chris, and Ashley throw the water at one another.

Everyone was saturated except Lucas, who stood near the sink wiping at a plate with the tea towel, unamused. Each of them attempted to wet him but they weren't able to get close enough. Their flickers of water stopped mid-air, sliding down what I guessed to be his Shield.

Now and then it would pulse the splashes of water back into Ashley's face as Lucas shot him disapproving looks. It was the first time I'd seen a Shield. It was strange to watch, as it wasn't actually visible; the only thing that could be seen was the water stopping mid-air at an arm's length in front of Lucas. Everyone called him a party-pooper but he wasn't fazed.

I was so astonished by the invisible barrier that I began creeping closer, and poked my finger into it. I slowly probed my finger near him until it came to a stop. It was like trying to drill my finger into a cement wall. I stopped putting pressure on my finger because it actually started to hurt. I raised both hands to it, enjoying its smooth texture. *The invisible wall that comes between us,* I mused.

I forgot that I wasn't invisible, and Lucas was looking at me amused by my astonishment. I froze and smiled, embarrassed at my intrusion on his personal space. My hands went through the Shield as it evaporated into nothing and my weight had nothing to support itself on. My body fell through the air into Lucas's arms. He caught me with both arms, smiling at my blushing face. I quickly stood tall, distancing myself from him.

As Lucas smiled at me, Ashley pounced on him raising a handful of suds to his mouth. He coughed at the bubbles before gathering a heap himself and throwing them back at Ashley. After wrestling Ashley to the ground and forcing suds into his mouth, Lucas quickly jumped at me giving me little time to defend myself. I coughed and spluttered the overpowering taste out of my mouth, noticing the hint of lavender in it. I scratched at my tongue, trying to scrape the taste off my offended taste buds.

Lucas laughed at my awkward attempts to remove the suds while I coughed and spluttered. I scraped a small portion of bubbles from the ground—only half the amount he put in my mouth. I rubbed my hands through his hair, squashing the bubbles. He gave me a disapproving look while I slowly let my smile creep back, enjoying myself. Lucas's dark brown eyes softened as he gave me a small smile back.

Everyone clapped and laughed as Ashley crept up on us with a bucket full of water, throwing it over Lucas while he was distracted. His black long sleeved shirt instantly turned skin-tight. He shook his soaked hair and left my side, chasing after Ashley who was already sprinting out of the dining room and down the hall. Lucas quickly followed behind while his shoes squashed under him. Suzumiya and Chris clapped while laughing and shortly after started cleaning the bigger mess they had just made. They appeared to me then as one big, happy family.

Chapter Twelve - Life, Death and Dreams

$\mathcal{S}$hortly after everyone had finished cleaning, Kurt, Helena, and Seth, came to collect me. I followed them into the lounge-room and sat next to Kurt who was on his usual couch next to the unlit fireplace. Helena and Seth sat hand in hand on the long couch, looking at me seriously.

"Karla we want to take you back to your home for a little while," Seth announced. "But before we take you back, we need to make sure you can defend yourself in the case of an ambush."

Tears welled in my eyes instantly at the thought of seeing my parents. I tried my hardest to supress the pain I felt from being so far away from them. The weight seemed almost overbearing. I was still very uncertain as to where I was and the ending in store for me. I was studying in school only a week ago and now I was being forced to make life and death decisions.

I still breathed the same air on this land yet everything felt like a completely new world to me. *Is there really a possibility of going back to my hometown and continuing life as normal?* I was being forced to believe in a world where Shielders and Starkorfs existed. I was being educated on a war that was alien to me; trained to participate in it using a skill that I wasn't sure I even had. *How much truth can really be in these words? I have seen Lucas's Shield, I know it is there.* And yet, believing I had the same ability seemed beyond comprehension. *I am just an ordinary girl.*

"It is for your own safety," Kurt said, abruptly interrupting my thoughts. "Depending on how quick you're able to learn, you could be seeing your parents in no time. Then we can assess if they are in danger and if they need to be brought back here with us. We do have their best interests at heart, Karla, and we will look after both you and your family."

"We just want to make sure you're safe first, sweetie," Helena said, stretching over to pat my hand reassuringly.

"I don't understand," I said quietly, looking down at my fiddling hands. "Can't we go get them now if they're in danger?"

"You were the Starkorf's target—not your family," Kurt said, rubbing the stubble over his jaw. "We have already discussed this and find it to be the best option for now. The fact that Raven and other Starkorfs were in search of you near here is alarming. We must refrain from leaving for a while in case they have the woods and surrounding areas on surveillance. If they find out where we are hiding, we would be in a bit of a pinch. Our main focus right now is to find out why they are after you and to protect you from them."

"This is what your parents would want most Karla," Helena said, placing her hand to her chest. "Any mother or father would just want their child to be safe and this is what we think is the safest option for you."

"In only a short time Karla, we will reunite you with your family. Please be patient with us for a little while longer. For your own sake let us help and teach you to defend yourself," Seth said, rubbing his thumb along Helena's hand affectionately.

The thought of seeing my parents was a painful reminder of everything I had once took for granted. I realized how much I appreciated my family and friends, especially Sarah and Paul. Now I was being given the chance to go back to my home and to see my parents, to be reunited with them.

Shouldn't I be as civilised as possible and agree to do some training so I can see them? Why would I say no to that? I am too fearful to run away again and if this were my only option, then why would I disagree? Is it because I am scared of the ability they tell me I have? Could it be all the fear and uncertainty I now carry? Or is it because slowly everything they speak of—Lucas's Shield, my healing hand, attacking Starkorfs—I have now all witnessed for myself. Maybe I am simply trying to avoid the evidence that I too might have the ability of a Shielder. Because if that is proven, then I cannot deny the words they speak or the reality of this world I have been dragged into. If I can produce a Shield, I am exactly as they say I am and there will never be a normal life for me to go back to, I thought in despair.

I simply nodded my head, almost dazed. I felt like a child being told what was best for me. *But I am still a child with the chance to see my parents again,* and that thought alone drove me to agree to their plan. "The sooner I learn, the quicker I can go to my parents?" I asked, still clutching at my chest in pain.

"Yes Karla, we promise," Seth answered, determination in his hazel eyes. "And we will all help you."

Helena stood, raising her hand in a gesture for me to join her. She gave me a gentle hug, making me feel somewhat better as she embraced me. I slowly raised my hand to her back, finding myself to be almost crying. It was like the touch of my mother—only Helena was slightly smaller. I could still find the same concern and comfort radiate from her as her jasmine perfume brushed past my nose. Seth placed his hand on my shoulder, giving me a small nod of reassurance before putting his other hand on Helena.

"Stop smothering her, muffin," Seth gently teased, taking his hand off my shoulder. Helena released me, nodding in agreement. She gave me a faint smile as she blinked back tears. Her eyes reflected my own. I gave her a small smile in response, trying to make it look as convincing as I could. The pity in her eyes however made my lips go crooked as I tried not to cry. Still, the thought of my past life now seemed so distant, and I buried the memories as I tried to regain control of my composure.

Suzumiya walked into the room looking between everyone guardedly. "Come on kid, you're with me," she said, hands on her hips. Chris stood not too far behind Suzumiya chewing idly on gum and blowing bubbles. I wasn't sure whether their relationship was of the romantic kind or simply friendship, either way they seemed very close.

Suzumiya followed Chris as they walked towards the training room on the left. After one more reassuring look from both Helena and Seth, I followed them. The large room appeared the same as it had the last time I saw it, except now it seemed even more intimidating. I looked over the equipment as I stood on the first step. After walking down the stairs it seemed even larger than it had when I was looking down on it. The room echoed as Suzumiya directed Chris to put certain things in their specific places.

I felt out of place in the room as I looked over the fitness equipment. I found it difficult hitting a ball with a tennis racket let alone punching a small sack of sand. The little bumps in my arms were a sad excuse for muscles and I only felt worse when I gazed at Suzumiya's toned figure—she looked like she was a world-class boxer.

"For the first week nobody will be interrupting us, so it's all ours," Suzumiya mused.

"In other words *you're* all hers!" Chris teased. Suzumiya looked at him and his grin vanished within seconds.

She took her red jumper off revealing her toned stomach in a fitted orange tank top that cut off at her belly button. Every muscle in her stomach was perfectly aligned, making me feel insecure instantly at the sight. She placed her jumper down on a chair and gazed at me, annoyed as I stumbled further into the room. I tried stretching the purple sleeveless shirt I wore, hoping it would cover my not-so-chiselled stomach.

I wrapped my hands around my stomach feeling insecure and intimidated as Suzumiya fluttered about carrying heavy equipment. Chris sat down, tapping along to his own beat with low thuds on the back of the chair.

"Okay, let's get started," Suzumiya ordered with hungry eyes, reminding me of a tiger ready to pounce on its prey.

Suzumiya instructed me to do a variety of exercises I was unfamiliar with: push-ups, crunches, and weights. She continued this for the next hour, demanding more and more from me as I struggled under her watchful eye. If I collapsed on a certain routine, she would then tell me to do it twice more until I perfected it. Sweat soaked my purple sleeveless shirt and long dark pants. With only a moment's break, I consumed as much water as I could from the bottle Chris handed me. I emptied the bottle and looked around the walls for a tap.

Chris knew what I was after and pointed me in the direction of a tap, his arms folded in amusement. I gulped from the stream, not even bothering about my manners. It tasted a little muddy so I assumed it was tank water. I didn't care though. I knew little about exercise, but one thing I did know is that if you drank too much water you'd get stitches. However my body thirsted for water and I couldn't stop.

Suzumiya clapped her hands together and I knew my short break was over. I finished gulping and quickly let the gushing stream pour over my face and soak into my hair. I tried ringing my hair out while walking the gruelling steps over to Suzumiya. My legs felt like weights and my arms ached from just raising them above my shoulders. I twisted my hair draining as much of the cool water off as I could. Now my head felt as heavy as my legs did and my body was slightly swaying, unbalanced.

"Chris, your hair-band, please," Suzumiya demanded. Chris's snoring stopped with a loud snort and his beady eyes were dazed as he focused on us.

"My what?" he asked rubbing at his green eyes and thick eyebrows.

"Your hair-band!" Suzumiya repeated with impatience.

Seth walked over to us fidgeting with the back of his hair and pulling at his locks. He handed it to Suzumiya and his dreads unfolded down the sides of his face. She passed the hair-band to me and I hesitantly took it out of her hand. It was slightly dampened from what I assumed to be sweat. I looked back over at Chris who was in a new position: sprawled out across a mat trying to get some beauty sleep.

"Come on now, let's start your actual training!" Suzumiya exclaimed slyly, picking up a pair of boxing gloves.

"Let's... what?" I asked, feeling the color drain from my face in fatigue.

"Training?! We were only warming up before," Suzumiya replied coolly. My body buckled with despair and defeat. At the thought of giving up, I visualised my parents. *I must do my very best so I can see them soon,* I reminded myself. I dragged my feet as I traced her footsteps over to the punching bag, thinking of a reunion with my parents. *This is what I must to do, if only to say goodbye to the life I once knew.*

By midday it was lunch, and I needed Chris to carry me up the stairs. "I didn't know she was working you so hard. Maybe I should've said something," he admitted faintly.

"Next time stay awake and plead my case," I answered, only half-joking.

He responded with a cheesy grin, then, "sorry little buddy."

We made it to the top of the stairs where he let me go. I followed them slowly into the dining room, dragging one foot in front of the other. Whatever was cooking smelt great and I realized how hungry I really was.

Chris made his presence known, bouncing around the kitchen happily. "Please tell me you're making some 'Macaroni Hell's'?" he mused, like a little kid.

"Only for you," Helena answered, peering around the corner with a bright smile. I reached the door and placed my hands on the frame, dragging the rest of my corpse-like body up to it. I somehow managed to walk to a chair, collapsing into it like a slinky. I sat in an awkward position, too tired to even make myself comfortable.

Everyone else had started drifting into the kitchen, laughing and teasing each other. Lunch was served in the center of the table and consisted of salads, sandwiches, homemade biscuits, fruit, and Chris's own special serving of macaroni. My stomach growled at the sight of the food. Lucas was last to arrive and took his seat next to me. Chris was on my other side with his face full of cheesy spirals and a little bit of the sauce in his hair. I stared at him in amazement wondering how he could chow down so quickly when he hadn't done anything but sleep all day.

"Don't stare for too long or he'll eat you too," Lucas said, somewhat seriously. My trance shattered, I turned to look at Lucas.

"Is this coming from previous experience?" I enquired.

"No, but I'm not stupid enough to sit close enough and take that risk," Lucas retorted. He took a plate and selected a little bit of each of the foods on display.

"How's your training going, love?" Seth asked as he passed Suzumiya a bowl of salad.

"She vomited like two times," Chris erupted, smothering the whole table with macaroni while he laughed at me.

Suzumiya was quick to correct him: "actually, she threw up *three* times. You were asleep most the time."

 I slid down in my chair, ashamed of how limited my fitness level was. Everybody started commenting on the first time Suzumiya personally trained each of them, so I didn't feel as embarrassed.

"Here." Lucas slid his plate over in front of me and began piling food onto another plate for himself.

As I thanked him I noticed dirt smudged across his face with a small leaf poking out from his sandy blonde hair. I pulled the piece of leaf out, examining it and showing it to Lucas. Lucas simply shrugged, unfazed, and continued piling his plate with food. *Has Lucas been in the woods?* I wondered.

I looked around the table, eager to understand how their group functioned. Kurt sat at the end of the table with a book in one hand and his fork in the other, reading intently. I could see that he was ultimately in charge, but it was Helena and Seth who had taken the role of the parental figures to the group. Everyone had a role to play, and I had already learned the hard way that Suzumiya was the trainer. Chris seemed to be wherever Suzumiya was, whatever his role was. I had no idea what Ashley did yet as I had only spent a brief amount of time with him. For the rest of the lunch I stayed silent, trying to understand how Lucas fitted into it all.

Once everyone had finished their meals, Helena and Seth began collecting the plates. I dreaded what would be expected of me next, but thankfully it was Kurt who summoned me. "Come with me Karla," he said, guiding me back to the training room. "I am going to start teaching you how to use your Shield," he continued solemnly. I followed him down the stairs and stood in front of him, unsure what to expect. "Producing your Shield is a stimulation that begins in the mind," Kurt explained, raising his hand to his temple. "You must first imagine and visualise your Shield surrounding you before it can physically manifest itself. At first it may be extremely difficult and tiring, but you will grow and adapt with practice."

He took a measured breath before continuing in a sombre tone. "Don't show anyone your ability that isn't a part of this household. Strangers do not take well to our ability. Now I want you to try it but remember this is only your first time—your Shield will probably break the first few attempts."

I stared at Kurt, trying to absorb his words. The enormity of my situation swirled in my mind, making it difficult to focus on his instructions. *I hope they are wrong,* I thought. *I hope I can't do it. I don't believe in such a thing. I can't possibly have some ability like theirs. But if they are wrong, can I simply go back to a normal life? Will everything be the same as it once was? How could I possibly be the same after all I have seen?* I shuddered, remembering the violence I saw before, closing my eyes and pushing the images away. *If I fail I cannot see my parents,* I reminded myself. Now calm, I opened my eyes to find Kurt staring at me intently. I nodded my head, agreeing that I was now ready to attempt the task.

"Think of it as a big rubber band spreading over your body. Visualise it. As soon as you do that it will manifest," Kurt explained calmingly.

I closed my eyes, trying to imagine a bubble around me. I heard an astonished gasp come from Kurt as I continued visualising the bubble. My head felt heavy like my mind was made from metal. All noise was blocked out, leaving me to concentrate in silence. I felt the weight of my mind get heavier as I focused.

I opened my eyes as Kurt's voice finally broke through to me: "Stop, Karla. Stop it!" He was yelling but he sounded distant. I began to drop the image of my Shield from my mind, struggling to take in his words. My Shield stayed projected with brown ripples surrounding me. I stared at them in astonishment as the Shield combust outwards from me. The windows near the ceiling on the right shattered onto the exercise equipment beneath. Kurt held his hands in front of him protectively as he was thrown back into the air. My knees collapsed under me and Kurt's figure slumping to the ground was the last thing I saw before everything turned to black.

The walls were a dusty pink, complementing the roses that scented the air. The floor was made up of white tiles and the roof was comprised of mirrors that shone down on me, reflecting my astonishing beauty. My hair was arranged in a neat bun, with a few strands of hair blowing against my face. The dress I wore flowed out to my ankles and the green gem that was glistening on my necklace was all that adorned my shoulders. The strapless green dress wrapped itself around my body, complementing the brown of my hair and the green that shone in my eyes. I radiated a beauty that was not of this world.

"Karla, my dear, you look stunning." Uncle Kyle crossed the room elegantly in a white suit with his red hair slicked back tidily. He grabbed my arms and started spinning me in circles, dancing slowly to music my ears could not hear.

"Thank you, Uncle Kyle." My voice was clipped and proper, as if I were royalty. "And to what do I owe this honour?"

"Can an uncle not request the presence of his niece after so long a separation?" He swept his arm over my head gracefully and I spun under it like a fairy.

"Not when he has not seen her for ten years because of an argument he had with her parents."

"I've come here to mend what I have broken, my dear Karla."

"Then you should make amends with my parents. Their acceptance of your apology will also be my own. It is them that have suffered because of this battle, not I."

"I had to see you first, child. They do not believe in my quest, Karla. If your uncle asked you to partake in one simple task could you complete it?"

"Dear uncle, have you forgotten the trust we once had when I was a child? I will do as you please, and with relish, to know that my uncle is back." My dress swayed around my legs, the unknown material shining with an unearthly beauty.

He pulled me closer into a hug and whispered kindly into my ear: "You must distance yourself from that boy my sweet, sweet Karla. He is not the one you seek." The elegant tapping of my heels stopped and I dropped my hands from his at the mention of Lucas.

"My dear uncle, I am not allying myself with anyone. I am like I

91

have been for the last century: alone, and keeping myself strong. I will not let any outsider take what is mine, nor take my heart."

"But he has already, child. You must stay distant or it will end badly and you will lose all memory of what you've been looking for all these years. It is impossible for you to be together. While you're blinded, others can see the fate of this union. Dear Karla, he is not like you. You must kill him sooner or later. Do not fall for your prey."

"Indeed I know what it is I seek uncle. I will find Aeisha and if it is he who can help then I will accept his services."

"While you seek the Immortal Blades of Aeisha, they also seek for Borac and Sheliste. When you find Aeisha, your journey will have to stop… you cannot have him Karla. Aeisha will stop you before you have the chance and savour his blood when you cut a wound deep into his chest. Leave him now," my uncle said to me pleadingly. I thought of the three Immortal Blades that he referred to, unconcerned about his warning. Aeisha, Borac, and Sheliste will all become my property very shortly.

"Karla," Lucas's voice brushed past my ears like the whisper of an angel. I looked behind me to find Lucas in a green suit made of the same material that I wore. A black rose was poking out the pocket of his vest and he held a red one in his hand. His sandy blonde hair brushed against his pale face when he stepped into the glow of the moonlight. "Karla my love, let us go."

I looked back at my uncle but couldn't find him anywhere. I walked over to Lucas and accepted the hand that he offered. He presented me with a red rose, which I accepted with a light kiss, wrapping myself around him longingly.

"Where were you, my love? You have been gone for a long time," I said, eloquently.

"Nowhere, my love. Let us leave," Lucas said with a smile.

A loud bang had shattered the glass above us and a familiar looking man dropped onto the floor silently. He wore a black jacket with his torn up jeans, showing a bare chest with many scars. I saw that it was Lucas. There was two of him.

"What are you doing here? You are not meant to be here!" the Lucas by my side exclaimed— my Lucas. The other one had pulled a sword from the sheath he held. The blade was pure silver and a red gem sparkled on the handle.

"Borac!" I gasped. I instinctively reached for Aeisha, my Immortal Blade, but she was not there. The blades that I have been searching for—Aeisha—had not yet been found. I was defenseless against the Immortal Blade he held: Borac. I could no longer even visualise what my two blades looked like: their fine details and ornate carvings.

There was a silent scuttle and my hand had left Lucas's while the other intruder plunged Borac into his chest. Lucas was thrown to the floor with a loud gasp. The other, evil Lucas smiled over him, pleased. When the sword was pulled from his chest, blood filled the tile cracks and seeped over to my white heels, staining them red. Lucas's body was motionless on the ground and his eyes were dull. He gasped for air one last time, and then there was no movement.

Without hesitation the other Lucas ran over to me while I simply stood there shocked. Borac pierced me in the chest, piercing right through to the skin on my back. I felt my heart being pierced by the metal and the sword pulsed with my dwindling heartbeat, draining me of life with a savage hatred. The dark brown eyes of Lucas were wild as he smiled.

"Now I come for Sheliste," he whispered.

But Sheliste no longer exists… I thought, as I hit the ground.

Chapter Thirteen - Accusations

"*H*eisha!" I gasped, clutching at my chest where I had dreamed of Borac so vividly piercing into me. I pushed back my long hair that was plastered to my face with sweat and tried to take in my surroundings. I was hunched over on the floor of the training room. Kurt lay far across from me against a wall, gasping as he also clutched at his ribs. I saw that his eyebrow was bleeding.

Suzumiya and Chris came running into the room, their faces a mixture of horror and confusion. Suzumiya's eyes fell upon Kurt. Her eyes narrowed as she looked between us in anger.

"What have you done?!" Suzumiya yelled, gesturing at Kurt. Within an instant she had jumped over the second floor, landing on her feet in a cat-like stance. She ran at me while pulling out a knife that was strapped to her thigh.

"You're one of them!" she screamed wildly. I quickly found my feet and scurried towards one of the hanging punching bags. I moved just in time before Suzumiya was slamming every bit of her body into it with loud forceful blows. She swept against the ground gracefully and flipped back through the air effortlessly.

A forceful flick of her arm sent her knife slicing through the air. She had a grace in her movement like a dancer rehearsing her steps. The knife punctured the punching bag, narrowly missing me. I couldn't see any part of the blade, only the handle that was sticking out.

She ran to the knife, dislodging it viciously so grains of sand began to pour out. "Stop this Suzumiya!" Chris was yelling. I was vaguely aware of other voices in the background, but I had to give Suzumiya my full attention as she lunged at me suddenly. With an impossible speed, she closed the distance that was between us, forcing me to dodge violently from left to right in an effort to avoid the knife she thrust in my direction. Before I knew what was happening, I jumped over her. I was now behind her standing in a defensive stance, surprised that my body had reacted in such a way. One of my fists was in front of me, the other at my side.

She traced my jump and was already moving towards me. My body moved before I even knew what it was doing. She swept the blade in front of her, aiming for my chest once more. I felt the tip of the blade graze my chest vertically, tearing my shirt into two pieces of fabric that hung in tatters by my side. With one big lunge I was near where the chair was, grabbing it by the leg and forcefully smashing it into the ground so one splintered leg was left in my hand: *a weapon*.

"I'm not one of them!" I shouted in a pleading tone.

I didn't understand any of the things I was doing until my body had already done them for me. I was now near the punching bag where Suzumiya had thrown her knife. It still spilled sand, bursting like a fountain. She took another stab at me and before I knew it, I was hanging from the chain that attached the punching bag to the roof. I had nothing to stand on—I was only relying on one arm—yet somehow I was perfectly upright and balanced.

"Liar!" Suzumiya shouted savagely, as she threw the knife up towards me. I swept the wooden leg over my face and the knife hammered to the ground. She grabbed me by the leg, pulling me to the ground. A loud squeal echoed through the large shed as we rolled onto the ground. Suzumiya took the opportunity to attack, but somehow she was thrown off me with a heavy smack. I grabbed the wooden leg in my hand ready for her next attack. Instead of Suzumiya, it was Seth standing in front of me—protectively. His face was hard as he towered over Suzumiya. It was so odd to see such an expression of disgust on the usually smiling gentle-giant. His eyebrows knitted together and his lips tightened into an expression of contempt.

Suzumiya was on the ground in front of him, slowing her breathing as she looked up in confusion. I dropped the piece of wood and stared at my hands, replaying in my mind what I had just done and what I was capable of. My chest was bleeding slightly from where she cut it previously, and a few black bruises were rising in my arms from where she must have hit me.

"Enough, Suzumiya!" Kurt yelled, as Helena helped him from the floor. He still clutched at his ribs, wincing in pain. I looked around, finding that nearly everyone else in the group had been there the entire time. Chris stood shocked with his hands on his head, before slowly walking over to Suzumiya.

"Kurt!" Suzumiya exclaimed. Her voice was filled with panic. Ashley ran down the stairs, unaware of what has transpired between

Suzumiya and I. He came to Helena's side and collected Kurt's weight from her, supporting him effortlessly.

"Here," Lucas said, standing next to me. He looked away as he offered me his leather jacket. I looked back down at my chest, realising my shirt had been cut open, exposing my pink bra. Embarrassed, I took the leather jacket and wrapped it around myself. His dark eyes froze on Suzumiya angrily for a moment. He looked down at me trying to soften his eyes, but his jaw stayed clenched.

Lucas offered his hand to me. I looked between Suzumiya's disorientated face and Lucas's soft eyes as I accepted his gloved hand. He helped me stand, as I stayed silent, still trying to absorb all that just happened only a few minutes ago.

"Suzumiya, get out," Kurt ordered authoritatively, hovering over her like a black shadow.

"But Kurt, she is one of them! She hurt you—..."

"Get out!" Seth interrupted, still standing in front of me protectively.

Chris went to help her stand but she simply slapped his hand away, storming out of the room. On her way to the stairs, she picked up the knife she had tried plunging into my chest and looked back at Kurt.

"Kurt. You saw what she could do. She's not what she says she is," Suzumiya said, forcefully trying to regain the control she once had on the situation.

"What I saw, Suzumiya, was you trying to kill my guest. If you ever try to harm her in any way again, I will kick you out of this house. Understood?" His voice was tainted with frustration when he spoke, an unusual tone for him.

"Understood."

She left the room silently and Kurt didn't turn until she was gone. He looked at me as if I were a lost puppy he had just found—as if he was wondering what to do with me.

"I want you to be honest with me Karla. No lies," Kurt said. Ashley, still holding him up, looked intently between his mother and father. Seth had moved to the side so he was not in Kurt's view, leaving me vulnerable in front of their peering eyes.

"I'm not lying about anything. No one is more shocked about what just happened, than me. I don't know how I did any of that," I exclaimed defensively. Kurt's eyes held mine for a long time.

"You've never trained like this before?" he questioned, though it sounded like he was working some other equation out in his head.

96

"Never. I've never even taken a self-defense class before." I looked back at Lucas who also stared at me intently. I looked down to my hands, trying to figure out how I was capable of such movement.

"You mentioned Misfeata's Blades. What do you know of Aeisha?" Kurt questioned.

"Aeisha? I don't know. I just had a dream about my uncle speaking of Aeisha to me. I don't know..." I said, puzzled by all the questions. The dream I had woken up from suggested to me that Aeisha was not one sai, but two: a pair. The blades had a green gem between the blade and the beginning of the handle. I remembered Uncle Kyle warning me of Lucas. I hadn't seen my uncle for years, since I was only little. My hand clutched at my chest again remembering the other Lucas who had put Borac—Tyran's blade—into my heart. I looked at Lucas, desperately trying to understand the message of my dream.

"All three Elders had their own blades. As you know, the youngest—Sebastian's—vanished when he did and over time no one can remember what it looks like, but it is remembered by the name of Sheliste—..." Kurt said, before I interrupted.

"*Sheliste*. He mentioned he was after Sheliste in my dream. He had Borac and Aeisha and now he is searching for Sheliste," I said, trying to be helpful so as to deter their accusatory looks.

"Who was looking for Sheliste?" Kurt said, slowly pushing Ashley away so he could stand on his own.

I looked down, confused as to who it really was that was after the Immortal Blades. I then looked at Lucas sadly, remembering the dream vividly. "You were," I said to him quietly. Lucas's gaze froze on my face. He simply stared as if his spirit had left his shell. Finally he blinked, his jaw tightening in anger at the accusation.

"I think that's enough for today," Helena said, wrapping the jacket around me tighter and edging me onto the steps.

"Are you alright, love?" Seth asked with concerned eyes.

"Yes," I said hesitantly, remembering the gentle-giant throwing Suzumiya off me for my protection. "...Thank you Seth," I continued, dipping my head in gratitude before leaving the room.

Helena escorted me to my room and found me another shirt. She began to clean the scratch that was on my chest.

"What happened?" I asked Helena, rubbing at my temples. I had a pounding migraine as I remembered the nightmare. I was attempting to project my Shield.

"I don't know. When your Shield was projected, it was visible. I have never seen a visible Shield," she answered, wiping at my chest with a cotton bud.

"You mean I actually did it?" I was torn between emotions; mostly I was relieved that I was actually capable of the ability everyone said I had, but I was also scared of it. *How can I go home now for good if I too am a Shielder?*

"You don't understand Karla. Shields aren't visible. We have never seen anything like that," Helena said, fixing a bandage on my chest.

"So what happened after that?" I asked, confused at this revelation.

"Your Shield shattered as if you had no control of it. It was too overwhelming for Kurt's Shield and he couldn't protect himself fully. After a moment of your Shield combusting, you fell to the floor unconscious—but for only a few moments" she added quickly, gathering the used cotton balls.

"Will Suzumiya come for me again?" I asked coarsely, as it began to sink in that she actually tried to kill me.

"No love," she put her hand to my face reassuringly. "Suzumiya will not come near you. She was very much out of line. Everyone will look after you. I'm going to let you rest, but if you find you can't sleep feel free to look through the books in the lounge-room. Perhaps you will find something interesting," she said with a faint smile. After giving me a new, long-sleeved, blue shirt she left the room.

I tried to sleep but with little luck. My body ached from the training I endured that morning, and my mind replayed the memory of my fight with Suzumiya in an endless loop. The capability that my body possessed frightened me.

I walked to my mirror, lifting my shirt and peeling the patch off. I have not yet seen the damage Suzumiya left. To my surprise, there was nothing. No scratch, no scar. I frowned at the sight, questioning how it was possible for me to heal so quickly. Remembering Helena's suggestion, I slipped through the hall to the lounge-room in search of a book. *Perhaps one will contain the answers I'm looking for*, I thought to myself. I searched through the books in the living room, listening to the clatters of dishes coming from the kitchen in the background. A lot of the books were the size of encyclopaedias and I could only imagine Sarah laughing at me for considering a book so thick.

My shoulders sagged at the thought of my friend. I missed Sarah's rants about her love life; I missed her attention-seeking ways. I always frowned upon her antics, but now I felt a smile tug at my lips. I missed Greg and his awkward companionship. I missed Paul—all those years I had known him as nothing more than an acquaintance. I had distanced myself purposefully. I smiled again. Maybe I was so cynical towards him because whether I wanted to admit it to myself or not, I was attracted to him.

My fingers trailed along the spine of each book, savouring their individualistic design. Every book I touched resonated with the feeling of knowledge, importance, and age. I flicked through one book, which was someone's journal. It was a Shielder's journal from the 1760's, talking about the raids her group had been involved with whilst killing the Starkorfs. One page I had flicked to spoke of when her son had been murdered and his blood had splattered across her face. Every night she felt it on her. Every night she tried to scrub off the blood that wasn't there, the blood she could still feel. Some of the pages spoke of when she battled alongside Misfeata, admiring how graceful and wise she was. Eight pages spoke about the battle she had witnessed between the siblings—Misfeata and Tyran—and how neither of them won, nor came out of it unwounded. Within minutes Misfeata would heal. The last page spoke of how Misfeata suddenly vanished. No one had known it but through the war Misfeata was pregnant, something that was thought to be impossible. When she delivered the baby she gave it to one of the other women in the group to look after. Two days after that Misfeata and Tyran had left, giving the impression that they would be back to fight their war.

The woman that wrote the journal was called Myra and her last words questioned whether they would indeed be back. Myra had been given the ability—Shielding—yet she was still scared of being slaughtered in this ongoing massacre of a war. Her group was having a confrontation with the Starkorfs the next day and she feared for her life even though it's what she had been doing for years. I flicked through the pages for further entries, but there were none.

I put the book back in its position and continued scanning for something I could read in my room.

"What was in your dream?" Lucas asked, startling me. He was slumped casually against the wall behind me, his hands in the pockets of his dark blue jeans. My dream was vivid but I couldn't bring myself to try and interpret its meaning. I looked back into Lucas's dark eyes, almost ashamed that I had seen his death. Flashes of his stabbed body along with Uncle Kyle's words of warning drew pain to my face. I looked away, putting my head back in the books and reading over their labels.

"You died..." I said, saddened. "I died."

"How did we die?" he asked, taking a bite into a red apple. The crunching noise filled the room with sound.

"You killed us. Well it was someone who posed as you. But he looked like you," I said, recalling the two separate versions of Lucas. As I talked, I noticed the books were in chronological order. Over the years, the more recent books had gotten thinner and weren't as nicely decorated or preserved as the rest.

"Why was I asking for the three Immortal Blades?" he asked, taking another large bite out of the apple.

"I don't know, Lucas," I said in reply, somewhat frustrated at his probing questions. "I don't want to talk about it anymore."

"Well, I do. You were trying to suggest something in there, accuse me of something..."he trailed off, annoyed.

"No, I wasn't," I said angry now. "I told them what I saw in my dream. That is all it was, Lucas. It was a dream." I picked one of the books from the shelf and stormed past him. I wrapped my hands around the book, holding it to my chest as I brushed past him. His face was hard as he moved to the side, letting me push past him with no further questions.

Chapter Fourteen - Imposter

I walked down the hallway, savouring the flickers of sunlight shining in from the small windows. I looked down at the book I had picked from the shelf and thought of it as a mockery of my situation: *Romeo and Juliet*. I threw the book onto the bed and flopped down next to it in defeat.

I stared out the window, trying to ignore the conflicting thoughts fighting for attention in my head. *I feel like I am going insane without all the answers I need. Why is this all happening to me?* The sunny day was too good an opportunity to miss. I walked to the lounge-room where Seth and Kurt were deep in discussion. They both looked up as I came to a stop in the hallway.

"Can I go outside to think for a little while? I won't go far," I promised, fidgeting with my hands. Kurt gave me a small nod and Seth also nodded with a light smile and warm eyes.

I walked past the training room and saw Chris and Suzumiya sweeping pieces of glass and arranging the broken things into a pile. Chris looked between Suzumiya and me with worry. She narrowed her eyes on me before continuing what she was doing.

After opening the door, the sun hit me and the feeling was like electricity on my skin. It had been such a long time since I could enjoy such a simple thing. I lay in the grass like a snake trying to heat its body. The sky was cloudless and there was little wind to scratch at my face, making it as peaceful as I hoped it would be.

"You must distance yourself from that boy my sweet, sweet Karla. He is not the one you seek…" Uncle Kyle's warning resonated in my head. *What does that even mean? Why was there two of Lucas in my dream? Is there another person out there that looks like Lucas? Am I meant to be seeking out someone…?* I worried. The sun's light was suddenly blocked, leaving me in someone's shadow. I sat up only to see Lucas looking up at the sky.

"What are you doing?" I questioned, moving myself back into the sun. He sat down where his shadow was, dropping to my side.

"I'm sorry about before," he said, stretching his legs and placing his hands behind his back for support.

I accepted his apology, annoyed at myself, as I knew I too was out of line. "No. I may have been in the wrong too and I am sorry for that. All of this is still so overwhelming for me." I curled my legs up to my stomach, letting my chin rest on them.

"I know," he said, his eyes sad. They looked light brown— almost golden— in the sun, compared to their usual dark shade.

Lucas stood up, looking at the sky again. "Karla," he began gently. I opened my eyes and propped myself onto my elbow so I could look up into his gentle face. He offered his hand to me. "I want to show you something."

I brushed the grass off my legs, accepting his hand.

"I want you to try to project your Shield again. It's not something you should be scared of. I can help you learn to control it," Lucas offered soothingly, as he took in my worried face.

"But I hurt Kurt last time," I said, ashamed.

"You won't hurt me or yourself," he promised, grabbing my other hand. I looked down at the leather glove that held mine, comforted as his right thumb traced over the side of my hand.

"Visualise it," Lucas said.

I gave him a faint nod, remembering how Kurt tried to teach me before. *Think of it as a rubber band. Visualise it.* I closed my eyes, trying to visualise it in my head. *Think of a bubble that's wrapping itself around me.* The weight in my head started getting heavier and all sound was lost. The bubble was getting bigger, wrapping itself around my body slowly. The weight was getting heavier, compressing on my brain. I felt a heavy yank on my arm and the weights were lifted. My ears regained hearing.

"Karla. Stop... Stop!"

My body was being rocked back and forth. Lucas's face was close to mine, worry leaving his face as I opened my eyes. He was so close. When he took a breath his chest was close to mine. He gave an exasperated breath of relief, blowing the smell of mint into my face. "Karla..." Lucas loosened his grips on my arms, relieved. "Karla?"

"What is it?" I said, leaning my weight backwards so I wasn't so intensely under his gaze.

"Oh, thank goodness. Why didn't you stop the first time I told you to?" he asked sternly.

I looked around, unsure what he meant. I hadn't heard him say anything.

"I only heard you ask me once," I said, looking over his shoulder at the wind rustling through the tall grass. I felt the irritating buzz of my headache coming back.

"You think I told you to stop only once? I have been asking it of you for the last couple of minutes. You seemed to be unconscious, but with your Shield still projected."

I slowly sat down on the grass again, hearing drums echo in my head. "I didn't know," I admitted. *Why am I losing consciousness if I use my ability?*

Lucas sat beside me picking at the long green grass. "When Kurt told me your Shield is visible and colored I didn't believe him but now I have seen it myself. I've never seen anything like it." He was ruffling up his hair, deep in thought.

"Karla...you're amazing," he said evenly.

I blushed at the compliment, dipping my head as I felt my cheeks go red. For some reason my heart now pounded at Lucas's words. I looked back over him, taking in all of him: his sharp squared jaw, prominent cheek bones, tensed shoulders, deep, dark brown eyes, and sandy blonde hair. Even the masculine tone of his voice; when he was angry it was rough and dominating but when he is with me as of late, it seemed to be that of an angel's, ringing in my ears soothingly.

"I don't think so," I shyly disagreed before he noticed how entranced I was by him. *Why is my heart fluttering like this?* I asked myself. Then, I had another question: "How come you were able to touch me? You were shaking me while my Shield was up...how?"

"What do you mean?" Lucas looked over his shoulder as if he were scoping out the area to make sure no one was near.

"Well, I thought no one would be able to penetrate a Shield." I felt childish asking.

"It's not completely impenetrable—like all things, the strength of your ability is based on practice. If another Shielder is stronger, they can use the energy of their Shield to overpower yours. I'm sorry I had to do so with you but I didn't know what else to do. It is why you probably have a faint headache now."

"How did you know that?" I asked, rubbing at my head. I smiled shyly at the thought that Lucas could read my mind. "The great thing about being a Shielder is our capabilities of recovery. A massive amount of energy is stored in our bodies as a result of our ability to Shield. Energy has healing properties and propels our healing process if any harm is done to us. Your headache will be gone in no time," he said reassuringly.

"Come on, try it again. You won't learn if you don't try!" Lucas continued encouragingly. He turned himself so he was now facing me, with his legs crossed. "Give me your hands." He held his hands out to me.

"What? Why?" I pulled my hands up to my chest, embarrassed at how quickly my heart jumped at the suggestion.

"I want you to put pressure on my hands when you start to project your Shield so I know when something's changing. If you go unconscious like you did before your grip will loosen," Lucas explained.

I turned myself towards him, placing my hands in his. His leather gloves felt warm as I took them gently, preparing myself for another attempt.

"Okay," I said, closing my eyes as he squeezed my hand tightly. I tried to pull them out but his grip was too firm. "What?" I stared at him, still trying to pull my hands back.

"Don't close your eyes. Keep them open. Be conscious and aware of your surroundings. Concentrate on me." He readjusted himself into a straightened pose. I stared into his eyes, trying to visualise the Shield at the same time. I felt the pressure of the weight resting on my head again. A thin piece of plastic wrapped itself around where I sat—only letting Lucas's hands enter. The thin veneer of plastic pulsed with purple ripples instead of the brown ones from before. I instinctively felt that the color was based on my mood. And right now, I was content, calm and mesmerised by the beauty of what I was producing.

I looked at Lucas; the Shield cut off around his hands and wrapped back around mine, forming an oddly shaped ball around me. It was amazing. Lucas looked over it from the outside, just as mesmerized as I was. I squeezed his hand gently, biting my lip. The pressure started getting heavier so I concentrated more on keeping up the fragile layer I had around me.

"Now release it," Lucas instructed, giving me a small nod of reassurance. I concentrated on the energy of my Shield, pulling it back into me. It felt like I was doing some form of exercise. My Shield disappeared silently. The wind picked up its pace once more, lifting my long hair.

I smiled and looked around where we were sitting. It somehow looked different even though I knew it hadn't changed. I feel like I was experiencing such a beautiful thing; the experience changed how I saw the world. Even the small, yellow flowers on the hill glowed with a radiance I hadn't noticed before.

"Did you see it Lucas? I did it!" I exclaimed excitedly, remembering the beauty of the colored ripples pulsating around me. I smiled at the memory. *That beauty came from me.*

"It was amazing. I've never seen anything like it," Lucas said with admiration. For once everything didn't seem so surreal to me. To have created such a beautiful thing from my core...it gave me an unfamiliar sense of belonging. Questions began to form in my mind, invading my sense of peace, but I pushed them away. I wanted to enjoy this moment. *This moment I have with Lucas.*

I gave him a sheepish smile, pulling away from his hands that still cradled mine. A low grunt came from Lucas as he regained his expressionless mask, but I noticed a slight shade of red across his cheeks.

"I think we should take you to Max. He might have a few ideas about your case. If he can help out or lend us some of his books, we might know what's different about you." He stood up, rubbing his hair.

"Who's Max?" I rose to my feet sleepily. Practicing my Shielding really drained a lot of energy from me.

"Max Jacket. He's an acquaintance of ours. He knows a lot of things that might come in handy. He could probably tell us why you're Shield is visible," Lucas said, as he stopped rubbing vigorously at his hair. *I wonder if he knows that is a habit of his when he is deep in thought.*

He looked into the distance before continuing. "Kurt might not go for it. Kurt and Max aren't exactly friends. They only go to each other for advice when they are desperate, but most of the time it's Kurt going to Max. They're not friends and I don't think they ever will be in this lifetime. Let's just say Max is highly untrustworthy and has cost us dearly in the past when we've approached him for favors," Lucas said, crossing his arms and looking out towards the woods intently.

"It doesn't matter. Now that I can use my Shield I want to see my parents. It has almost been two weeks now," I said as I began walking towards the house, pulling at my long fringe that blew in my face from the wind. Lucas was already by my side, still in thought. "I'll try again tomorrow. I'm kind of exhausted today."

"First can I show you something? Come on." Lucas grabbed my hand, pulling me slowly away from the door.

"Where are you taking me?" I asked, as Lucas led me to the side of the house.

"Just wait," he commanded.

I stared at Lucas's defined back beneath his black shirt as I followed him. Eventually he came to a stop at a large room next to the house. It had aged over time, with peeled paint and rusty nails holding it up. There were a few holes in it where it looked like pieces of wood had been kicked out.

Lucas opened the door with a serious expression on his face.

The room was dark and devoid of sunlight. He flicked on a switch and the room shot up with a florescent red light. The room was full of blades, crossbows, knives, daggers, bows, arrows; things I had never seen in my life before. Lucas's face was anxious as he looked to me for a reaction.

"A weapons room?" I asked, spinning myself in a slow circle. Lucas picked something up, examining it. It was something I had never seen before. It was a long stick with a blade at one end and a sphere on the other. I looked at the other sharp objects that were in the room and picked up something that was familiar to me. There were eight of them all different sizes, nicely polished.

"Nunchucks?" I asked surprised, letting it swing in my hand as if it were an extension of my fingers.

"They're Chris's. It seems like a stupid choice of weapon but he makes them look easy to use and he can actually inflict some serious damage with them," Lucas said, putting down the weapon he was holding and grabbing another. He now held a knife that was split into three sharp points, like a fork.

I hung the nunchucks back up, grabbing the next thing that caught my attention. It was a tiny knife, small enough for me to hide in my shoe. I touched the tip of it realising why it was in the weapons room and not in the kitchen. My finger started bleeding and I cursed under my breath for not taking my mum's lectures seriously. 'Don't touch the sharp ends,' she had always told me as a child.

"They say behind every great Shielder there's a weapon that defines them. Perhaps it's somewhat traditional because the three Elders were defined and recognised by their blades," Lucas lamented, putting down the oddly shaped blade he was holding and going over to a large collection of swords that were neatly hanging from the wall.

"Like Aeisha?" I asked curiously, thinking of the blades in my dream.

"Yes, like Aeisha. Most Shielders come across a weapon that they're drawn to, and that's the weapon they choose to partner with.

Shielders have a great bond with their weapons, like the three Elders and the three Immortal Blades. Our Shield is used to defend ourselves but the ability to draw energy from your weapon is truly the art of being a Shielder. So, most find it easier to bond with one weapon which is accustomed to their energy flow. The more you entwine your own energy into it, the easier it will become to use, and over time it will act as an extension of your arm... like an attachment of your soul and being." He cut the sword through the air and let it sway with his fingers, making the sword look as if it were dancing. He flipped it into the air before catching it by the handle, placing it respectfully back on the stand where it hung from the wall.

"Do you have a weapon yet?" I asked, still looking over the various items in the room.

"For now, no. I'm actually looking for my father's sword. The Starkorfs that invaded our home and killed my father and brother stole it. I want that to be my chosen weapon," Lucas said with determination, propping himself onto one of the benches in the room. Surprisingly, the room was quite large despite its deceivingly small exterior.

"What happened to your mother?" I asked quietly, pulling myself up onto the bench across from him.

"She died giving birth to me," Lucas said sadly, as he dipped his head to ruffle his hands through it. "Anyway, that's why I brought you in here." Quickly he changed the topic of his family and continued as if nothing was even said on the matter. "I wanted to see if you were drawn to anything. You don't have to choose anything from here. The item you're after might not even be in this room." Something in his tone sounded like an interrogative. My stomach turned at his words as I contemplated what he was really asking me. *Was he asking about my dream of Aeisha? Does Lucas suspect I know where Aeisha is because of my dream?*

He jumped off the bench and began pulling the drawers out revealing more blades, bows, even small spears and weapons.

"I don't plan on hurting anyone," I said, dazed by all the weapons that kept getting dragged out of their hiding places in the drawers. The room had gotten smaller as more weapons were sprawled out across the room. Too many, making me feel uncomfortable.

"Yeah, that's what everyone thinks. But when push comes to shove you'll be glad you have it with you," he said, offering his hand to me.

I scanned over all the sharp sticks, bottles of liquids, and blades;

not finding anything that took my interest. I walked back to the spot I first started from and looked back at Lucas who was tapping his finger on his mouth.

"Nothing," I said, overwhelmingly happy to know that I didn't desire something that could hurt another person.

"What about this?" Lucas asked, grabbing a blade that split into three points like a fork and offering it to me. "This is a sai." It looked very similar to Aeisha, who was also a pair of sais. I frowned looking at it. *Is Lucas suspicious that I am somehow involved with the missing Immortal Blade? Is this a mere coincidence or is he trying to dig for something?*

"It'll do you for now. I want you to have it everywhere you go— even when we see your parents." He rummaged through another drawer and pulled out what looked like a belt with hoops and pockets. "Don't worry. You won't be walking around with it in plain sight because this will be strapped to your hip. And I want you to have this in your garter at all times too." He picked up the little knife I had pricked my finger with and offered all three items to me, looking around to see if there was anything he had missed.

"Lucas I feel uncomfortable with all these," I said, looking over the weapons he offered. I rolled the sai around in my hand, turning it side to side, looking at the tips of it where the red light glinted. *This is very similar to Aeisha.* I looked back at Lucas, almost accusingly. Lucas stared back at me, his hands strapped across his chest.

"Is this a test?" I said questioningly. *This is to somehow test whether I knew anything of Aeisha's location*, I realized. I found guilt in Lucas's eyes and I knew I had guessed the truth.

I threw the weapons onto the bench in disgust, leaving the room and slamming the door behind me angrily. *Why is Lucas pestering me for information on Aeisha?*

Lucas followed me around the house, keeping at the same pace as my own. He was now at my side, trying to push himself in front of me in an effort to stop me. "Why won't you take this seriously, Karla?"

I looked up at the now cloudy sky, trying to block out the annoying buzz of his voice.

"Stop!" He slammed his hand against the side of the house. He was blocking my way, his face flushed with red. I tried ducking myself under his arm but to no avail. His faced leaned in to mine and I registered that his breath still smelt of mint; once again his lips were so close to my own.

"I just wanted to see whether it seemed familiar to you," he said, trying to reason with me. I tried to go around him but he was already a step ahead of me, blocking me once more.

"You are the most arrogant, inconsiderate person I have ever met," I said harshly, throwing my hands up in anger.

"Only an arrogant person can see the arrogance in someone else," he said childishly, before closing his eyes and reaching his hands out to me. "Wait, no, I didn't mean that, I am sorry Karla."

I raised my face to his, inhaling the mint that scented his mouth. "Leave me alone," I said, now sad at having trusted him.

Suddenly, my chest froze as if the air had been knocked out of me. I shrieked in pain. My lungs blistered and I heard the crack of one of my fragile ribs and clutched at it as I fell to the ground. I couldn't hear anything, but I felt Lucas picking me up. My heart squeezed under an unknown pressure, sending a blazing fire though my throat. I vomited over Lucas's shirt, seeing the red stain I had left on it instead of my stomach acid. Lucas was screaming out to me and was already running with me tightly folded in his arms. He ran me into the house as I continued to cough and splutter red on his face. *I can't breathe. Is it happening again?* I coughed another patch and felt a rupture in my head, my eyes showing me nothing but red and then black. *I am dying. Again.*

"Dear Karla, see what happens when you show affection to your prey? You cough your own blood instead of seeing theirs." Uncle Kyle looked the same as he had when we had danced so elegantly together in my previous dream. Everything was the same except for my dress, which was no longer a radiant green, and instead looked a misty black. Even my hair and lips were black, making my skin look like moonlight against the blackest of nights.

"What is it you wish to say to me now, Uncle? I told you once and I shall tell you again. He is no use to me dead, nor is he more to me than a companion." When I looked up at my uncle, I saw my own reflection in his eyes. It was not my voice that spoke. It was that of an older lady's.

"Karla, you have been distracted, you have forgotten. What do you plan to do if they get Aeisha? Can you handle being alone in this world? Not having Aeisha in your life would make you weak and vulnerable. Not to mention unrecognizable."

"I will find what is mine Uncle; I will be triumphant."

I tried to shout out to Uncle Kyle, to tell him it wasn't me. I felt like I had no control of my body, like I had been trapped in a glass box. Every word that passed through my lips silenced into nothing. I couldn't move or feel my body. "Let me out!" I shrieked. "Let me out!"

"What will you do if you can't find her though, Karla? What will you do then, if they have all three Blades? Your life is pointless."

"Dear, dear Uncle. It is my blood they seek, as I seek theirs. They will not curse me with everlasting death. No Starkorf, nor Shielder, shall take my life. I shall be..." my words finally came through in sync with the impostor's, the woman who had taken possession of my body: "...forever immortal."

Chapter Fifteen - Entrapment

"Leave me be!" I yelled, upset by the intruding hands that poked at me as I woke. Seth and Helena had their hands out towards me, both obviously concerned. I even saw a tear fall down Helena's face. I jumped up, unsettled by the grabbing hands. I was now standing on my bed, leaning back against the wall defensively. My shirt was covered in blood. I put my hand to the patch, staring at it, disorientated. *This is my blood.* I took the first deep breath I had taken since I came out of the darkness. As soon as the air hit my lungs I dropped into the bed; coughing out all the anger, frustration, pain, and uncertainty I felt overwhelm me.

"Karla," Seth soothed, slowly coming closer. I threw my arms around my body sobbing, trying to find an explanation to what my body has just endured.

"She just wouldn't stop," I coughed out in a huge, jagged breath. I thought of the woman in my dream that had possessed my body to speak with Uncle Kyle. It was my body, but I was an onlooker, trapped in my own mind. Everything that was said, were the thoughts of the unknown woman in my head. "She wouldn't leave me alone. I wanted to come out but she wouldn't let me!"

Seth stroked my hair and patted my back while I tried choking in burning breaths. Kurt burst through the door and was now by Seth's side with medical equipment. The room seemed so small it was tiny. I stared at it, feeling claustrophobic as I imagined the walls closing in. *Like the small glass box I was just trapped in.* Seth started patting down my forehead with a damp cloth while Helena took over comforting me. I flinched away from all of them who were trying to look after me. *No. This isn't what I want. I cannot trust these people.*

"Stop!" I said, flinching under Helena's embrace. "Just don't. Please."

"Karla we just want to help you," Seth said compassionately. I crept away from them, finding my back to the bed's frame. I clutched at my mouth, trying to steady my breaths as I felt they were escaping too quickly. I found myself panicking and gasping more and more for air. *What is happening to me?*

"Karla, please..." Seth pleaded, reaching for my hand as he tried to come closer.

"Just stop!" I spat out savagely, feeling the explosion of my uncontrolled Shield erupt from my body. Everyone was thrown into the wall across from me. Black ripples pulsed around me like suspended knives searching for a target. I felt no strain in my head and yet my Shield was no longer a little layer of plastic but a thick, glass ball.

Ashley burst into the room screaming for his mother. Both Kurt and Seth had been thrown through the wall, and I saw no movement from them. Ashley looked at me frantically and took in my Shield with a look of disgust.

Everything was wrong. He found his mother and quickly ripped the debris of the wall away from around her. "Mum, are you okay?" Ashley asked, pulling the plaster away from her hunched figure. She was bleeding from her arm. She strained to see her son; her glasses had been thrown off in the explosion.

What am I doing? I tried to stop, I tried to move my gaze, even my finger, but nothing would move. Suzumiya, Chris and Lucas came running into the room with knives. Suzumiya directed her gaze on me and took aim at my chest with her knife.

"Suzumiya!" Lucas shouted, standing in front of me protectively and using his Shield to throw her knife off course.

Uncontrolled, my Shield threw a forceful pulse in response to the knife Suzumiya had aimed at me. Chris and Suzumiya were thrown into the wall, yet its force only budged Lucas slightly. He held his hands in front of his face as his feet dragged back because of my angered Shield. "Karla! What are you doing?" Lucas shouted, holding his knife close to his face in defense.

"Lucas, I can't take this: the dreams, this ability, everyone...you. Lucas, *look* at me!" I screamed, finally feeling in control of my body once more. "Lucas, damn it, look at me! What is this?" I wailed, feeling a tear slide down my face.

"Karla. Calm down," Lucas said, staring at me with soft eyes. He lowered his hands and placed his knife slowly on the floor as I felt the presence of his Shield disappear. "You can control it!" he reminded me. "I believe you can."

I stared back at him in horror, knowing how monstrous I must have looked. Slowly I felt the presence of my projected Shield dissipating. The ripples of my Shield turned to red and then powered out with no sound.

Lucas examined me for a little longer before cautiously walking towards me. *Does this mean I will be able to control my ability now?* I thought, fear clutching at my heart. Tears flowed as I battled the rising questions in my mind. Lucas came to my side and took a seat on the bed next to me, cradling my face in his chest. I buried my face deep into his warmth.

I turned my head at the sound of Suzumiya dragging herself out of the small hole she had been thrown into. She had another weapon in her hand: a small knife like the one Lucas had asked me to wear.

"I told them you're not like them," she wiped away the blood from her mouth, smiling as she threw the dagger. Lucas placed his hand in front of the dagger creating a small Shield to throw the knife off, just as he had before.

"What the hell, Lucas! She's one of *them*, can't you see it?" Suzumiya shouted angrily.

"She's not one of them," Lucas said confidently, his hand on my head as he nestled my face back into his chest.

"Why are you so blind?"

He flinched at the insult Suzumiya had thrown and his muscles tensed tightly underneath my hands.

"Don't," I whispered. He didn't look at me but I knew he had heard.

"You can't handle meeting someone new, because you're so scared of an infiltration of the creatures that slaughtered your father. Instead of killing them out there, you're trying to kill your own kind in here," Lucas said calmly.

For a long moment she was silent. "You are not my kind," she said coldly. "You and I will never be the same."

I looked away from her angered face and surveyed the room for the others. Kurt was now grasping at the doorframe to support himself, whilst clutching at his ribs with the other hand. Seth had slipped through the door behind with a small cut across his forehead. Helena was shaking Ashley, who was on the ground, unconscious from the force of the second explosion of my Shield. I still hadn't seen Chris. I had no control of my Shield and the damage it could cause. *I have had no control of my body, like I have been trapped in a glass box.*

"It wasn't her fault," Kurt suddenly said, breaking the silence.

"That's a load of lies Kurt and you know it. You saw it yourself," Suzumiya said, throwing her arm at me accusingly. "She's not what you've been looking for Kurt—she's a monster!"

"That's enough Suzumiya. Go wake Chris up!" Kurt ordered.

"I'm so sorry," I said, letting more tears pour over Lucas's chest.

Seth stepped forward. "This has gone on for too long Kurt. We need to see him." He spoke quietly but firmly.

"We don't need him, Seth. She's fine," Kurt said simply, panting as he slid to a sitting position against the frame of the door.

"Damn it, Kurt. *Look at her*. She's not fine! Her body is shutting down on her and we need to know why," Seth shouted. He moved back to Helena's side and began to check over her injuries.

It happened again. My body shut down on itself, and quicker than before. This is now the second time I have died. Yet once again I am revived—alive. Is death too good for me?

After a long pause Kurt raised himself to his feet once again. "Fine. Tomorrow is when we leave." He stormed out of the room.

Seth picked up Ashley's unconscious body and Helena followed him out of the room, closing the door behind them. Alone in the room with Lucas, I surrendered myself to my emotions—weeping over all that has occurred. That night, Lucas did not release his grip of me as I burrowed into him tightly.

One thought clouded my mind, chasing away sleep: *Is death too good for me?*

Chapter Sixteen - Elemental Breathers

*T*he tinted windows showed me little of outside except the same thing I'd been seeing for the last ten hours: *trees, road, and more trees.* No one had really spoken to me since the accident. Only Seth and Helena were kind and forgiving. I didn't deserve their forgiveness, yet they still tended to my wounds. They took the courtesy of driving me as I sat in the backseat by myself. Kurt, Suzumiya and Chris were in the car in front of us, leaving Ashley and Lucas to follow on their motorbikes behind us. Helena played low classical music as no one spoke in the car, only giving one another the occasional reassuring smile.

Today was the day Kurt decided we would travel to see the mysterious Max Jacket. I hadn't heard much about him but Lucas said he was an acquaintance of Kurt's who was considered untrustworthy. Seth also said that Max was my only hope of figuring out what was wrong with me. The road had turned to dirt about an hour ago and it appeared to be rarely used. The only break we had was when Suzumiya's car got a flat tire, but Ashley fixed it within minutes.

"Why are they turning left?" Helena questioned. It was the first time the silence has been broken since we left the gravel road.

"I don't know. But you know what Max is like. He's probably changed it to be precautionary," Seth answered, indicating left.

I looked back through the back window of the car at Lucas and Ashley. They stayed in close proximity to one another, taking up the majority of the man-made road. Ashley wore a helmet and a dark navy leather jacket. Lucas wore no helmet and his blonde hair flashed like wild fire in the wind.

"Why are they stopping here?" Helena asked, sounding panicked. I turned around in my seat properly, finding myself surrounded by trees on either side of the car.

"I think we're walking the rest of the way," Seth said, turning the car off. Ashley and Lucas had pulled up on both sides of the car and were greeted by Kurt. Seth and Helena got out and stretched their legs while Suzumiya and Chris walked to the edge of the trees, examining what lay beyond them.

Everyone was outside the car now talking amongst themselves in a low, serious tone. Even Ashley was nodding seriously. I sensed they were all tense at the prospect of having to walk the remainder of the journey. Lucas opened my door. "Come on," he said, gesturing for me to get out of the car. He left the door open for me and walked over to Ashley who was fumbling with a belt at his waist. I shielded my eyes from the light that glinted from the metallic weapons that were attached to it. When I looked around, I noticed that it wasn't just Ashley who possessed a belt full of oddly shaped objects. Suzumiya tucked a small knife into her leather boot as well and secured a smaller one to a strap near her chest. After readjusting it, she quickly zipped her red leather jacket up and fiddled once more with her boots. Everyone was wearing leather and even the fragile Helena had a belt strapped to her waist with a few knives on it.

I looked down at my own deep green leather jacket and tight-fitting black jeans. Shuffling the leather jacket off, I was instantly cooler. I felt better wearing only my black sleeveless shirt. The heat of the day felt like it was melting me in such attire.

"Okay guys," Kurt said, clapping his hands together to get everyone's attention. "We're walking from here. Now we all know what Max is like so be on your guard." I wondered what this Max looked like, trying to envision such a man that everyone would fear so much. I pictured a heavy, tall man, with bulging muscles, dark features, and piercing red eyes.

"I don't see why we should risk it..." Suzumiya started, pointing her chin towards me in disgust, "...just for her." Everyone was silent. Even Kurt didn't disagree with her statement even though it was he who has allowed the mission. They shuffled around one another and I felt the disgust some of them held for me like a slap in the face.

"Because she needs our help," Seth said with soft eyes on me. "We do not dislike you Karla. It is simply that Max is someone not to be trifled with. Everyone must be on their guard." He looked between us all, his eyes flashing with annoyance at Suzumiya's unhelpful comments.

"This way," Kurt instructed, pointing into the surrounding trees. We moved forward without hesitation.

"Take this, sweetie." Helena slowed her pace so that she could stand by me, and was holding out the same small knife that Lucas had previously offered to me. "Take it. I know it's uncomfortable to have.

Even I feel uncomfortable with it, but you need it. Max is…oh, how would you describe him? *Unpredictable*. You need it," she said. Her blue gaze looked wise, making me clutch the little knife slowly. *If this man is such a danger to visit, why are they all going to so much trouble for me?* I wish I could say the knife felt out of place in my hand, but it didn't, it was almost comforting.

I held it close to my chest even when I pulled myself over rocks. I had to keep my pace or I feared they would have left me without hesitation. Lucas kept looking back to make sure I hadn't strayed that far. I kept raising my hand to tell him I was okay and that I didn't need his assistance.

The distance between us had me pushing aside my own trail of branches on my lonely path as slowly they crept further and further away. They were always just in sight, so I could hurry behind the path they've just made. Our hike lasted no more than thirty minutes, but at a slower pace, it could have very easily been hours.

I eventually made it to where they were all standing like towering statues. A girl no older than me stood in front of the door to a little cottage behind her. She was shorter than me with fiery red hair tied back into two long ponytails. Her eyes were almost black, just like the unusual black material she wore which was fashioned into a short dress. The pattern on her dress reminded me of tiny curls connecting like vines. The top part fitted so tightly that it could pass as a corset. From the waist down the dress puffed out with curled edges, which looked like rose petals. Her black boots stopped above her knees showing little flesh between the height of her boot and the end of her dress. She radiated with an unearthly beauty. I watched in confusion as she tauntingly removed her silky black glove off. She thrust her hand towards the sky, dragging a blue flame from her fingertips.

"Get down!" Lucas yelled to everyone.

I was pushed back into the trees alongside Helena and Kurt. Suzumiya, Chris, Seth, and Ashley, stood behind Lucas as he took lead position in a structured triangle. Another blue flame shot from the girl's hand with an elegant flick of her wrist. It burst in front of Lucas's face and ashes flicked from the sides of his Shield. A scream left my mouth before I even registered my fear. Both Helena and Kurt held me to the ground, as they covered me protectively.

Suzumiya cast out a huge chain at the girl but she simply grabbed the end of the chain, letting it wrap itself around her fragile wrist. Her hand burst with another flame, which traced blue fire the length of the chain down to Suzumiya's hand. Suzumiya ripped her hand from the flaming chain, clutching at her hand that had just been burnt.

"Trish, we're not here for a fight. We just need to talk to your father," Lucas shouted over the commotion, placing himself in front of the injured Suzumiya and Chris.

"Not a chance," she said with authority. She flicked her wrist again, sending a wave of flames to encircle the four. She slowly raised both of her hands, squinting as she concentrated hard. The circle started slowly closing in on the four as they shouted to one another while throwing knives and daggers at the girl. I could see their faces contort in fear when the flame extinguished and then lit up again in front of my face.

The weight that had been smothering me on the ground wasn't there anymore, giving me the chance to turn around to face Kurt and Helena. Helena had tears in her eyes and was screaming out Seth's name, trying to get to her feet. Kurt's hand was digging into her shoulder holding her down and staring at me with grave eyes. "You want to help them, don't you?!" he shouted over the crackling of the flames.

I quickly scampered to my feet and instinctively ran towards the flames. *If I can control the strength I had in my Shield, like last night, I might be able to help them... help Lucas.* I imagined my Shield, feeling it project instantly at my calling. I was surprised at how little pressure it now put on my mind. *Did my outburst last night allow me to gain some control of my Shield?* Focusing on Lucas, I jumped into the flames and found that the circle was much smaller inside than how it looked like from the outside. I kicked dirt from the path as I sped to Lucas's side. He was sweating and yelling at the others to huddle together. I searched over the blue flames that rose over our heads, which looked now to me like a fountain of fire. The girl was still in sight, concentrating as she slowly closed her hands together.

Suzumiya was still cradled on the ground, clutching her blistered hand. Ashley threw a dagger into the flamed wall that melted instantly on contact. Seth held two knives closely to his chest in a futile attempt to fight the flames.

Lucas now noticed me, surprised that I was inside the circle of flames with them. Helena's voice echoed out for Seth and Ashley, crying for them and pleading with Trish to stop. *I need to help them.* As if reading my thoughts, Lucas ran through the flames and they washed over his Shield, enclosing into a solid wall once more. *I must protect the others and help Lucas fight.* I followed him, clutching the small knife in my right hand. The girl instantly dropped her hands and the projected wall dropped.

She jumped back as Lucas swung a sword near where she stood. Her speed was incredible and her position was hard to trace. I ran beside her, trying to keep up with her speed. Everything I did was a reflex, and somehow my body instinctively knew what to do. I threw my small knife down on her as she raised her hand to the weapon and squeezed down on it, melting it into a pile of ash.

She abruptly stopped, digging her feet onto the ground as she spread her hands onto my Shield. Through her firm grip, fire was shot onto my Shield, sending me back with a blast. My Shield around me was pushed back taking me with it, as I had no choice but to drag my feet in an effort to stop the force.

Lucas was directly in front of her, jumping as he tried to bring down the sword he held. She jumped over Lucas, dodging the blade and dropping on the top of his Shield. Both of her hands combusted into two blue flames as she punched fiercely into it. I could sense the presence of Lucas's Shield wearing thin. Lucas rolled himself on the ground, throwing the young girl off, as she stood unscathed on the ground.

"Elisabeth?" an old crisped voice rang out.

Lucas raised his head as I did, watching an old man in a wheelchair come to the side of the young girl. He stared out into the trees, searching over all of us blankly. "Elisabeth?" he asked again.

Seth quickly picked up Ashley, whose knuckles were bleeding with blistering wounds just like Suzumiya's. Helena ran over to them crying at the sight of Ashley and Seth. Kurt came out from the shrubbery dusting his shoulders off. He came to my side, clutching at his belt as the man approached us, his daughter following closely behind.

When the man had stopped in front of us it was obvious he wasn't looking out to the trees because he couldn't see. He was blind. His gaze wavered over me unsteadily. My knees buckled as I felt myself losing control over my Shield. I retracted it and fell to the ground, exhausted. Perhaps it was adrenaline keeping my Shield projected.

"Elisabeth?" he said, reaching his hand out to me.

Kurt moved to hold a knife to the man's throat. Both the old man and the young girl were unfazed by his actions; the young girl only looked over the damage she had done around her. The man looked as if he were over eighty; he was bald and slumped into his wheelchair wearing a green suit with the same material as the girl's dress. The old man still had his hand extended towards me, but it was in Kurt's direction he next spoke: "I didn't expect to see your face around here after last time, Kurt."

"Get Trish to heal them," Kurt ordered, pointing his other hand to where everyone huddled together. "I know she can fix what she's done. Make her do it. Now." Kurt's blade edged deeper into the old man's throat, grazing his vulnerable skin, but he only smiled in response.

"I've raised her well if she can handle your people so easily in only a few minutes. She was only doing her job, I told you that you were never welcome here again," he said. "Trish, fix them up."

Trish's black eyes were boring into mine but at her father's command they filtered into a light brown shade. "She does not look familiar, father," she said as her eyes still assessed my face and figure. Both of them were still apparently untroubled by the blade itching at the old man's throat.

"I do not expect you to remember Elisabeth—she is an old friend of mine, Trish. Go to the others now." The man reached out for my face again with a withered smile. Trish nodded and left without hesitation, ignoring the fact that Kurt still had his blade against her father's throat.

"You call her Elisabeth. Why?" Kurt demanded. The man's hand that was searching over me froze with a stillness that matched his creamy blue eyes. Kurt pulled his knife back to his side, watching over the man warily. "Max. Why is it you call her Elisabeth?"

This is Max Jacket? The man I had visualised was very different to the old blind man crippled in a wheelchair before me.

"This is Elisabeth. I would know the scent of her blood anywhere," he said, frowning. Max lowered his head as if he were hearing something we could not. *The scent of my blood?*

"Her name is Karla. She is why we have come to see you. We require your knowledge," Kurt said intensely. His tone has changed into one of politeness and yet it was domineering at the same time. Seth walked over, showing me that his back was now fine. There were no burns to be found, only the hole that had been burnt through his jacket. Seth stood on the other side of me clutching at his belt and dangling his fingers over the large knife that was hanging off it in an alarmed fashion. I looked back at Max who everyone had feared so much. He seemed even more helpless than I was.

"Give me your hand, child," Max requested, raising his hand out to me. He paused as Seth raised his knife in front of me protectively. "Give me your hand," Max demanded again.

Kurt shook his head at Seth, exchanging an uncertain glance. Seth slowly put the knife back into the pocket from where he grabbed it. The man's hand was still outstretched, seeking my own.

"*Give me your hand*!" Max bellowed. His eyes flashed with a deep black just as his daughter's had done, showing no pupil before returning to its natural creamy blue. Both Seth and Kurt had their weapons out in front of me, forcing the man to close his eyes until he could reopen them again calmly. Smiling at no one in particular, he continued: "Some old traits never die, isn't that right Kurt?"

"And some are easily fixed with death. It was you who always told me that," Kurt said ruthlessly.

Trish arrived behind her father's wheelchair, taking her glove off at the sight of the weapons while her eyes flickered black, and then disappeared into light brown once again. *Like an animal giving a warning signal before a fight.* Both Ashley and Lucas arrived beside Seth. Ashley also no longer had any visible injuries.

I noticed a bit of red on Lucas's cheek: a kiss mark that was the same color as Trish's lips. I was disgusted in myself when I felt anger flickering through my body, all over one little mark. The blind man peered down at me with an amused smile. "It seems like I'm not the only one with a temper problem," he said with a wide, cracked smile. Everyone looked down at me confused, though still on guard. "Give me your hand child. I will not hurt you." He raised his hand out to me more slowly than he had the other times.

"Don't touch him," Lucas warned quickly.

The old man looked up at him with flickering black eyes. "I would not hurt her. Even if I wanted to, I could not." Max picked my hand up with a speed that shocked me into releasing a sharp squeal. Everyone had their weapons out but it was Lucas who was by the old man's side with his knife wrapped around his throat. Trish also had a firm grip, but not around her father, but around Lucas. Her eyes burned black while both of her bare hands and perfect nails clutched into Lucas's arms. Everyone froze with a rigidity that couldn't even be deterred by the whistling wind against their eyes.

The old man hummed a mellow tune to himself as if he were calming some conflicting thoughts in his head. He gently released my hand and for the first time became aware of the knife that was wrapped around his neck. He spluttered a cough of amusement to himself.

"Be careful. You might hurt someone with that knife, little Starkorf," Max said amused. Lucas flinched and took the blade away from Max's throat. Trish loosened her grip but left her hands to linger on Lucas's tense arms, her eyes finding their pupils once again.

"We are Shielders, old man," Lucas said angrily, letting his knife dangle from the belt it was originally strapped to. He looked down at Trish's hands, which clung to his skin. "Ah, of course you are. My mistake," Max said, turning his wheelchair around and revealing the back of his bald head. "I wish you didn't, Trish."

Trish smiled at her father brightly while she clutched at Lucas's biceps. He slowly pushed her away as I felt myself burn with anger. Everyone else was now relieved and released their hold on their weapons. Max wheeled himself towards the small cottage that looked like it had been made from the wood that surrounded it.

"Come in, come in. It's too cold out here," Max mused politely. Trish was behind him, grabbing Lucas's arm flirtatiously and pulling him in with her. I felt my face fluster red and my hand clutch at the dirt more than what was needed.

"Come on," Ashley offered his hand out to me. The melted skin that covered his knuckles was gone, showing no wound. "I've met them before. Trust me, it's easier to keep her happy—she has a terrible temper."

I accepted his hand, trying to contain the unwelcome feeling of jealousy. Holding Ashley's hand, I was mesmerised by his smooth skin, and I kept looking back over his knuckles. "Your hand; it's healed!" I said quietly, in disbelief.

"She made the wounds." Ashley gestured to Trish who was still laughing at Lucas and telling him how funny he was. "She can fix it. They are Elemental Breathers and are in complete control of one element. If they inflict it, they can reverse it as well."

"Elemental Breather?" I questioned, as Ashley helped me up.

"Are you guys coming?" Lucas interrupted, looking over at our hands, annoyed.

"Long story. I'll tell you later," Ashley promised, ignoring Lucas. "You did well out there by the way."

Max was waiting near the door as we approached. "May I speak to the young woman alone?" he asked.

"Not a chance," Ashley replied as he escorted me to the cottage, slipping me past Max and through the front door.

Chapter Seventeen - Elisabeth

$\mathcal{T}$he cottage was surprisingly enormous compared to its exterior appearance. I considered it to be a trick of the eye, as it seemed double in size inside. The room we walked into was massive, and we were surrounded with bookshelves. Candles flickered with flames in a giant chandelier that hung from the ceiling. There were candles placed in enclosures close to the wall and a fireplace that was brightly lit. The room radiated with soft light.

The chandelier hovered above the mat that we now stood on, showering the room with dull colors; the brightest being maroon. A large coffee table was placed in the middle of the room with a dozen black couches surrounding it. Everyone had claimed a chair, Trish choosing to sit next to Lucas. She played with his hair, laughing at him while he pulled his face away annoyed. "I told you I'd beat you some day. Dad trains me every day," she said, bragging to him. He grabbed her stroking hand away from his leg, nudging himself further away from her in his chair. She pouted her lips at him childishly. Her eyes flickered black as her father interrupted her angry stare.

"Trish, can you get our guests some tea?" Max waved his hand for Ashley and me to join everyone else on the couches.

"You okay?" Ashley asked me as I flushed red with a built up anger I held for Trish. She had tried to kill us not five minutes ago, but somehow everyone was calm and understanding about that. *On top of everything she will not stop touching Lucas*, I raged inwardly.

I gave Ashley a harsh stare and then softened my eyes in apology when I remembered my anger was focused on Trish and not Ashley. "I'm fine," I lied. Trish led Lucas into one of the hallways, nudging him to the side in a playful tease. Lucas gave Kurt an angry glance but Kurt only nodded in return, urging him to go with her. "Trish, keep the door open," Max ordered, while placing himself between the couches Ashley and I sat on.

Trish giggled to herself. Actually *giggled,* and left with Lucas strapped to her side.

"Kids these days," Max mused. I rolled my eyes in disgust and looked over the books that surrounded us.

"I must admit, Max. You have raised her well; she's a lot more powerful than I expected her to be," Kurt admitted from where he sat across from Max.

"Of course she is. She's my daughter," Max simply said, proud.

A huge bark echoed through the room and a huge flash of grey forced its weight on top of me. I cried out for help before I realized it was a dog that had jumped on me and nothing else. The dog was as big as… a wolf? I questioned, concerned. Its tongue trailed the length of my face with breath that smelt of mince. One eye was blue and the other was brown; its coat was the lightest of grey—almost white.

"His name's Sam. He won't bite," Max answered coldly, disapprovingly of the dog's presence. The wolf's weight pressed me into the couch while it panted over my face.

"That's a lie," Lucas said, panting at the doorframe. Trish stood behind him, clutching at her necklace in frustration. "He bit me last time I was here!"

Ashley pushed the large wolf off me. Sam bolted past Trish as she kicked him with an angry expression. The wolf made a small yelp and left my sight.

"You pulled his tail," Max accused Lucas. "Trish the tea, please, and chain that dog up."

"Yes father," Trish said, nodding her head as if it were a serious demand.

"You don't have to tie him up. I was just a little surprised," I said, plucking at the grey hair that I was covered in.

"How did you come across her?" Max asked, his eyes hovering over Kurt. Somehow Max knew where everyone sat. I looked over at Seth and Helena, who were huddled closer than usual, hand in hand. They were obviously uncomfortable.

"Two weeks ago we found her. Some Starkorfs were following her," Kurt said, not giving away too much information. "You called her Elisabeth when we arrived. Why?"

"I thought it was Elisabeth because it's her blood this one carries," Max explained, before turning himself to Lucas. "I thought it was Elisabeth so of course I wouldn't kill her."

"Karla has Elisabeth's blood?" Kurt asked, looking over at me, surprised.

"That's what I felt pulsing through her veins. How could you not know this Kurt? Why would you need this information from me? I haven't heard from Elisabeth for quite some time, and never heard of her having a child," Max replied.

"Wait, who is Elisabeth?" I questioned in frustration, not understanding any of their conversation.

"Neither one of her parents are Shielders," Kurt said as if I hadn't spoken. His voice sounded like it was trying to measure up another unspoken question.

"Who's Elisabeth?" I said again loudly, so everyone would focus their attention on me.

"Elisabeth is Misfeata's descendent; the last of her kind that held the pure blood of a Shielder. Having such blood in her veins connected her to Misfeata, inevitably making her one of the strongest Shielders in all of time, just like all those who once possessed the same blood before her," Max answered. "You really don't know of her?"

My choked out answer was more than enough for him to understand that I really didn't.

"Why is it you come to me then?" Max asked as his eyes waved over me unsteadily. *How does he know where I am and how can he look me directly in the eye?*

"Her body has now shut down on her twice. Every organ in her body completely stops. On top of that, her Shield is visible and she has little control of it," Kurt answered abruptly. Trish sashayed in with a tray full of teacups.

"Perhaps she is a very ill child. Ill children go to hospitals, not to me Kurt," Max said coldly. Trish handed cups of tea to everyone, and presented the biscuits as if she had just made them herself. *She probably has, she can probably do everything*, I thought to myself spitefully.

"When she projects her Shield, it is visible with colored ripples pulsating through it," Seth said, before having a sip of his tea.

Lucas opened his mouth as if to say something, I imagined it to be about the dreams I have been having. I gave him a wary look, begging him with my eyes not to tell them. I didn't want them knowing about them, it felt like a secret I wanted to keep to myself. *Well, at least between Lucas and myself*. He closed his mouth around his cup and took a sip of tea.

"That is interesting," Max said, placing his cup down on the coffee table and staring directly at me. Everyone was quiet; barely anyone had spoken other than Max and Kurt.

"That's not all. Twice now her Shield has burst, like a huge shock wave. Both times it's slammed me into the nearest wall and it forces her to pass out. It's like she can't control her own power. I've never seen anything like it before," Kurt said scooping and stirring sugar into his cup.

Trish found her seat beside Lucas again, swirling her hand through the tips of his hair. He grabbed her hand, giving her a warning look. *I cannot understand the relationship between these two. If Lucas has no interest then why does she continue to do these things? Trish is completely unfazed about how she welcomed us.* I let out a long sigh of frustration. *Why am I getting so annoyed by this?*

"I would like to see this projected Shield. Not today of course, I can feel the girl at her energy's limit. Clearly she has only recently started using her ability," Max said.

"You wish for us to come back again?" Seth questioned. His voice sounded different, misplaced in a conversation that was between Kurt and Max.

"Don't be silly, the drive is too long. You may stay here for the night, as long as your clothes are changed into more formal attire."

"We need to find somewhere to stay," Chris declined coldly.

"Don't be silly," Trish argued with a smile stretched across her face that was intended only for Lucas. "It's a great idea and we have clothes in every size for any formal occasion." *Why do they keep talking about formal wear?* I thought.

"It's how Elemental Breathers are. Normally you wouldn't even be accepted into their home in what we're wearing. Everything is formal and fancy—even their pajamas. It's their cultural custom," Ashley whispered to me, as he noticed my confused face.

"Then it's settled," Max said, clapping his hands together. "Tonight we have guests. Trish untie your—…" He paused, rephrasing what it was he was going to say. "Untie Sam. He will lead our guests around. We have four spare rooms, more than enough." *Fo ur spare rooms? The small exterior of the cottage was misleading indeed.* "Helena and Seth you may have the double. You two…" Max pointed to Suzumiya and Chris who were huddled together on a couch. Somehow he knew where everyone was even though he was blind. "…You two can bunk up in the other double."

"We're not together," Suzumiya said, flushing red in embarrassment.

"Oh. I'm sorry, my mistake. Then you may share the double with Karla," Max said impatiently.

"No!" Suzumiya quickly interjected. "It'll be fine, I'll stick with Chris." I didn't have to see Suzumiya's face to know her eyes were cold. *She still hates me, still thinks I'm a monster,* I realized.

"Lucas can bunk with me," Trish bellowed across the room with a squeal of excitement. *How generous of her.* I felt the acid of sarcasm burn the back of my throat. I pinched my lips together, avoiding the embarrassment of saying something I would later regret.

"No, Trish. Karla will be bunking with you," Max said smugly. He seemed undisturbed by his daughter's intentions of seduction.

"Don't bother on my account," I said coldly. "I don't mind where I sleep."

Lucas stared at me, confused. I looked back at the books that blocked us in, pretending to be interested. I would rather sleep with the dog than with Trish.

"See father, problem fixed. Now Lucas, don't make me angry in my own home," Trish threatened flirtatiously. "Now come!" she said, jumping from her seat and dragging Lucas behind her. Lucas was pulled into the hallway, staring at me as he was dragged away. The hallway echoed with Trish's giggles as they disappeared from sight.

Max yelled for his daughter to return but neither she nor Lucas did. All I could visualise was my hand openly slapping Lucas across the face. *I feel so betrayed.* I caught that thought, infuriated by it. *Why am I feeling like this towards Lucas?*

Sam came bursting through the hallway again, stopping at Max's side. The wolf sat beside Max obediently.

"I wish for some privacy in my room, Max. I'm a light sleeper," Kurt stated.

"There's only one room with a single, and the other remaining room has two singles," Max said, looking over at Ashley and I. "You two don't mind staying the night in the same room together, do you?"

"I'm okay with it. Lucas is a big enough girl to share a room with anyway so I'm sure I could handle the real thing," Ashley said, looking at me with a sheepish smile. "That's only if you're comfortable with it?"

"I'm okay with it," I said, admiring Ashley's thoughtfulness as he asked for permission. He was much like Seth in that sense, a gentleman.

"Excellent. Sam will show you all to your rooms and then shortly come by with your formal wear for dinner," Max said as he rounded up the cups of tea that he instinctively knew were there. Sam nuzzled at my leg, baring his teeth into a smile.

"I think he wants us to follow him," Ashley said, standing up.

When we arrived at the room Ashley claimed his bed by jumping on it childishly, while I examined the small bathroom we had to share. The rooms were made with the same wood as the outside of the cottage, and the floor was polished and varnished. There were no windows, only candles and a small chandelier hanging from the ceiling that gently lit the room. There was nothing but two beds in the bedroom and a shower, sink, and toilet, in the ensuite bathroom. The mirror that hid behind the bathroom door showed my filthy brown hair and smudges of ash across my face. I quickly rubbed at my face to clean it.

"So Trish and Lucas, huh?" Ashley said from his bed, fiddling with the metal that was hanging around his waist.

"Yep," I answered angrily, feeling the taste of rage on my lips. I wanted to hear nothing more on the topic. "I'm going to have a quick nap; can you wake me when something happens?"

"Sure can," Ashley said. He stopped fiddling with his belt, giving me the peace and quiet I needed to get some sleep after my exhausting day.

"Why do you fight against me?" she asked. I was encircled by a mirrored room—I could see nothing but a reflection that was not my own, yet somehow it spoke to me. I looked down at the leather I wore; just like we all had been wearing today. Weapons were strapped to every part of my body, yet the weight of all of it had little effect on me. When I looked at my reflection, a woman stood in the mirrored glass staring back at me, her movements mirroring my own.

She looked as I did the first time Uncle Kyle came to me in a dream to warn me of Lucas: the same green dress, with her hair pinned back, letting the fringe flow down the side of her face. The green gem sparkled on her more than it had on me, shining so brightly I couldn't even make out the most dominant features of her face. I couldn't see how old she was, what she looked like, anything. It was all blurred, and my attention fixed on the dress that flowed out in the mirror elegantly.

"Because it is my body. My soul. You can't take whatever you please, whenever you please," I said, clutching for my belt at my waist.

"But it's my blood you carry," she said, her voice echoing around the room. I could not fathom a face to match the voice that resonated with such dominance.

"It's my blood I carry. My soul I carry. My body. None of it belongs to you," I said, striking my hand out and watching her do the same.

"And it's my fate you carry. Let me take the burden off of you, let me finish what needs to be ended," she offered, her voice swirling around in the room.

"Your fate and my fate are nothing alike, nor will they ever collide. This is my life and you will never be welcomed into it," I said, pulling a knife from my belt—Aeisha. She was strapped to where she belonged: at my side.

"And what is it you will do? Lead them? Fight amongst them? Make them sacrifice their life so you can have control over yours? Selfish is it not?" the elusive woman asked.

I cut through the mirror with one easy strike of Aeisha, watching the mirror shatter to my feet. "I'm here to help." I said placing Aeisha back to my side. The outline of the stranger's figure fragmented with the shards of the mirror.

"You're here to help yourself. You can't have him, nor can he have you," she said, partly amused. "You can take your vision of me away, but you can't take my vision."

"Why can't we be together? Enlighten me!" I screamed, angered as flashes of Lucas's smile came to my mind. 'Why can't I be with Lucas?' I thought to myself. The mirrors around me showed her flowing green dress, and the room was now flooded with the green material.

"Because it is my blood. No Shielder, nor Starkorf, will take my life. To take my heart would be to take my life, entwining my soul with someone else's would be to take my life. It will not happen," she said domineeringly.

I grabbed the silver whip that dangled from my belt and cracked it around where I stood, shattering glass and mirror alike. Shards of glass pierced my skin, cutting open my lip. I licked the metallic taste of my blood.

"My blood, my life," I asserted, as the image of her disappeared as the last of the glass broke.

I woke up to find myself sitting on my bed with my fists clenched. Ashley stood over me, his hand to his jaw. "You're awake! You've got a punch and a half on you for a small thing," he said as he stopped rubbing his jaw and revealed a red mark—the mark of my fist. I wiped away the hair that stuck to my face and neck, breathing heavily as I now noticed I was safe and no longer in that mirrored room with that woman.

"I'm sorry," I whispered covering my mouth in disgust.

"It's alright. Were you having another nightmare? You were pretty restless," Ashley asked, now sitting at the end of my bed and straightening out the blanket.

I nodded in response, curling my feet under me and smothering my face into the pillow with stress. "They're getting really weird now and more real. It's like I can never go to sleep because she's always there."

"Who's always there?" Ashley asked. He had stopped straightening out the blanket and sat like a shrink would, well postured, formal. He actually was presented well with a purple suit that contrasted nicely against his black hair. The only thing seeming out of place with such formal clothing was his silver eyebrow bar that still stuck out, glinting in the candlelight.

"I don't know," I answered absentmindedly, still glancing over the clothes he adorned. It was the same material Trish and Max wore. "What are you wearing?"

He looked down at his clothes, almost embarrassed. "My evening wear. That's why I woke you up. You have something to wear as well; Sam brought them in for us." Somehow the choice of their clothing didn't appeal to me nor did the fact that it was presented by an enormous wolf that they kept as a house pet.

"Why do they have a wolf in this house?" I asked suddenly, remembering the anger they held towards the animal.

"I don't know, but he has been here for as long as I can remember, and he has always been able to guide us to rooms, bring us things and do other odd jobs. I never understood it much myself but it just has always been like that," Ashley said, looking over his shoulder as if someone were listening.

"I see," I said lightly, inwardly questioning such a capability in an animal. "I don't have to wear something like that, do I?" I scrunched my nose up at the thought of wearing what he had to.

"I don't know, I didn't open your package." He gestured to the box that was neatly placed on his bed. A black box, neatly tied up with a red ribbon, my name written on an attached nametag.

"Why are they so formal at dinner?" I asked, still torturing myself over what could be in the box.

"Right. I owe you an explanation."

"Damn right you do. Nothing has made sense to me since we got here, starting with the fact that she can shoot fire out of her hands."

"Well you know how in the old days there was the burning of witches. Well mostly Elemental Breathers were the reason behind that. Humans were the ones that labeled them witches."

"So they're witches?" I interrupted abruptly.

"Sort of. They're Elemental Breathers. When they're born, they can channel and command a particular energy. They can control that one form of energy—that element they control—and use it in any manner they wish. Whether they choose to train to strengthen that one element is their choice. They also live twice as long as humans and Shielders, so Max is really over one hundred and fifty years old. They also have great knowledge on other things as well, that's how they healed us within minutes. They are somehow connected with nature so with their ability, they can always reverse the damage their own energy has caused; whether that damage was to humans or land. They think of themselves as the Gods of their ability because no two Elemental Breathers can harness the same energy or present the same form of created element. That's why it is vital that in their presence you must be formally presented. It is extremely disrespectful to be in front of them without doing so. Powerful beings, but very short tempered and untrustworthy."

"Do their eyes turn black because they're angry?" I asked, remembering Max's and Trish's eyes turning into a deep black.

"Yeah. That's why we try not to get involved with them. They're as untrustworthy as any Starkorf and they'd hand us over just as easily for a piece of knowledge. But their knowledge is great and gets passed down through generations, and these days they're harder to come across. Trish and Max are the only ones we know."

"You came to them to ask about me?" I asked heavily, hoping they would risk their lives for other reasons than just me. *Why would they put themselves in danger to understand what is happening to me?*

"Yep. We were talking a little while you slept. Your biological parents are human but you're a Shielder who carries the descendant blood of Misfeata. They guessed that is the reason as to why you can't control your Shield. Having the same strength, energy, and ability as Misfeata would be too powerful for an amateur to control. But we still

132

have no idea how you have that blood in you and why you're Shield is visible. On top of that, we don't understand how and where Elisabeth is involved. You're a mystery and a half." He jumped off the bed, grabbing the box that belonged to me and passing it over. "You better get ready, dinner's soon. And yes, you do have to wear it," Ashley said giving me a small smile.

"Hey, Ashley?" I said, grabbing his attention before he left. Ashley stopped at the door before opening it. "You said they possess their own elemental power. What is Max's?" I'd seen his daughter burst flames out of her hands but they all seemed to fear Max the most.

"Electricity. That's why it's always outcast out here. On top of that, our bodies create electrical signals, which are the reason why he can always sense who and where we are. He may be old but he can pack a punch. He killed Tim, one of the guys who used to fight with us. Max only glanced at him out of anger and a bolt of electricity burned him alive, leaving his ashes to blow in the wind," he said, shuddering to himself grimly. "He was the first person I watched being killed, and I was only seven. But he sure as hell wasn't the last."

"That's so sad," I said remorsefully. I didn't know if I could handle seeing that now, let alone at the age of seven.

"Get dressed. We're just meeting up where we were before and then we'll be escorted..." he pulled a twisted face at the word 'escorted', "...to their dining room."

"Thank you for everything Ashley. Listening to my issues, and being the first to actually explain something to me even after all I've done. I'm really sorry about everything," I said, dropping my head in shame.

"It's not your fault. We will find a cure for you Karla." Ashley gave me a small smile of reassurance before slipping out the door.

I snapped the seal of red ribbon off the box that belonged to me. The large box felt fairly heavy, and dropped to the floor twice before I could open it. When I finally managed to open it, I glimpsed a red material neatly folded in the box. I stretched it out, taking in the material. The red dress was made of the same fabric Max and Trish wore. The pattern of it curled around just as theirs had. I held it up to myself in the mirror, seeing how short it actually was. It was hemmed about two inches above my knees, as short as Trish's black dress was.

"No way," I whispered to myself. I couldn't wear this. *It's so short and revealing.* I scurried through the box, only finding a pair of red heels, a red necklace and some earrings. "No, no, no, no," I whispered to myself in panic.

They want me to get out of a pair of jeans for this? Ashley said I had to look formal but I wondered how something so short could be deemed acceptable. Ashley's voice of urgency kept repeating over and over in my head. *I have to wear this. I have to.*

Chapter Eighteen - Possession

*T*he shower lasted longer than it probably should have. I tried to waste time; to delay when I would have to put on the dress. When I finally slipped the dress on it clung tightly around my waist, making it hard for me to breathe. I added the accessories and quickly slipped on the pair of red heels.

When I reached the mirror I was shocked at the transformation. *I have a waist, an actual waist.* The long red necklace draped elegantly over my chest, clumping like a bunch of neat vines. The earrings dangled ostentatiously, complementing the radiant red of the dress. The dress itself wasn't as short as I had originally thought it would be, and it flowed out like a blooming flower at my knees. I swayed back and forth in front of the mirror, reveling at the figure it reflected. I had a waist, and it enhanced what little chest I had. It wasn't me at all. It was another girl completely staring back at me with confused eyes. My brown hair flowed over my shoulders in little ripples.

There was a low growl that came from the other side of the door and then a quiet, surprised gasp. I opened the door, looking down at Sam who was sprawled out in front of my door. Helena stood to the side, looking at me with surprised eyes as she took in my appearance.

"You look *stunning*. Absolutely stunning. You're beautiful," she smiled brightly. I looked back down at the dress fidgeting at the tight waistline. *Do I really look stunning?* Helena's dress was just as beautiful as mine, with the same material, but it was strapless, yellow, and it came down to her ankles. She bloomed like a sunflower. It was an unusual color to see on Helena but the warm tones made her eyes appear to sparkle. She adjusted her red glasses that had slipped to the tip of her nose.

"Thank you, and you too. This material's something, isn't it?" I said, still admiring the yellow Helena wore. Sam let out a low howl that made me jump in surprise.

Helena smiled again. "Looks like you have an admirer. He hasn't let me near your door since I got here. Now come on, let's go, everyone's wondering where you are," she said, grabbing my hand and leading me down the hall, Sam panting behind us.

The room looked the same as it had before only with a spark of elegance floating through the air. Everyone sat around in the fire lit room looking as if they were born to wear the clothes they adorned. Suzumiya wore a pale maroon dress, which was split to her thigh. Her short hair was pinned back, revealing deep blue earrings that dangled to her shoulders. The dress clung to her figure more sharply than it clung to my own.

Chris, for the first time looked like a gentleman, waving his glass of wine around in his elegant green suit, he even had a deep green tie to complement the outfit. Seth and Kurt sat uncomfortably, twitching and pulling at their suits, which seemed too small for both of them. They both wore the same gray. Neither held a drink in their hand and seemed to be having a serious discussion. Neither Trish nor Max was present, making everyone a lot more relaxed in the spacious room.

Sam released a loud yawn and everyone looked up at the whining wolf, noticing Helena and I were with him. Everyone went quiet, staring at me. Helena walked to her husband's side and looked back at me with a bright smile. Yellow did suit her—her personality.

"You look beautiful, love," Seth called out with a bright smile.

When I looked over to Lucas I saw that his jaw was tight. He looked away from me, blushing red. He wore long black pants with a white shirt tucked in neatly and buttoned, and a tie that had not yet been done up. His hair seemed lighter than it normally was under the chandelier, making it look golden blonde and perfectly styled.

Sam nudged his large head into my side, searching for attention. I swept my hands through the large wolf's fur while he panted contently by my side, looking over me with his mismatched eyes.

"I think I would have looked better in the red," Ashley teased, leaving Lucas to examine the bookshelves.

"I think I would've coped better in the suit," I said honestly to Ashley. I could hardly breathe and I was relieved when everyone started talking again.

Trish entered the room, instantly jumping at Lucas, who had only a few seconds to project his Shield. Her eyes flickered black as she stopped at the Shield. "Do not use that in my home."

Lucas dropped his Shield after Kurt gave him a disapproving expression. She smiled sweetly, pulling a piece of her fringe away from her eyes and giggling.

She wore a red dress that barely covered her thighs and a

simple red choker designed to take as little attention as possible off her strapless dress. Her hair was pulled into a neat bun that spiked out through the back, with a red flower nestled in her fringe. Her red heels had straps that crossed over her legs like vines, stopping at her knees.

I pulled on my dress self-consciously; compared to her I seemed underdressed even though this was over the top for me. Max followed through the door more quietly and elegantly than his daughter had. He wore the same clothes as when I first saw him: a black suit.

"Lovely. All of you are decently dressed, finally," Max said. "Come through, come through." He waved everyone through to the hallway he had just made his appearance from.

Trish walked in front of me, nudging my shoulder as she walked past. I held my shoulder angrily where she made contact. Her eyes flickered with black and then changed to their natural color of brown. She looked over me for the first time since she came in and smiled slyly, pulling Lucas to her side. She held his hand tightly, showing most of her glove and hiding Lucas's underneath.

"Well, isn't that unfortunate. We're wearing the same color," she said as she took in my attire with an amused giggle. She covered her mouth while pinching her lips together. *Yes, how hilarious*. "If I had known, I would have selected something a little better fitting for you."

Lucas shook his head and mouthed '*don't*'. I felt anger boil in me as I looked at the hand that held his.

"Yeah. I considered just wearing my jeans, they were a little more fitting, maybe next time I should offer them to you though, you look like you need something to cover up your—…"

"Come on Karla," Ashley interrupted, pushing me along before I could voice the acid I felt in my throat for a sentence.

"Cover up my what?" she asked angrily, standing in front of us, and towering over Ashley and me. Her eyes danced with black and her hand was still tightly clenched around Lucas's hand.

"Trish, don't worry about it," Lucas soothed, trying to pull his hand out of hers. She clamped her hands like iron bars, weaving her fingers through his like a snake.

"Not a chance. If this little washed-up impurity wants to say something in my own house, then I invite her to try," she spat, her eyes now stained with black.

"Impurity?" I repeated, infuriated. *I don't think I have ever hated anyone more than this woman who now stands in front of me.* "Impure, like your intentions?" I gestured at Lucas. I felt his gaze bore into me like lasers. *Could I possibly be jealous because of Lucas?*

Trish ripped her hand away from Lucas's, pulling off her glove. Her hand burst into a blue flame. "Jealous much, mongrel?" she yelled, her voice echoing through the room. She only gave me a second to prepare myself for the blue flame that spat from her hand, aimed at my face. I pushed Ashley into one of the shelves, blocking him from its path. The flames turned to ash in front of my face as they made contact with the tiny black ripples pulsating around me. I felt a desire at one with my Shield—I pulsed with the desire for her to be hurt.

"Your little carnival tricks aren't going to work with me, sweetie," I said smiling. I felt my hand move back and my posture move into a kind of crouch. It wasn't my crouch, it wasn't me telling my body to do that, and it wasn't me who said that. Trish unsteadily took a step back before reclaiming her posture.

"What the hell is this?" she bellowed. Everyone had returned to the room.

The voice echoed through my head like pounding drums, making no sense to me. *None of it made any sense to me. Who was it that had used my lips to speak? Was it the woman from my dreams?*

Max quickly barged past Kurt on his wheelchair, grabbing his daughter's arm angrily and lowering her to his eye level.

"Do you want to end up dead? I said *don't*." He slapped her across the face and the room reverberated with the sound of the smack. Lucas caught her before she fell to the floor. She looked up at me as her eyes flickered from brown to black and then regained their brown shade.

"I am sorry, father," Trish quietly said, adjusting her dress and standing tall without Lucas's support.

I looked around to Ashley who was sprawled across the bookshelf I had thrown him into. Books were scattered all around him. *I must have thrown him into it pretty hard.* My vision of his outstretched hand was distorted with tiny ripples of black. I gathered control over my Shield, feeling the small combustion of it make a light breeze shoot through the room; the wind flickering through the pages of a nearby open book. I looked back at everyone's terrified faces, seeing my own emotions reflected in theirs.

"I'm sorry," I said shakily. *I've been apologizing a lot lately for things I couldn't control.*

"Don't be sorry. Trish has a short temper and must accept that she can't shoot up flames every time something happens," Max said

138

clapping his hands together, breaking the tension in the room. "Let's all go eat."

Trish was looking down at the ground, holding her face. She placed her hand on her chest, giving a small fake smile. She grabbed Lucas's arm and took him through the hallway. I hadn't even had the chance to get a glimpse of his face to see whether he was disgusted in me or just as terrified as everyone else.

"What happened?" Kurt demanded, watching as everyone quietly took their leave.

"Trish got agitated and started shooting flames for fists. Her temper's worse than her father's," Ashley said, picking the books up. I stroked through Sam's hair, he hadn't left my side through any of the argument.

"Karla?" Kurt looked at me coldly.

"I don't know." *What am I meant to explain? That there's a voice in my head other than my own?*

Ashley offered his arm to me in a gentlemanly manner, pulling me away from Kurt's anger. Sam panted by my side, following us into the dining room. I avoided looking back at Kurt, feeling frustrated at his lecture and not wanting to say anything that would worsen the situation. All I now felt was anger—it was swallowing me whole and becoming my complete being. *Is the woman inside of my head taking over? Is she igniting my feelings with her own?*

Dinner was presented elegantly and everyone was pleased with their plateful of food. I only had small portions of everything, as my stomach couldn't expand anymore through the tightly fitting dress. Surprisingly, Chris also ate little, using his serviette when needed and chewing with his mouth closed.

I had to look away when Trish attempted hand-feeding Lucas, who looked as if the novelty of his new 'girlfriend' was wearing off. I burst with satisfaction when he pulled his face away from the food she held out to him. Her eyes quickly flickered with black and then she changed her choice of food, shoving a different morsel in his face as if it were the food that was the problem.

Sam sat by my side through the dinner and was pleased when I flicked the food off my plate for him to eat. Everyone spoke amongst themselves quietly, politely pushing the plate in front of them when they were finished.

I left dinner early, and entered my room to find they had already placed a pair of pajamas for us on our respective beds. I lifted the second dress they offered to me as a nightie: a silky blue mid-length dress to sleep in. They obviously didn't realize how uncomfortable I was wearing a dress for a few hours let alone sleeping in one for the whole night.

On my way back to my room from dinner I searched over the books, sneaking one into my room to read. I felt appallingly rude taking what I haven't asked for but I would return it in the morning. Sam rested his head on my stomach while I flicked through the hard-to-follow book. I thought it was a spell book of some kind.

Sam howled at the door before it even opened. Ashley crept through quietly before realizing I was awake. "Oh. You're still awake," he exclaimed, shuffling to his bed and looking at the silken material he was expected to sleep in. He looked back at me; looking over the jeans and black sleeveless shirt I had put back on and then looked at Sam, who was snoring contentedly. "You two have gotten pretty attached." He clicked his fingers at Sam trying to get the animal to walk over to him. He clicked and whistled and even made little kissing noises but Sam didn't move.

"Yeah. He seems like the only sane being around here, might as well keep him close," I mumbled, combing my fingers through his thick fur.

"Back there with Trish...?" Ashley asked.

"It wasn't me," I said, pleading with him to believe me. I paused when I saw his confused face, and turned another page of the book while trying to think of something reasonable to say. "Well, it was me. I'm just not normally like that. That's what I meant."

"Oh. Okay," he said throwing his pajamas to the floor.

"You're not going to change?" I asked, closing the book and putting it on the floor next to my bed.

"Nah, one of us has to stay awake. All of us are doing it. The invitation to sleep here might sound like a nice offer but it's stupid on our behalf to actually go to sleep."

"I can stay up instead," I offered. I repositioned myself beside Sam. He lifted his head, waiting until I was settled in a comfortable position before shifting his head back into my lap with a wide yawn.

"No, I'll do it," Ashley insisted, walking into the bathroom.

"Seriously, Ashley. I'll do it. I'm not tired; I've had plenty of sleep." That was partly true, but the main reason was that I actually feared going to sleep. I didn't want her to come back. "Besides, I know everyone didn't get much sleep last night. I'll do it."

Before he could argue there was a low knocking on the door. Sam jumped towards the door with a large growl, baring his teeth protectively. "Sam!" I moaned, losing my comfortable position. "It's settled now. I'll stay up."

Ashley walked away from the bathroom, shooting me a look of disapproval. He unlocked the door and opened it, revealing Lucas who was scrunching up his hair in a confused manner. He still wore his black pants but with his white shirt now half unbuttoned, revealing his bare chest. I cast my eyes away from the beautiful sight. Lucas looked over Ashley's shoulder at the growling wolf beside me.

Sam jumped from his protective crouch, shifting his weight onto my lap while still baring his teeth. I nuzzled him lightly in the neck, quieting the tense wolf.

"That wolf really doesn't like you mate," Ashley said seriously. "Why are you here anyway? Don't you have plans with Trish?"

Lucas looked down at the pajamas that were sprawled over the carpet: both mine and Ashley's.

"So, what happened?" Ashley continued, picking up the pajamas under Lucas's interrogative stare.

"I could ask you the same," Lucas said gesturing to the pajamas.

"What happened?" Ashley groaned, ignoring Lucas's accusing tone.

"I don't know, she blew up into flames like a phoenix when I told her I didn't want… what she wanted," Lucas admitted, annoyed.

"Oh yeah, you're a keeper," Ashley muttered to himself. Despite their squabbling I could feel Lucas's eyes on me. I couldn't stand looking at him after watching Trish bop around him like a slinky. Even if he had to keep the peace by doing so, I hated watching them play with one another's hands, seeing the evidence of her poisoned kiss on his cheek. It made me feel ill.

I felt like crying: because of how betrayed I felt by Lucas; and the little control I had over my own thoughts and body. I shifted Sam's weight from underneath me, picking up the book I had borrowed.

"Are you okay, Karla?" Ashley asked as I opened the door.

"Come on, Sam," I said, waving to the massive wolf that stood protectively behind me. Sam was now growling at the two boys that had stopped talking. Sam slipped through the door and I felt relief at being alone.

Chapter Nineteen - Knowledge

I walked to where I had picked out the book, finding the space for it easily. Sam ran to the open front door nearby, looking back at me as if he wanted me to follow him outside. The cold breeze from the night licked my face as I approached. The night was overcast, just as Ashley said it would be. The shine of metal caught my eye before I noticed Max was there. Sam walked to him warily, coming to a stop by his owner's side.

"Join me, Karla," Max said, offering his hand out to me.

"How'd you know it was me?" I asked politely, cautiously taking a seat by his side on the gravel floor.

"I've told you before: I'd know your blood apart from everyone else's any day. I was by Elisabeth's side for many years. We fought together hunting Starkorfs for a very long time. You carry the same blood as her, and I need no sight to know your burden."

Max swiveled his wheelchair to face me. Sam howled nearby at the roaring winds as it pushed his fur into knots.

"Burden?" I repeated, almost crying at the thought of someone understanding my pain. Sam left his position by his owner's side and gently rested his head on my lap where I could pat his fur.

"You were forced amongst them were you not? You feel hatred, especially towards the young one. Lucas?"

"I don't hate him," I said, blinking in surprise at his accusation.

"They treat you like a monster, a burden to them. They feel nothing but disgust when they see you, yet it is you who suffers. Why should someone as powerful as you suffer; someone with as much potential as you? Why do you allow yourself to suffer because of them?"

"I don't suffer!" I said, feeling acid burn at the back of my throat.

"They can't teach you properly because they don't know what you are. They can't give you the nurturing you need."

I jumped to my feet, catching Sam off guard and hearing a low yelp when I accidentally nudged my knee into his chest.

"You don't know what you are nor do you know what you're capable of. The years of knowledge, the—…"he continued.

"That's what you want from me? Knowledge?" I demanded. The sky roared with thunder and sparks of light filled the sky. I had only been sitting next to him no more than a minute and he was already manipulating me, trying to turn me against them.

"You do not belong with them, you never will. Stay with me, I will teach you… show you what you are, what you're capable of. All of the things they cannot offer you," he said calmly.

I felt the edging of my Shield, ready to project and burst, ready to lose control. As I turned towards the door I felt his withered nails dig into my wrist. "Let go," I shouted, trying to release his grip. He looked up at me with fierce black eyes, showing the anger he felt for me just as his daughter once had.

"You have no idea, do you child?" His tone was savage. "You have no idea how to control this curse and yet it is you who still maintains your body. Your soul will be taken if you don't learn how to control it—you stupid, ungrateful girl. I saw Elisabeth experience the exact same burden." His nails edged deeper and deeper into my wrist, piercing into my skin.

I felt threatened. I closed my eyes and tried to keep my Shield within me. *Don't lose control Karla, don't lose control.* I inhaled a deep breath. I opened my eyes feeling calm and in control. I grabbed his hand and threw it off from mine easier than I thought I could have.

"If I need your advice, I will come for it," I said, walking to the door and hearing his loud voice bellowing behind me.

"And I shall wait for your return; knowing it is your body, but not your soul, that you possess."

Chapter Twenty - Temptation

$\mathcal{L}$ucas was sprawled out on top of Ashley's bed, while Ashley sat on mine. They stopped their conversation when I interrupted them, closing the door behind me. Now that I was in the light, I could see the little bleeding marks on my wrist from Max's strong grasp.

"Karla," Ashley said in surprise, getting off my bed as if he had been busted for doing something wrong and quickly collecting himself. He stood in front of me, a little nervous. I took a few steps back clutching at the new book I had borrowed, unsure of why Ashley looked nervous when he approached me.

"Lucas wants to stay in here for the night. I told him I'd ask you first though—after all it's your room too." Ashley flashed all his pearly whites, stretching out a smile that forced little dimples into his chin.

"I...um...yeah. Sure," I stuttered. *I was to share the same room as Lucas?*

"You got another book," Ashley stated, as he tried looking through my clamped fingers to see the title.

"Yeah. Something to keep me awake tonight." The book was thicker than the width of my hand and heavier than a bucket of water.

"You won't have to do that tonight now that Lucas is here," Ashley replied. I pushed myself past Ashley, placing the book onto my bed.

"No I want to. It's fine. Besides, I can't sleep," I said, slumping onto the bed. I didn't want to risk dreaming of that horrible woman.

"Is it because of the dreams?" Ashley asked, leaning up against the bathroom doorframe and watching me anxiously.

Lucas shuffled himself into a sitting position, his eyes intent on me. "Dreams?" he asked coolly. I looked back over to Ashley who still had his arms strapped across his chest.

"Yeah," I sighed.

There was a scraping of the door and then a howl. I jumped to the door, letting in the large wolf I had abandoned. Sam came galloping through the room and took his spot at the end of my bed.

Ashley jumped on Lucas while they tugged and pushed at one another's faces. I picked up the book I had taken, while the two fought playfully between themselves. Sam looked at them as if he were an old man watching two immature grownups play.

A part of the book was in English, and the rest was a foreign language that had small scribbles down the page, alongside images of what looked like plants. Words were misplaced and jumbled, making the words into tongue twisting sentences that I couldn't understand, yet somehow still found interesting. Within the hour Ashley had fallen asleep and Lucas sat on the floor against the wall throwing his knife into the air. I licked at my fingers before flipping to the next page, finding an animated picture of what looked like a large bowl on stilts.

Sam's weight had numbed all feeling in my leg. His snoring was nowhere near as bad as Ashley's though. He snored like he was trying to blow the cottage down, with a ringing noise at the end when he took another breath.

"Did you ever have a dog growing up?" Lucas asked. It was the first time Lucas had spoken to me in what felt like a long time.

"Once—a Labrador. Her name was Francessca." I looked back down at Sam. Although he was a wolf, he reminded me more of a simple house dog: small and grumpy from old age.

"What happened to her?" he asked catching the knife again and flicking it through the air as gracefully as he had caught it.

"She got taken away. We couldn't keep her, she was too expensive," I said, saddened by the thought. The memory of my childhood friend getting taken away cast a grim shadow over the memories of my childhood; she really was my best friend until Sarah came along. "Did you?"

"Never. My father always told me anything that wasn't raised in our family was untrustworthy; could viciously lash out at my brother or I whenever it pleased. The closest I came to a pet was a stray kitten I found. I was only seven when I found it. It was stuck in a log and I helped it out. It was only a few weeks old, maybe five tops. It was all white with a black blotch over its eye. I decided to call it Pepper, an original name," he said, smiling to himself at the thought. "I kept it hidden away from my father and brother for a few days, feeding it left over food from my meals and giving it milk. On the fifth day of keeping it secret I was training with my father, learning how to use my ability. After I had finished I got to my room, hoping to find Pepper curled up in his box, but instead I found a massacred kitten with dislocated limbs. My brother had tortured it to death while I trained."

"That's horrible." I whispered, closing the thick book I still had in my hand.

"When my father found out that I kept a kitten in our house, he was furious and hit me five times. It was the first true punishment I've ever had. My brother was always his favorite. Shortly after that, they were killed."

I had no idea what to say, so I conveyed my sorrow through my saddened face. I looked at Lucas with pity. What a terrible and lonely childhood he had. He must have felt so very alone. Sam moaned as I shifted my weight under him, trying to adjust myself so I could feel my legs.

"They were killed by Starkorfs. The only reason I survived was because I had disobeyed my father once again and ran away. Shortly after that Kurt found me and brought me back to Seth and Helena," Lucas said grimly.

Before I could say anything, Lucas placed his finger to his lips for me to be silent. He listened intently, his head turned to the door. Lucas flicked his hands up gesturing for the both of us to rise. I got up; feeling frosty pinches as I tried to walk a few steps. Lucas quietly rose to his feet with the knife held tightly in his leathered hand.

"What is it?" I asked, slowly dragging my numb legs to where he stood.

Lucas grabbed my hand and quietly guided me to the door. He continued walking me deeper into the hallway and came to a stop at one of the doors, raising his hand for me to be quiet. He popped his head around the corner, looking into a room that flickered with shadows. I couldn't squeeze my head around his but I could see the reflection from the large mirror that hung from inside the room.

Trish and some foreign man were kissing between Trish's giggles and the man's deep moans. He was the same build as Ashley but with dark blonde, almost brown hair. I couldn't see his face because it was covered by Trish's hair. He wore all black with a grey leather coat over the top.

Lucas pushed me back, looking everywhere but my face, he was scared. He finally looked at me with panicked eyes. "Lucas what is it?" I said, brushing my hand over his face in concern. He looked like he was going to throw up, he was so pale and his lips looked blue. He grabbed my hand tighter and pulled me behind him.

"We've got to go," he whispered.

I slammed into his back when he abruptly stopped. I braced myself when it was Sam I saw blocking the hallway with his teeth bared, growling at us with his fur stiffened along his back.

"Sam," I said, pushing myself in front of Lucas so he could recognize it was me behind Lucas. The giant wolf lunged at me. Before I could hold in my scream of terror Lucas had me up against the wall. He quickly grabbed my hand and led me through the hall again, while the large wolf howled behind us.

"Get out!" Lucas screamed down the hallway.

Ashley burst through the door holding a knife in his hand. "Wha—…" Before Ashley could finish Lucas had a firm grip on his leather jacket, dragging him to follow us.

"They're here!" Lucas bellowed.

Ashley's face turned as pale as Lucas's. He took Lucas's hand off his shirt and ran ahead of us. When we reached the living room, Suzumiya and Chris were already there, raiding the room. Ashley dashed into one of the other halls.

"Here, here?" Suzumiya pointed to the floor.

"Here, here darling," an unfamiliar voice called out.

Lucas threw me behind him, accidently slamming me into one of the bookshelves. Trish and the man stood in the hall. Sam howled like an alarm ringing when there's an intruder. Sam plunged himself into Lucas's chest, baring his teeth towards Lucas's throat. Chris and Suzumiya were already jumping through the air with swift kicks and punches at the man's satisfied smile. Trish quickly took her gloves off, thriving in the enjoyment of what she was watching. A flame burst over Lucas as quickly as Sam had jumped on him.

Flames roared over my Shield as I had my hands protectively outstretched over Lucas. Ripples of purple flustered over my Shield, like water reflecting a sunset.

"You!" Trish bellowed, slamming her hands together and producing a huge shock wave of flames in front of my face as my Shield protected me.

"Karla, let's go," Lucas said still behind me, ushering me out. Everyone was scurrying out the front door. Helena looked absolutely horrified. I grabbed Lucas's hand, following his lead through the doorway. Max sat contently in front of everyone, blocking the way to the woods. His eyes blistered with black while his cracked smile started to bleed.

As soon as a strong breeze of air brushed past my nose, I felt my blood pulse with the strongest shock it has ever felt. It hammered repetitively under my skin like drums. It was something in the air, the calling of my name; the frailness of the breeze. The other three had boxed us in leaving Max to smile in pleasure.

I focused on the direction we had to go to. Thunder roared around us, streaking the air with flashes of light around us. "Go to the cars." I screamed. "I've got this." I felt my mind drift as if I were in another dream, dazed by how real it all seemed. *What am I doing?* It was my thoughts, but it wasn't how it normally was; like I was in third person.

"Go," I shouted. It was my voice shouting but it wasn't me. *It was her.*

"Karla, I'm not leaving you," Lucas said. I felt his leathered hand tighten around my arm before I realized that I have pushed him into the trees forcefully. It wasn't me that pushed him. It was she.

"Don't you know you shouldn't play with fire, little girl?" I said, feeling the twitch of my lips turn into a smile. Black ripples shaded around me like thriving blades.

"What do you know? The little one has a back bone after all," Trish laughed to herself. I crouched into a sitting position, hovering over the ground like a cat.

"Oh it's not the little one any more, sweetie." I slammed my fist into the ground, sending a huge pulsating shockwave over the ground, knocking them all off their feet. Max was thrown from his wheelchair into the trees.

"Father!" Trish screamed, picking herself up from the ground. Her body flared into flames with a simple burst, and I could see nothing other than her arms, legs and enriched black eyes. Everything else fluttered with blue flames.

I don't want to do this, I cried internally.

I'm keeping them alive, isn't that what you want? She answered angrily to me in my head.

Flames circled around like a cyclone compressing itself onto my Shield.

"That's a nice party trick," I mused. "Play time's over, sweetheart." I jumped through the air, letting ten meters come between the ground and I. I flew past the smothered flames. I couldn't find the man anywhere. He has left Trish.

That's when I realized the woman's intentions. My own hands were going to be the cause of murder. *My hands, although not my will.* She wanted Trish dead. As soon as a ripple of my Shield pulsed towards her, I took control of what was rightfully mine—my body. Trish got thrown back into her small cottage where Sam lay as if he were still sleeping.

The trees, you stupid girl, she yelled at me angrily after I had forcefully ejected her from my mind. Lucas jumped out from the trees, lunging for my hand and leading me through the forest as fast as we could run.

When we burst through the forest I saw at once a fight was taking place. Chris was slammed into Seth's car, caving in the roof while he cried out in pain. Suzumiya jumped onto a mutated woman, smothered in dirt like a cat. With one quick flick of her blade, the disfigured woman collapsed to the ground. Ashley blocked the sword that kept trying to slice through his neck, stabbing a small dagger into the man's own neck in return. Seth and Kurt protected Helena as she wailed in fear. There were so many of them, at least twenty.

"Don't leave my side, okay?" Lucas said, pulling me towards where everyone fought. I was pushed into the ground, and then something cut at my hair. I looked up and I searched over the man's face—it was as dirty as the ground beneath me—and I saw he was choking because of the knife Lucas had stabbed into his stomach. The man had no nose, nor a scar in its place.

Lucas pulled my dazed body up, cutting and slicing at random attackers that jumped from all angles. He took his place by Kurt and Seth's side, throwing me into the protected circle with Helena.

"There's too many," Kurt bellowed. It was the first time I had seen the old man fight but it was obvious why he didn't do it often, his old age has withered him, and he obviously found it hard to keep up with the onslaught of attackers.

"Ashley, Seth, and I will stay, you get the others to the car," Lucas ordered as another woman screamed, lunging at Lucas like an animal. He punched her in the stomach, watching her fall to the ground as she gasped for the air she had lost.

"Right," Kurt said grabbing Helena and I. He quickly ran with us to the car where Suzumiya and Chris had already started the engine. They were revving and ready to go. Ashley, Lucas, and Seth, stood around the car protectively throwing off any intruders.

Seth threw Helena into the car, and as I entered behind her I was suddenly pulled out of the car and slammed against the car's door. A man scratched at where I had once been with his deformed fingers and razor sharp nails. Lucas hit him with a jaw-breaking punch. Lucas had lost the knife that he had, and now had to fight with his bare hands. He pushed Seth into the seat where I was meant to be, closing the door as the car screeched away and swerved through the jumping Starkorfs.

Lucas grabbed my hand and led me through the pile of attackers, while Ashley stayed close behind swinging his knife. Lucas threw me onto his bike and was sitting in front of me within seconds. There was a jolt of power from underneath, and the bike roared with a humming noise that beat in time with my heart. He grabbed my hands and wrapped them around his stomach tightly as the bike gave a jolt of power in acceleration. Ashley was ahead on his bike. Somehow he had managed to get out of the dangerous environment before us. I turned around, looking at the few deformed creatures that ran after us, losing all sight of them when the trees covered the road when we turned onto it.

2

Misguided Curse

If I were to fight everyone's battle,
I would never have time to fight my own.
If I were to fight everyone's battle,
I would be forever at war.
If I were to destroy all enemies and burdens,
what would my purpose in this lifetime be?
Am I a pawn of destruction?
Or simply a misguided girl tortured in the night?

Chapter Twenty-One - Memories

*L*ucas placed his hand over mine and tightened them around his stomach every few minutes so that I wouldn't lose grip. Without him I think I would have fallen off the back of his bike from being so numb. My mind had drifted from any sense of reality and taunted me with the memoires of the war I had just witnessed. The war *she* has dragged me into.

I visualized all the power that came from my body and somehow I sensed even at that level of strength she forced through me, she was holding back. I could feel the immense experience and skills that she had, coupled with an intense desire to see Trish dead. I thought of Trish and the anger she displayed which incited my murderous rage. Compared to Trish, and the woman in my mind, I had no idea what I was capable of. *She* knew though—she knew how to manipulate my body to her advantage. I was nothing more but a prisoner in my own mind; an onlooker watching from afar. She hadn't spoken to me since I took back control of my body. She was now silent, leaving me to my own reflections. Everything seemed like a blur; confusion smothered reality.

Lucas's hand wrapped around mine again, tightening the grip around his stomach, that I had obviously let slip without realizing. He left his hand on mine, stroking it with his leather-gloved hand that was now sticky from blood—the blood of people whose life he took. *Not people: Starkorfs*. It reminded me of the first time I was attacked by Raven. She had looked ordinary, unlike the other mutants who had since attacked me. The child looked no older than twelve, and all that she possessed out of the ordinary was her crystallized blue eyes and pointy teeth. *How is such a beast contained within that mask of innocence?*

My surroundings were familiar: the same small, deserted town that was no more than two hours out of my hometown. My parents were only a couple of hours away. I wanted to cry; to release the build-up of poisoned emotion in my body, but no tears would leave my eyes.

My face held the same shocked expression that it had for two hours now.

Ashley overtook us and went into the small fuel station that was deserted by the left of the road. Only a small neon sign flashed red then black: 'Carl's Corner Open.' Lucas pulled into the same fuel station and parked next to Ashley's bike, which was covered with dirt and splashes of blood. Looking at his injuries I saw that the blood was his own.

"We'll fuel up here. That should be enough fuel to get there," Ashley said, as Lucas and I stared at the mark of blood. Ashley tried rubbing it off but gave up within moments. Lucas slowly pulled my hands from his stomach and pushed himself off, waiting for Ashley to finish putting fuel in his bike.

Everything still seemed so distant to me that even the fuel station seemed out of this world, an abnormal thing to take in. Lucas pushed back the hair that had flopped in front of my eyes. Without the force of the wind pushing my long hair behind me, my dirt stained split ends were whipping at my eyes. It took me only a few seconds to crash back to reality under his cold, leathered touch. Finally I noticed Lucas, the one that saved my life.

"You alright?" Lucas asked stroking my cheek slowly, reassuringly. I nodded, grabbing his hand and embracing it.

"Where's everyone else?" I asked, searching over the road we had turned off.

Ashley stretched the nozzle to the side of Lucas's bike and watched the price rise as the tank swallowed greedily.

"We will meet with them soon; they had to go a different route. Come on, you need to get cleaned up," Lucas said as he waited for me to walk towards the store with him. Before we entered, he tried rubbing the dirt off his face and combing through his hair to make himself look half presentable—trying to look like someone that wasn't smothered in blood and that hasn't just been in a fight. A pretence any sane person would see through if they stared at his blood soaked, torn, and unbuttoned shirt for long enough.

I pulled him back from the entrance as he went to open the door and swept my fingers across his shirt, pinning up the buttons from the bottom up to his chest. His stomach and chest were so hard against the touch of my soft hands. I left my hand to linger, feeling the beat of his heart thumping through his shirt. He placed his hand over mine, forcing my hand firmly onto his chest. To my surprise the beat of his heart doubled, matching the beat of my own. He pulled our hands to our side and let go of mine as he opened the door.

It was a tiny shop that had two shelves in the middle with a few packaged snacks and a counter in the corner with an old man sleeping behind it. "Do you want something to eat?" Lucas asked. I shook my head slowly; food was the last thing on my mind. "Ok. Go clean up a little," he said, pointing me to the direction of the bathroom. He watched over me warily as I walked forward without him. I felt just as unsafe as I had when the Starkorfs attacked us. *I wonder if it is possible for them to break into this stall right now...*

The mirror reflected a cut across my cheek that had almost completely healed. The time it now took me to heal was quicker than before. More so than what it used to be like before *she* came, the woman from my dreams. I tried gently rubbing off the dirt and splatters of blood from my skin without much success. The blood was stained just as vividly as the images in my mind. Eventually I was able to scrub it off.

It was hard to see the surroundings in the night, but the sun began to creep up readying to break dawn. It has been almost six hours since I saw any sign of Suzumiya's car which had me concerned as to whether they had actually made it out safe or not. We continued along the road; Lucas still reassuring me with comforting embraces of his hand and only letting go of mine when he needed both to steer. I knew how unsafe it was for him to steer with one hand but his reassurance was too much for me to deny. *I needed it.*

The breeze against my arms was colder than it had been previously in the night and my body longed for rest. I nuzzled my head into Lucas's back, grateful for something to rest my head on. Looking at the sky that now broke out with bright colors as the sun slowly rose, I tried to evaluate how I was feeling: *Who is this woman that possessed me? Is all this fighting what I now have to do? Do I have to be a part of this war?*

Lucas's thumb rubbed over my hand, softly waking me from my eerie thoughts. I nuzzled my face into his muscular back. *Lucas saved me. Lucas is protecting me.* I felt ashamed of how wrongly I had judged him, thinking that he was trying to trick me or do wrong by me. As different as he and I seemed to be, we were also very much the same. *And if anyone can help me, it will be Lucas: my protector.*

Although rest was what I longed for I could not give my body that satisfaction. I knew when I slept *she* would be waiting for my

154

arrival. Instead I gazed up at the sky, watching as the moon's surface and the stars slowly lost their shine as the sun began to rise.

An hour later, we arrived in a town that the rising sun helped me recognize: the small corner store, the video shop next to the fish and chip shop, the only shopping centre in town. It was my hometown: Roperia. I sat up straight, feeling the tears trail down my cheeks as I began to cry. Ashley and Lucas have brought me to see Mum and Dad. I turned around to see Ashley's hard eyes as he concentrated on the road, and then on me. Words and feelings that I thought would bubble to the surface when I would finally see my parents again, vanished, leaving me breathless.

When we pulled into my house, I stared at it, dazed. I have never cherished its old humble exterior so sentimentally in my life. Lucas had hopped off the motorbike, offering his hand out to me. I accepted it, moving my shaky legs towards the footpath. *Why are my legs shaking?* Ashley stood in front of us near the mailbox, also staring at the house. Excitement and relief straightened my legs as I drove away my body's odd and eerie feeling. I quickly paced towards Ashley, intending to walk past the door but he stopped me, outstretching his hand in front of me so I couldn't walk any further.

Ashley slowly took steps towards my home, searching over the surroundings with his big, bulky shoulders, tensed and ready to fight if even a shadow moved. His pocket began to vibrate and he looked at the mobile's screen. His tense, muscular shoulders dropped as he answered it. "Hey Dad, we just arrived," Ashley said, as he walked away.

Looking back at the door, I flooded with emotion. *Mum and Dad are behind this door. I will finally be reunited with them. They will make this better and know what to do. They will be able to tell me what they know and how they knew the Starkorfs would come for me. I will finally have my parents back.*

"Mum? Dad?" I bellowed, banging on the door. There was no reply.

"Do you have a key?" Lucas asked, standing behind me and searching over the small house. I looked over the rose bush Mum always loved and watered. It looked almost dead, with a withering leaf ready to fall off. I looked under it where the key was usually hidden to find the space empty.

"Mum?" I called out, slamming my fist down on the door. "Dad?" Still, no answer.

I lead Lucas around the house to my room. It was only three stairs high, so the window was reachable. I lifted the window up and dragged it across, pushing it open.

"Let me go first," Lucas said, as he easily lifted himself through the window. Ashley jogged around the corner, putting the phone back in his pocket and cupping his hands together. Ashley supported one of my feet so I had extra help to climb through the window. I shifted my weight through the window as Ashley gave me an extra push. I flopped onto the bed head first, losing any steadiness or aim I had before the unexpected boost. Lucas looked around my room, staring at the posters on my wall and picking up the unfinished book that was on my bedside table.

Lucas walked in front of me checking each room before I did, making sure no Starkorfs were present. After opening all the bedroom doors he looked back at Ashley and me with uncertain eyes.

"Mum... Dad?" I called in suspense, waiting for them to welcome me home. I flicked all the lights on, searching over the furniture frantically until Lucas and Ashley walked into the kitchen where I now stood dazed.

"Karla," Lucas said, offering his hand to me. I stroked my hand through my long hair, upset and frantic. *Where are they?* I took a few steps back, rejecting the hand Lucas offered me.

"They're not here," I said my voice seemed distant, unrecognisable. *They're not here.* "Why aren't they here?" I demanded angrily towards both Lucas and Ashley.

"We don't know," Lucas said quietly.

I used the bench for support, trying to keep my limp body standing. "They should be here!" I said, yelling at no one in particular. My legs gave in, slowly sliding me to the ground. The reunion I thought I was so close to obtaining was now gone. *I miss my parents so much.*

"Maybe they're staying over at someone's for the weekend," Lucas offered.

"They wouldn't have, they work pretty much every day," I said trying to find a reason as to why they weren't here. I felt a build-up of grief rise from my stomach, creeping through my chest.

"They thought they lost you, I'm sure they would have taken days off," Lucas said, crouching to my eye level. I held my hands to my mouth trying to cover the gasping, hyperventilating breaths I was sucking in. "Karla I need you to breathe."

I peered at the knife that was closest, knowing too well what I could do with it. *Do it. Do it.* The voice echoed in my head. *Do it.*

Visions of her hands stabbing into people's bodies flickered through my mind in a quick flashback of memories. I felt the pulse of Aeisha—Misfeata's Immortal Blades—awaken and indulge in Starkorfs blood. Every time it was Aeisha that took the lives. Stabbing into chests, legs, lungs, arms: the images flipping through my mind as if it were I who committed the acts.

"Stop it!" I screamed, clutching at my head, trying to shake away the images I have seen; the memories of the woman in my dream and all that she has done. The images were all I saw now. The gasp for air, the struggle for life, their eyes flutter and then fade into nothing but eternal sleep. I saw everything but her face, the woman who lay dormant in my dreams, waiting to take over my body. These were all the woman's horrendous memories.

"Lucas. Leave me," I said, trying to push the woman's thoughts from my mind as she bombarded me, trying to take control of my body. I had already plunged something into Lucas's chest before when he saved me from Raven and it was something I never wanted to do again. *To anyone.*

The worst part was that I could see the images in my head. I could imagine being the one to take Lucas's life. When I looked at the knife I measured how many ways, how many angles I could use it, to commit the murder. My body willed me to take his life with anything but remorse, leaving me to feel sickened.

"Karla," Lucas said steadily. I flinched under his touch as he placed his hand on my shoulder. "Karla, breathe. It will be fine. When day comes we will ask your neighbours. We will ask whomever we must. Just breathe."

Word by word, I inhaled his calming influence. *Calm. Breathe.* I felt the stirring of the woman in my mind cease as I collected myself. My chest rose and fell steadily as I regained my composure. I stared into Lucas's dark brown eyes as he watched me breathe in and out slowly. I nodded my head vigorously as I continued to follow his lead. *I need to be calm. I will find my parents.*

"It's only a few hours until the neighbours will be awake. Why don't you rest until then? We won't do anything until you wake," Lucas said soothingly. I gathered my sinful thoughts, erasing them until I was once again in control.

I walked over to the stacked knives and one by one slowly took them out of their holders, placing them into the drawer where all the blunt knives were kept. One by one I felt the temptation leave my hand as the knives sunk to the bottom of the drawer. As each one fell, I realized how much I wanted that blade to stay in my hand, I felt like I needed protection. *But from what?*

My bed felt like a foreign object to rest on. Something I haven't felt for a long time. As tired as I was, I couldn't sleep. I would rather not sleep than get tortured in my dreams. I haven't spoken to Lucas since my temptation to take his life.

Even though they didn't say it, I knew neither of them trusted me by myself. That's why he insisted my bedroom door stay open so he could hear me from the lounge-room in case 'someone intruded', or in other words, in case I tried to escape. As my mind bounced from one thing to another, my eyes grew heavy and my mind was taken into a deep sleep.

I wore my leathered protection, strapping the weapons firmly across my body. I checked the aim through my cross bow, displeased. I threw it to the ground in frustration. "Argh, is there a decent one around here?" I demanded. I scurried through the wardrobe in my hidden stash of weapons.

"Karla sweetie, please stop," Lucas said as he came to my room, wearing black jeans and a white shirt, half buttoned.

"Don't Lucas," I said, raising my finger to him as a warning, without flicking my eyes to see his face. Crossbow, knife, dagger, gun... Gun? Why do I have a gun in here? I threw the gun onto my bed. I'll discard it as soon as I find something appropriate.

"You know most women scurry through their closet for clothes, yet you scurry through yours for objects that can kill people," Lucas said to me. I smiled, giving him the attention he wanted from me.

"Well if it's clothes you're concerned about, I could easily fix that problem," I said as I wrapped my hands around his neck, smiling into his beautiful dark brown eyes. I gently brushed my lips past his, teasing him. Instead, his lips were more of a tease to me, as I wanted every part of his mouth desperately to melt into mine.

I searched over his expressionless face: "Lucas?"

Lucas slowly tilted his head down, removing his dripping hand away from his stomach to reveal the gun I held against him. I didn't realize I had reached out for the gun while my other hand was still wrapped around his neck. The hole seeped out blood, staining the green dress I now wore; the same green dress I wore when Uncle Kyle had given me the warning in my first dream of Lucas. The same dress the woman wore when she tortured me in my previous dream of the mirrored room.

He opened his mouth but no sound followed. I hadn't even heard the fire of the gun. Lucas dropped to the floor, filling the pale blue carpet with a dark red. His eyes rolled into the back of his head showing nothing but ghostly white.

"Well that wasn't what I was expecting at all." Uncle Kyle stood at my door, unperturbed by the murder I had just committed.

"Uncle?" I said, unfazed, as if I didn't care about what had happened either.

"You could have at least waited for Aeisha," Uncle Kyle said in a condescending tone.

"You have her?!" I shrieked in joy, jumping over Lucas's corpse. I hugged Uncle Kyle in pleasure, knowing he had Aeisha—my two blades—that I've longed for.

"Of course I do!" Uncle Kyle smiled, as he unwrapped the covered blades he now held and presented them to me in the same way as he had when he offered me my Christmas presents as a young child. A cough was spluttered from the ground, distracting me from the beautiful Aeisha that was within my grasp. I searched over Lucas's grovelling body as he tried to push himself up.

"Karla…" he choked. "It's either…." He took another shallow breath, "…Aeisha or me." He splattered blood across the carpet while his eyes rolled over the room like a puppet, he was barely conscious.

"Don't be stupid, boy," the woman inside me laughed to herself. It wasn't me: it was her. She had once again returned to my dreams. She controlled my body, moving me over to Lucas, and I could only watch in horror as she lifted her heel above his face and slammed it with force making it—

"Lucas!" I screamed. My hair was now stuck to my face in sweat. I felt a firm grip around me, trying to squeeze as much pressure into me as it could, crushing me. Ashley gripped me like an iron bar, trying to control my scratching hands.

"Shh, shh…" Ashley whispered, taking deep breaths in front of me like Lucas had earlier this morning. I took his lead, trying to stop my pounding heart from exploding. I closed my eyes, throwing myself into darkness once more. *It was only a dream. Lucas is fine.* I tapped Ashley's hand to let him know I was now alright.

"Thank you Ashley," I said straightening myself. I looked out the window of my room noticing it was dark outside. *Night again?*

"You slept all day," Ashley said as he drew back from me and sat on the end of my bed. "Lucas asked your neighbours. Nothing has been reported of your disappearance because your parents haven't been here either. On the same day that we took you, they told your neighbour on the left that some family issues came up and they had to leave town for a while. Lucas asked a few more people and it is all the same. Everyone thinks all three of you have left town because of family commitments."

My mouth opened in shock and then closed, as I had nothing to say. *Where have my parents gone?* Instead of crying I felt a pull of determination. *Where has this strength come from?*

"We will find them," I said, certain and determined. Ashley creased his eyebrows at me confused. *If all I do is cry then what will be resolved?* I took a long breath as I thought of who might be able to help, who might know where they had gone.

Lucas made his appearance known at the door as he looked at me with a hard face. He knew of the same person that I did. The one who might have the answers that I desperately needed and someone I have missed without understanding why, amongst all the havoc.

"Paul," I said. "He was the last person I saw before you took me, Lucas. Maybe he knows something."

"Paul." Lucas repeated the word bitterly. Ashley gave an odd glance between Lucas and me before nodding his head to agree.

"Okay, but after that we have to go. It is unsafe for us to stay here for so long. The others are at an old warehouse a little out of town. We have to meet up with them as soon as we visit this Paul person," Ashley said as he pulled out his phone and glanced at the screen. "I will quickly call Dad and let him know of our progress."

Lucas looked at me angrily. I pushed past him, not understanding the meaning behind his harsh glare. *What had I done wrong?* I quickly walked to the bathroom to wash my face and plait my long hair to the side.

I hadn't seen Paul since the accident. We left many things on uncertain terms as well. *How am I supposed to ask him where my parents are after I have gone missing for so long? Did he even care that I went missing, or did he too think I had left town with my parents?* My green eyes radiated with determination. *I can do this; I can confront Paul and find my parents.*

Chapter Twenty-Two- Confrontation and Goodbyes

$\mathcal{I}$ looked between the piece of paper Paul had once given me with his address and the house we were now parked in front of. Music poured out of the front door as many students from my school stumbled in and out. *A party?*

I got off the bike behind Lucas, giving him an uncertain glance. "This is his house," I said, walking towards the crowded party. I thought we would simply be able to ring the doorbell and ask to speak with Paul, find out the information we needed, and, unfortunately leave Paul behind forever.

I looked down at my leathered attire that clung to my figure as Ashley came to my side.

"Come on. We don't have much time. The others are waiting for us. Let's find him," he said, stroking through his black hair.

The music poured out of the door like a boom box when we got closer, playing some tacky beat with incomprehensible lyrics. "Hey gorgeous!" some guy said to one of the girls behind us—who then smiled wickedly in his direction.

"Thanks, but you're not my type," Lucas said, placing his hand against the guy's chest and pushing him to the side so he could walk through the doorway, shortly followed by Ashley, and then me, as the guy looked between us in confusion.

I searched over the dancing students, finding Sarah amongst all of them in a purple strapless dress. I walked towards her, excited to see my friend after what had felt like far too long. I was pushed and shoved in the crowd, losing sight of Sarah's blonde flicking hair. I never thought we had this many students in our school. Ashley and Lucas drifted apart, checking different parts of the crowded rooms.

"Karla?!" Sarah squealed. I followed her voice as she jumped past a few of the students beside her to hug me. "Where have you been? Is your family alright?" she asked, her breath reeking of vodka and strawberries. "I don't know why you haven't phoned me or anything. That's kind of weird. Especially after you had that car accident with Paul and everything…" she remarked, hugging me again.

It almost brought tears to my eyes to hear her rant. *How surreal it makes everything.* As Sarah spoke, I noticed some of her mascara smudged beneath her eye. I wiped it away for her, awkwardly smiling as she continued chatting and chewing bubble gum.

"Oh and what is happening with you two by the way?" she asked me. "Like I was surprised when Paul came to me and was really intense about you. Like he was really freaking out, and asking me if you were okay after the accident, and where you had gone and stuff. I didn't think he would be your type, but I give you my blessing. He is so much more handsome than that Greg guy anyway."

She looked at me again with a wide smile and big eyes, squealed, and then hugged me again. "Speaking of handsome…" She looked across the room at a guy who wore pink shaded glasses with long shaggy black hair. "I will bring him over to you. Craig is my new boyfriend. We have only been dating for two weeks but he's really sweet and we are pretty serious about it all. Wait right here," she instructed as she took an unstable step back and patted me on the hand. "I'll go get him." Sarah walked towards her new boyfriend Craig as he walked outside, not noticing her.

I closed my eyes, savouring the memory. *That may very well be the last time I ever speak to Sarah, and yet I wouldn't change it.* I wanted to chase after her to say goodbye, tell her how much she meant to me, how amazing she was, but my feet wouldn't move. *What would I tell her? If I say my goodbyes to everyone, does that really mean I am saying goodbye to the life I knew?*

"Hey darling," the guy in front of me said, he stopped jumping in front of me and swayed back and forth smelling so strongly of alcohol that I had to hold my nose. The guy started singing in a cracked tone, obviously forgetting the words. He paused, looking at the light and continued. I turned to walk on when he suddenly grabbed my hand and pulled me back. I tore at his hand, trying to get out of the creep's hold on me.

"Let go!" I shouted, but no one heard me over the loud music. The guy started singing to himself again, swaying back and forth. "Let go!" I yelled again. When I opened my eyes, only the music played and all the bouncing students had stopped and were staring at me with panicked eyes. The guy was now under my knee where I had him pinned at the chest to the ground, and I held a small knife to his throat with my hand. My firm grip around his wrist and his pinned chest made him disorientated, unsure of how he got to where he was.

I heard my name being called over the music but I didn't have the courage to look up through the people to see who it was that called my name. Lucas squeezed himself through the circle, coming to my side and slowly shaking the knife out of my hand. I was just as shocked as everyone else and at first I couldn't let go of the knife.

"Karla. Look at me," Lucas said. I looked at his hand which was covering mine, then into his eyes. "Let's go." He slowly helped me up as I looked over the terrified faces of those who I once went to school with. *What am I turning into?*

"Karla?" a familiar, sweet voice said. I turned, feeling shock and then shame, as I realized what Paul had just seen me do. I rushed out the door before I started crying in front of everyone, ashamed of what kind of monster I had become.

The cool air of the night swept past me as I ran outside. I held in the tears that threatened to break loose. *No, I will not cry anymore.* I dropped my shoulders, ashamed at the reflexes my body now performed on instinct. *I am that scared of others that I will instantly pull a knife on someone in my own defense. What kind of person have I become?*

"Karla?" Paul called, pushing his bulky frame past Lucas and Ashley as he ran to where I stood on the footpath.

"Paul," I said almost crying at the sight of his concerned green eyes. He had the same pensive expression he held before he was knocked unconscious in the car accident. A small pink scar was healing on his tanned skin near his chin, reminding me of when we last saw one another.

Paul hugged me tightly, and my hands stiffened at my sides in surprise. The tight embrace made it impossibly hard for me to say anything and even breathing became difficult. It was such a surprise. *Has he not seen what I have become? Did he not see what I did in there, to that person?*

"I've missed you so much," he confessed, tightening his grip around me and squeezing the air out of my lungs. He lifted me off the ground before releasing the hold he had on me. Paul cupped my face, searching it over as if it was of importance to him. I forgot how bizarrely close we had become.

"I missed you too," I admitted, now realising how true that really was. I had missed Paul Stuart like crazy without even knowing it. *How could I have forgotten his face?* I had to touch it to make sure it was real. I let my gentle hand linger on his chin as I felt the edge of the scar. *Thank goodness he is alright.* I held my finger to it, trying to remember the moment, for it was most likely the last time I would see him.

Lucas coughed to interrupt Paul's hold over me. My heart thumped as Lucas looked at me coldly and then looked back towards the party where the doors were now closed.

"Where were you?" Paul asked desperately. I eyed Ashley as he gave me a long look. I couldn't really tell Paul where I had been and what I had seen, he would never believe me.

"Paul." I grabbed his hand. Somehow not being with him for such a long time made me feel desperate to touch him as I felt it would be the last time I'd get the opportunity. "What happened when you became conscious after the car accident? Have you seen my parents since?"

Paul looked down at our entwined hands, confused.

"What do you mean? I don't understand," Paul said uncertainly. "I woke up shortly after the car accident; I was only unconscious for a few minutes. I looked around for you for ages and couldn't find you anywhere on the streets. I went to your house then, thinking you were either home or had gone to the hospital. I was going to go to the hospital next but you were already home. Well, your mum said you were. Your parents came to the door and said you were okay and resting. I was really worried about you. You looked so sick," Paul said, looking at me with sad eyes. "The next day when I came to see how you were after school, you weren't there. Your neighbour said some family issues had come up and you all had to leave the very same day."

Ashley gave Lucas a hard look before the phone in Ashley's pocket began to ring. He answered it without hesitation, walking towards his motorbike. "Yea, Dad?" Ashley answered.

"Karla is everything alright?" Paul asked, still holding my hand as he gave Lucas a sideways glance. "I thought you said you didn't know him?" I barely heard his annoyed tone as my mind tumbled over my parent's disappearance. *Why would my parents lie? And where have they gone...is it possible they've been kidnapped?*

The moon was smothered with grey clouds, only letting half of its shine seep through to fill the night with light. I stared down the street, watching one figure pause in the middle of the road while I was deep in thought. *Why would my parents lie? Or were they forced to?* The figure played with what looked like one long stick and a smaller one as they stumbled awkwardly down the road. The figure wobbled from side to side, making me think it was a drunken person stumbling to Paul's party.

A car turned the corner, shining its headlights onto the wobbling figure. I only saw hair flash across her face and within the second I blinked my eyes, the car had passed over where she once was. I screamed before I realized I could see no remains of the girl's body.

"What is it?" both Lucas and Paul said, giving one another a territorial look, sizing one another up. I pointed in the direction where I saw the unsteady figure.

"Someone was standing in the middle of the road," I breathed heavily, still searching over the road. "She vanished just like that." I clicked my fingers.

"Did you hear that Ashley?" Lucas called out.

"We need to go," Ashley answered from his bike.

Both Ashley and Lucas were fully alert. Lucas walked over to his motorbike. When I searched back over the road I saw the figure again, this time realising it wasn't an intoxicated teenager playing with two sticks but a deformed woman with a bow and arrow.

I threw myself onto Paul pushing him onto the road, just as I felt the arrow's breeze brush past my back. 'Starkorf,' the woman in my head confirmed.

By the time I looked back up at the Starkorf's location Lucas had already jumped onto the screeching woman. I witnessed Lucas twist her neck in one clean break, and listened to her screams descend into silence. Lucas came pounding down the street with the body flopped over his shoulder. Just like that, she was dead. I then realized it wasn't just my dreams that I dreaded—it was simply walking down the street doing an everyday normal human thing.

"What was that?" Paul asked, mortified. I quickly looked away from the dead body and stared down at Paul who I was awkwardly on top of. "Did he just murder someone?" Paul accused with wide eyes.

"No. It's not like that," I said panicking as I realized what he must have thought. "She wasn't human... she would've killed us," I explained desperately.

"We don't have time for this, we need to go!" Ashley shouted as he clipped his helmet on. "Either he comes or stays. I'd recommend he comes so Kurt can decide what happens to him."

"What. Why? He hasn't done anything wrong," I said alarmed.

"Well he *did* see a Starkorf," Lucas said coldly.

"Not in that context," Ashley gave Lucas a harsh glare. "If your parents have been taken, there is a possibility they might come back for Paul for whatever reason. He might become a liability."

"We put Paul in jeopardy?" I asked, mortified that my own selfish desire that had now put Paul in harm's way.

"Karla. What have you gotten yourself into?" Paul asked, looking over me with an unreadable expression. His eyes were large and his jaw was clenched. *Does he now hate what I am and what I am involved with? I too hate all that I have now become. I will not cry, I cannot cry anymore…*

"I'm sorry," I said, still holding back the tears I so desperately wanted to release. Paul stared at me for what felt like an eternity. *What is he thinking? What can I say to make any of this better?*

"If you're in trouble I want to help you," Paul said. He cupped my face so he could look into my eyes, before looking over at Lucas angrily. "But I'm only coming to help you get away from these people, no matter what the reason is that you're with them. But I need you to tell me everything. Like what that *thing* was that tried to hurt you." He gestured with his eyes at the dead body still over Lucas's shoulder.

I was bewildered. Paul wanted to help me? He had now seen the monster I had become—a monster with a raging temper. The things and creatures I was involved with! This would threaten his own life and yet he accepted it within moments, just wanting to help me. *Paul wants to help me get out of this situation,* I thought in amazement. *Is that even possible? I don't want to risk his life but I cannot leave him here either if it will put him in jeopardy. If this is his decision, do I have the right to take it from him?*

Lucas positioned the corpse on his bike. We had to dispose of the body, as we couldn't leave it in the middle of a street.

"We need to go," Ashley said as he pulled up beside us on his bike. "Karla you can come with me?" He was looking between Paul and Lucas. I could feel the tension between them as they locked eyes and looked away from one another in disgust.

"Hurry up. We need to go, stop wasting my time," Lucas said angrily to Paul. Paul and I scuffled off the ground. I placed myself on the back of Ashley's bike as Paul quickly came over to me.

"I will get you out of this mess. I can tell this isn't what you want," Paul said, peering into my eyes deeply. He pressed his lips to my forehead, sending a shudder of warmth through my whole body. He stroked my cheek before hopping on the back of Lucas's bike so that the dead Starkorf lay between them.

I stared at Paul's broad back, trying to comprehend how he could still view me as innocent. With only a few questions about what had happened in front of his very eyes, he believed in me, and my innocence. *He trusts me that much that he has no issue with hopping on a stranger's bike and following me to an unknown destination. I wonder if he will truly want to save me after I tell him of this other life I am now forced to live. Will Paul still want to protect me when it is not only the Starkorfs I need protection from but myself as well?*

Chapter Twenty-Three - Identity

I held Ashley tightly as I looked up at the full moon, before the clouds once again covered it. It has been about fifteen minutes now since we had left everything behind, including Pauls' party. *What will I say to him? What will the others think of Paul when they meet him?* I looked over Paul's large frame that held onto the back of the motorbike, and then over to Lucas's smaller frame sitting in front of him. It has only been two weeks and I couldn't believe how much I had missed Paul. Yet at the same time, I have become close with Lucas in such a short time. *Is it because it all seemed like a matter of life and death that I find myself relying so heavily on both?*

Looking between them I saw how completely different they were, and how they clearly did not enjoy one another's company. *How am I to explain this world to Paul? It seems in two weeks I now live a completely different life. And I now must question whether that life will ever be able to include Paul. Is that selfish of me to want to involve him in this kind of life? But haven't I already...?*

I looked at my right hand while holding tightly onto Ashley with my left. These hands now have the ability to take a life. *But I also have the ability to protect.* Paul's dark brown hair fluttered in the harsh wind. "I will protect Paul," I whispered to myself, determined. *I will protect him until I know he is safe and then I will have to leave him behind. I cannot be so selfish as to try to drag him into this war because of my own pain and suffering.*

Will that not be the same for my parents though? What will I do when I find out where they are? Will I run away with them? Can I protect them if I am followed again? Do I have the strength to live a life where I am hiding and watching those that are around me constantly, living in fear that I could not only be hurt myself, but that my parents could be hurt as well?

I looked over at Lucas, examining him from behind. *Would Lucas be able to help me? Will he help me find my parents and help me protect them? Can I depend on Lucas? I have only known him for two weeks and yet I have such a pull toward him. Can he help me transition into this being I am to become? Can my two worlds still coexist or is there no going back?* I frowned at the pounding thoughts that echoed through my head. With so much to absorb and what seemed like so little time, I wondered how I could even begin to make choices. I could feel myself changing, but into what?

Lucas indicated to the right as we came across an old tattered warehouse that had Suzumiya's black car parked outside the front of the doors. Ashley and I got off the motorbike, quickly walking over to Lucas and Paul who stood staring at the car.

Lucas raised his hand to us to stop as he looked from the warehouse to the car. The car was empty and there was no sign of any of the others. In silence we all crept towards the car, looking around warily. The others have not come out to greet us. *Has something happened to them?*

The old warehouse door creaked open, slowly revealing Helena on her knees tied up with tape across her mouth. She was sobbing and shaking her head frantically at Ashley. One of the lenses on her red glasses was shattered, and her hair was plastered to her face in sweat. Blood glistened on the dark leather she wore as she continued to sob and shake her head frantically at Ashley.

"Mum!" Ashley yelled, as he began running towards her. As he ran past the boot of the car, Lucas grabbed his hand throwing Ashley underneath him onto the ground as it exploded into a large bomb of flames, throwing us off our feet and slamming us into the ground as a screeching and disorientating ringing filled our ears.

As my hearing and vision shook, other voices and images flashed in front of my eyes, taking me to a different place. I felt the call of the woman in my head as she ushered me into her world. A place where she finally felt she could reveal all that she needed to.

The wind blew my long brown hair into twisted knots, mixing and twisting the strands like the curling sensation I felt in my stomach. I clutched at my stomach in sickness and searched my surroundings, seeing that many people stood around me, all staring at the same thing I could not yet see. I wore rags for a dress, torn, ripped, and smothered in dirt—like all those who stood around me. The small village around me showed what a kingdom once looked like, with its malnourished people clustered around one another, some crying, some disgusted.

I adjusted my view, trying to claim the same sight that they did, but I found no success. I only saw a large wooden post reaching into the sky. It was the size of a two-story building, and it was in the center of the small houses. A large podium stood near the heightened post where a well-fed man sat indulging on the food his maidens offered. Gold cased every jewel he wore with the most dominant being the one on his head. A king, a bloodline of royalty watching over his people.

I shoved past the ill people that occupied the town center, trying to hear the king's words. Young children sat in front of me when I finally reached the front to see the commotion everyone's eyes were searching over.

The post that first hung over my sight didn't seem as tall when I reached it. The high post's floor was covered in twigs and planks of wood, forming a line at the base that could easily be lit. White flags hung down from the podium, and soldiers stood rigid in armored gear, holding their weapons straight. Black crows flocked around the sky, gawking as the town square stood silent.

"My good people," the king announced. His belly was as round as his eyes as he searched over the gathering before him. He was bald and looked fierce with his garmented wear, and the scar that blazed down his face melting somewhere into his second chin. "As your trusted King, I am to protect you from any harm and in return all are to respect and follow my law. If not, punishment is severe."

Everyone took a step back with frightened expressions. The women hid behind their men as the children ran from where they sat, straight into their mothers' open arms. "To show you how serious I am as your king, you are to all watch the consequences of disobedience. Many of you have seen your family members being lit alive for breaking such laws, and yet I sentence you to all watch it again. So you never forget," the king said, narrowing his eyes on the town's people.

The black hole in my stomach reappeared, forcing me to clutch at it in illness. Heavy armored men dragged two villagers out with potato bags over their heads, disguising the identity of whom it was who gasped and breathed beneath them. One of them wore a dress: a beautiful pale blue dress and it contrasted with her coloring the way the blue sky does against the clouds. A few gold charms hung from her wrists while a beautiful blue gem dangled from her neck, making the onlookers gasp as they recognized the jewels of the young woman who was condemned to death.

As words and mumbles waved over the crowd, the soldiers tied the two to the post where a fire was soon to be lit. Neither would have the opportunity to see one another's face as they were strapped to one another's back, only the post standing between them. The other that was sentenced to death was a male who wore the same clothes that myself and the crowd did, proving him to be a peasant, a servant under the king's order.

"If any of you think that I am weakening in my old age; if any of you consider I will be lenient in old age—consider again my good people. You obey my rules or die, and that stands for anyone in this kingdom, including my daughter," the king bellowed, seating himself in his gemmed throne while searching over his people with indifference.

"The King's daughter, Princess Carla Eleera Pholom, is sentenced to death for socializing with and bedding a witch; for having relations with him while unmarried; for stealing and defying King Pholom's requests and orders; for not proving her loyalty to her Kingdom or her people. Therefore she has demonstrated no honor or oath to that of her royal blood line." As the man, cheaply dressed in white on the king's side read the reasoning behind the prosecution, I searched over the frightened people. Some cried at the sentencing, others yelled and cheered as the potato bags were readily taken off.

Burns in my chest and acid in my stomach mixed, making me miss a heartbeat. A thick haze covered my vision as I stood in shock when they revealed who the condemned princess and witch were by taking the potato sack off their heads.

"No!" I screamed as few people cried out with me. My mother and father were the ones to be set alight and condemned to death. One man pushed through the crowd behind me, following my steps. A soldier let go of his arrow without hesitation. I quickly projected my Shield, ready to untie my parents who were held with ropes, ready to blaze. My Shield didn't work as if my ability didn't exist. The arrow struck me in the throat, clearing straight through to a man's chest behind me, who now dropped clumsily onto the ground. I searched over the man's face, feeling my hand around my neck; trying to comprehend how it went straight through my own frame.

"Although we were unreachable by their hand and weapons..." the woman suddenly whispered in my ear. I swung to see her face, seeing nothing but an empty space by my side. The smell of burnt wood and ash smothered and drowned my nose, snapping me out of my hallucinated daze.

"Mum! Dad!" I bellowed through tears. I pushed myself past the guards easily, and it was as if they couldn't see me as they looked past me to the crowded citizens. I reached past the flames grabbing the ropes that tied my parents together, frightened and scared. I desperately tried to set them free. The two creators of me, the two who gave me the characteristics I now claimed as my own, were now crying in front of me in pain. My father's head had already dropped, looking at the flames beneath him with dazed eyes. His hair blazed as red as the flames, his filthy clothes covered in smoke. I ripped at the rope, trying to free my loving parents.

"When we cared and wanted to free our loved ones so much…" The woman's compassionate voice rang again in my ear. I turned to see where her voice had come from, only to find the horrified faces of the townspeople. When I turned to finish my task to free my parents, I was blinded by a sky full of smoke. I now stood on a hill where the wind bled my eyes dry and the passing smoke stung.

"We could not help him for this was his choice to make," her voice empathized. Whose choice? Her green dress blew hesitantly against her skin, tugging away from her body just as our hair tugged and robbed us both of sight. The woman stood by my side.

"Why are you doing this to me?" I bellowed in agony. I hadn't seen my parents in two weeks—since the world I knew had been taken away— and they were whom I wanted to see more than anything, and she knew that. And yet this is the image she offered me.

"You don't understand this war, so why fight in it?" she said, ignoring my question. I looked at the black sky once again, remembering the squealing pitch of my mother's cry.

"Because I have no choice," I loudly said over the screaming howl of the wind. I pushed my hair away from my face, being bombarded once again with the light brown color of hair in my eyes as the wind tore at it.

"Why? Because they said so?" she said, meaning Kurt, Seth, Helena, Ashley, Lucas, Suzumiya, and Chris. "Those people are not trustworthy. They all have hidden secrets, ones that are capable of taking your life. None of them are trustworthy, including the one you are most fond of."

"Why do you claim Lucas as untrustworthy? He saved my life," I said upset at the suggestion that he might betray me.

"You cannot trust any of them. What I have shared with you was the images of how this war began. I see and feel what you do. I do not *wish to claim human life but I beg of you to let me possess your body to reinforce my brother's oath that he died for, the oath Sebastian died for, the same oath you should uphold, since you have now seen our world."*

How could she ask such a thing of me? How can she take lives so easily and claim she does not wish to do so? When I saw and felt the memories she showed me, she lusted for it, it was what her body drove for and all she knew.

Her long red hair blew and covered the front of her face, showing me not who she was, but the name rang in my mind. If Sebastian was her sibling, that meant that she was possibly the prophesied return of Misfeata. She was Misfeata.

As my thoughts narrowed down on whom the impostor of my mind was, her hair flew back revealing what she looked like. What Misfeata looked like. Her eyes shone with the most mystified strong hazel I had ever seen, streaking with a patch of amber across her right eye. Like the stories said she was the age of no more than twenty-five. Her lips parched a blistering red, too deep for anyone not to notice. Her hair flicked out, naturally coming to her waist and then flicked back into her face, covering her identity once again. Within a few seconds the wind had stopped, my breathing had stopped, everything had slowed down. I was now able to identify the woman who held me captive in my head; the woman who controlled my unconscious mind; the woman I fought with; the woman I hated... she was in fact the third of the reason I possessed such ability: because I carried her blood.

"You're Misfeata," I said in a choke of shock. The wind regained its speed, leaves and twigs wrapping around where she stood. When I opened my eyes to see her rippling dress I saw nothing, she had left, now that I could see who she really was.

Chapter Twenty-Four - The Façade

$\mathscr{I}$ opened my eyes as I coughed into the dirt. Slowly my vision faded in and out as I saw flames. My memory flooded back to me: *There was a bomb.* A ringing continued in my ears as I looked over at Ashley, Lucas, and Paul, in a daze. Placing my hand under me and trying to lift my head for support, I saw Helena tied up in the entrance of the old warehouse door. *Everybody else must be inside too.* I squinted at her; recalling the bomb explosion and being thrown back into a state of unconsciousness.

Still shaking from the explosion, I inhaled deeply; feeling like my head had been held under water for far too long, I refocused on the flames that thrived from the car. Lucas was hunched over an unharmed Ashley, who stared back up at him dazed. Lucas stood in front of Ashley projecting his Shield and therefore protecting him from the explosion. I looked to my left to see Paul cough into the dirt and clutch at his ribs.

Paul. I must protect him.

"Paul," I called with a dry mouth, as I dragged my recovering body over to him. Surprisingly my body ached but already I could feel myself recouping as I dragged my left bleeding leg. I ignored the sound of sirens that still rang in my head.

"*Paul*," a familiar voice mocked. I looked up to see Raven walking over to me, smiling and showing her pointed teeth. The Starkorf that appeared to be a young child with black hair and elusive blue eyes stared down at me as her lips stretched further into a grotesque smile.

But Lucas said he killed her.

"Paul," Raven teased again, his name echoing in the silence. "I only came for you, but if you want to be together I'll send you both to hell, child," she said, taking a few more steps while staring at the sword she carried. She looked at it as though she was reminiscing about all the times she had taken someone's life with it. She looked at me as if she heard my thoughts and smiled brightly once again, before breaking into a run in my direction. She jumped into the air and hovered over my figure, before coming to the ground beside me with the sword in her hand.

My head pounded as if a rock was being smacked into my head, but with every throb I tried to concentrate on projecting my Shield. Red ripples surrounded me just as her sword bounced back from my weak Shield. I looked back at Paul who was finally standing while looking around in disorientation. He took a step towards me, reaching his hand out before his leg buckled underneath him.

I must protect Paul from her. Why is Raven alive?

Her sword bounced off my Shield again. *'Defend yourself stupid girl,'* Misfeata echoed through my mind. Raven dropped her sword and sized me up. I felt the pressure of her Shield shred through mine. Her Shield was so strong, her being so overwhelming that my Shield shattered underneath the pressure of hers. The red pulsating markings of my Shield vanished. Raven wrapped her hand around my throat, choking me with a satisfied smile. Her touch blistered on my throat, and a trail of flames scorched at my neck as she drained my energy.

"Stupid Shielder," Raven's voice echoed through my head until I could register what it was she had actually said to me. The scorching flames took away my terrified cry and exhausted my struggling legs. My eyelids dragged over my eyes, which were moist with the same burning and exhausting liquid that pumped through my body. She was draining my energy. Her blistering hand throbbed at my pulsing neck, digging her nails in greedily.

Raven was thrown off me as Lucas now stood in front of me protectively, with his cold eyes narrowed on her. He picked up the sword as I clutched at my throat. Ashley ran towards Helena and fumbled to untie her. *The others must be in there too*, I thought.

'It's a trap,' Misfeata interjected.

I know it's a trap but I cannot leave them. I must save them. A thought of Seth came to mind, as I was frightened to see the gentle giant fall. I wondered if he could see Helena tied up and scared. *I must save them all.*

I ignored the pain of my blistering throat and stumbled to my feet, taking lengthy steps towards Paul who was still collecting himself. "Paul. I want you to drive as far as you can from this place," I said, catching his heavy weight on my shoulders as he fell onto me.

"I'm not leaving you," Paul said angrily, with fierce green eyes. He took one step towards the warehouse and then another as I quickly came to his side, watching him steadily. I didn't have time to argue with him as Ashley frantically cut through the ropes that tied Helena. She broke free, hugging Ashley as she cried over his shoulder. We quickened our pace towards Ashley and Helena, as Paul stumbled awkwardly from side to side.

I pushed Paul to the side, hiding him behind one of the stone poles that held up the old warehouse. The chains that hung from the roof rattled from the fresh breeze of wind that now swept through the room. The sound danced in sync with the few noises that creaked above me on the second story platform that surrounded the edges of the hollow room. I searched around the platform; scared that it wasn't the others who made the noise but an ambush of Starkorfs.

Paul's expression reflected my own thoughts: *we've got to get out of here*. Another large creek echoed through the roof as smudged and torn materials dropped from the roof.

"You make it too easy," a man's voice said charmingly. He flicked away his cloak throwing it to the ground in disgust. He wore black leather pants and a black collared shirt that was only half buttoned. He brushed his fingers through his hair before looking at me intently. It was the same man that was with Trish the night we got ambushed.

Raven's giggle echoed through the warehouse. The scar of her touch wrapped around my neck, reminding me who she was and what she wanted. Her poisoned hand had left its mark on my throat from where she had so hungrily drained me. Raven stood behind Lucas, pulling his head so far back I could only see his throat and the knife she had secured across it. She walked between Helena, Ashley, and I, to stand beside the man that had previously spoken.

"Don't even try—as soon as you move he's dead," Raven mused. Raven was so small compared to Lucas, reaching only his chest while maintaining the innocent look of a twelve-year-old. Her tainted black dress and coat only made her enriched crystallized blue eyes more horrifying against her deeply pale skin. If Raven weren't so powerful, Lucas would have the upper hand and would be able to penetrate her Shield, instead of her penetrating his.

I felt the presence of both their projected Shields fighting for dominance. Raven's Shield quickly splintered Lucas's—she was too strong for him. She overpowered him quickly and held him down. *I don't understand, why is Raven here and alive?*

Other Starkorfs now retracted the hoods from their heads, revealing their mutated faces. Some of them were staring at the pole Paul now walked over from. He squeezed his hands tightly releasing them, and walking carefully to my side while looking at them all grimly. *Why is he coming out to my side and revealing himself?*

Helena now stood strong and radiated anger at the sight of Lucas being held captive with a knife to his throat. Lucas had always appeared as an adopted son to Helena and Seth.

"We've come for you. You know that child. Leave with us and they survive," said the man who had previously spoken, raising his hand to me with a charming smile. He has nearly the same color of hair as Lucas, only a shade darker, and he had dark brown eyes. He wasn't a very large framed man but still he had broad shoulders. He looked like he was in his mid-twenties but it was impossible to tell as he was a Starkorf. After all, if they kept consuming the energy of the humans that they murdered they could live to be over a hundred years old, easily.

Before I could take any steps to surrender myself, Paul stood in front of me, cracking his knuckles as he searched over the Starkorfs that surrounded us. *How does Paul have such strength and determination to protect me? Didn't I promise myself that I would be the one to protect him?*

The knife was knocked out of Raven's hand and she was thrown back as Lucas projected his Shield. Raven flipped through the air before her feet dragged against the cement floor, bringing her to a stop. She adopted a crouched position, with her hand behind her for balance. Her pointed teeth were bared like an angry wolf's and her growl matched her hungry state.

"Kill them!" her voice echoed through the old warehouse.

I had already taken my place in front of Paul, wasting no time in standing in front of him protectively and projecting my Shield. Tainted ripples of red pulsated around me as I backed Paul against the wall so that the only way to him was through me: something I wasn't going to let happen.

The first two Starkorfs leapt for me, oblivious to my pulsing Shield, which knocked them off their feet as they bounced off it. *How could they be so stupid? Anyone can see my projected Shield—so why would they still run at it? Especially if they don't have the ability; why would they even bother?* I looked down at their curled, unconscious bodies, which looked to me like a dog would while sleeping. *Do the Starkorfs with deformities have a wilder, animal-like mindset than those who have the Shielding ability, like Raven?*

The presence of another Shield struggled against mine and I fought to heighten my ability. A woman thrust a knife at me, which grazed my arm. There was a cry as her Shield dominated mine, and as she reached her knife out to me in an attempt to stab me for the second time, I knocked the weapon out of her hand. As the knife sailed through the air, I punched her in the stomach, winding her. I jumped into the air, hovering over her hunched figure. I put as much force as I could behind my legs so that I could kick at her hunched back. She gasped for air, as she was smashed into the ground by my weight. Her head bled from the impact of the cement. She struggled to her feet, ready for another attack.

I was blocked by a Starkorf when I tried to follow Paul who had climbed the stairs to my right. Paul scurried up the ladder, and I looked up to see that the others were tied up and trying to wriggle out of the ropes that they were tied with. My heart sank. *They are in here.*

My vision of Paul was unstable but I was forced to focus on the new chain that wrapped around my ankle, pulling me to the ground. The back of my head smacked into the cement. My attacker pulled my stunned body to his side with rapid speed, toying with the other weapon in his hand. I could see he was ready to plunge it into my chest. I drew my knees close to my face and pulled my legs over forcefully, pulling the man towards me as he still held the chain. I sat in a crouched position. My body instinctively knew what to do to protect myself. Now when I fought, I could feel Misfeata pulsate through me with strength. She was channeling her ability through my own.

The man took no time to try and knock me off my feet again; ripping at the chain and making me do the splits. I hammered to the ground once again as he stood over me, looking at me with the one deformed eye he had. As the knife dangled over my head I quickly kicked at his ankle, catching the knife as he stumbled for balance. Without hesitation I sliced the knife deeply across both of his ankles, relishing his pathetic cries of agony.

My ears perked up as I heard Paul bellow in pain. A Starkorf stood over him, draining him from his back where he knelt beside Seth. One of the chains that hung from the roof was dangling near me. I swiftly collected the chain, swinging it and throwing its weight towards the Starkorf's neck. It wrapped around him, forcing him to release his hold over Paul. His deformed hands clutched at the chain that I held firmly. Seth's ropes snapped as he jumped on the Starkorf with a knife and stabbed it into his chest. The Starkorf dropped dead instantly and Seth ripped off the tape across his mouth and looked over the scene below him.

He gave Paul the small knife he held, instructing him to untie the others. He scrambled down the ladder and ran to Ashley and Helena, who both fought oncoming Starkorfs.

Another Starkorf jumped onto the platform near Paul. I ran to the ladder and jumped onto it strongly. She scratched her claw-like nails over Paul's chest, forcing him to bellow in pain and plunge the small knife into the side of her stomach. He then retracted it and threw her away from him with force. She stumbled and tripped over her own feet, causing her to fall over the edge.

Paul looked back at me with shocked eyes. He clutched at his chest where five bleeding marks trailed down to his chiseled, stomach. Paul just killed a Starkorf. He looked at me emptily, before composing himself with a shiver that shook his whole body. *How could I have forced him into such a position?* My eyes searched his green eyes; he was just as lost as I was.

He looked back down at Suzumiya, quickly cutting away at her ropes and then Chris's, and Kurt's, snapping them in seconds. All three of them ran towards the ladder, sliding down it and running towards the fight. The warehouse echoed with screams and the clashing of weapons. All three of them were heavily injured but swept through the Starkorfs as if they were unharmed.

I looked to Lucas, who was on the other side of the warehouse with Raven, fighting with a sword. My eyes searched over where the Shielders had been contained—there were small puddles of blood where they had been chained. I then turned to Paul who was looking over it all like I had, absorbing it all. *It is a very different world to the one in which we both have lived.*

We quickly slid down the ladder. *I must find Lucas amongst all of this.* Many Starkorfs surrounded Paul and me; they looked over Paul hungrily and were laughing amongst one another like a pack of hyenas. *There are so many.* Paul and I were back-to-back as he held his fists in front of himself defensively, giving me the small knife he had. I searched over them once again, overwhelmed by their numbers.

I felt Misfeata's presence once again within me as a sudden strength overwhelmed me.

Without realizing what it was I was doing, I swept my arms around me, spinning like a ballerina on the tip of my toes. My Shield spread past my body, expanding into an unimaginable size. As my mind caught up to my frozen body, I realized dizzily the strength of my ability, which was infused with that of Misfeata's. All the Starkorfs stood around hesitantly, not sure of what it was I was projecting, or if they should go near it. I held my arms out and looked over to Paul.

"Paul I need you to crouch close to me," I said, exhausted at the huge mass of energy I was holding between my hands. Paul quickly did as I asked, dropping into a crouch and looking up at me. He gave a small nod, signaling me to go ahead. I slammed my hands together, producing an explosion with a shattering bang. My extended Shield had burst, knocking everyone into the walls, including Raven who was greedily fighting over Lucas. I dropped to my knees exhausted by the sensation of my energy being drained. Paul caught me in his arms as he looked at me in bewilderment.

Everyone had been knocked off their feet, and they all slowly gathered themselves. Unfortunately it had been the same for the Starkorfs as well. I had no control as to whom it would reach. Helena, Ashley, and Seth, rose to their feet, looking over in confusion. Seth clutched his leg, as Ashley quickly came to collect his father helping him stand. Helena's hands were clutched to her chest, and she held a knife, which she kept on guard against every flicker of movement around them.

Suzumiya and Chris were quick as they scurried around; collecting as many weapons as they could and bringing them back to Kurt, Helena, Seth, and Ashley.

My eyes screamed out to Paul before my own voice had the chance. I pushed Paul out of the way, grabbing the sword that once plunged for Paul's back. I clutched the sword so fiercely it cut into my hands as I held it awkwardly.

I first mistook the man for Lucas, but quickly realized it was the man that was speaking to us earlier and that was a part of the ambush at Max Jacket's home. He was disgruntled that his blow wasn't fatal but still gleeful that he had an open strike as I struggled to hold the sword with my bloodied hands. *I may heal quickly, but not quick enough. I still feel pain, but now is not the time to be weak. I must protect them.*

Paul struck the small knife towards the man's chest, but he jumped back with the sword, smiling. Lucas ran from behind me and stood in front of me protectively holding his sword up high. Starkorfs coughed around us as they struggled to their feet.

"Lucas you always ruin the plans!" Raven said angrily, as she threw a piece of wood off of her from where she had been thrown. She slowly walked over to us, looking over all the Starkorf that still lay on the ground. Only a few got back up.

"That's my job," Lucas said, looking over at the man angrily. The man simply began to laugh at him. I unsteadily got to my feet using Lucas's bloody shirt for balance in helping myself up. Once steady, I released my grip on him, watching Raven steadily as she stalked towards us.

Lucas jumped, grabbing the chains above him and throwing a dagger towards Raven's face. The man cursed and swore as he swung his sword over his head, leaping for me.

I picked up a pitchfork from the ground; ready to defend myself. Lucas's sword blocked his, and quickly flicked his sword away from us, forcing the man to take a few steps back, away from me. I turned my back, holding the pitchfork high as Raven swept her own sword over where I had once stood, making me bump into Paul as I jumped back.

Suzumiya, Chris, Ashley, and Seth came to us, circling the others as Lucas, Paul, and I, stared at our attackers. We all needed to get to the bikes and car.

Raven and the man walked towards us smugly as another two Starkorfs encircled us. Helena and Kurt were still near the door, holding their weapons high above their heads. *We can't fight off this many. If I could do what I did before then that'd give us enough time to leave.* But the exhaustion my body carried gave me little hope. *It'll be too much for me.*

"These games bore me, Lucas," the man said, straightening his back and smiling at Seth, who was closest to him. "Like a father to you, is he not?" With rapid speed the man lunged for Seth and wrapped himself around him, Seth's eyes widened in surprise at the speed of the man as Helena screamed out a wail that echoed throughout the warehouse. Ashley stumbled back as the man had pushed him away from where he stood beside his father. The man plunged his sword deep into Seth's back making the tip of it appear through his stomach. Seth's hazel eyes dropped as he looked down at the sword that stuck out from his body. He did not cry; he did not wail. He simply stared.

The room was silent. I stared into Seth's eyes as he looked back up; death was reflected there. The man pulled his sword back out and kicked Seth away from him onto the ground. "I don't care what father says," the man said, opening his hand to Lucas. "I want you to come back brother. This has gone on for far too long."

Brother? I looked at Lucas, struck by the poison that rested in my heart. *Brother?* His eyes stared at mine blankly as his jaw tightened. *Brother. What does he mean by 'brother'? Is Lucas a Starkorf?*

I was thrown to the ground by Paul as he clumsily threw himself on top of me protectively. Raven had swung her sword where I once was standing, looking over Paul with an angry flicker of the eyes as she traced where we had moved to. I looked up at her, dazed. The end of her pointed sword sparked with blue as thunder ran up it and surrounded her. She squealed at the pain, clutching at her hands that were now burned. I felt her project her Shield in defense, stopping the thunder from harming her any further.

Trish and Max Jacket stood angrily near the doorway as they began shooting fire and electricity to the Starkorfs that rose.

"Retreat!" the man that claimed to be Lucas's brother announced. Lucas looked down at me before I felt the presence of his Shield project. His dark brown eyes held so much sorrow before he turned to run in the same direction as Raven.

My jaw opened and I felt I couldn't breathe. My body pained at the thought. *Lucas is a Starkorf. Lucas has betrayed us all. Lucas isn't who I thought he was.*

Helena's roaring wail echoed through the warehouse. She sat back on her knees holding Seth's face, cupping it and stroking it as she screamed into the chilled night air. Ashley held his father's hand, crying as he pressed Seth's hand to his chest.

Seth smiled at Helena, cupping her face and wincing at the pain he was in. *Seth is going to die.* I felt a burn rush through me like I had never known. Seth was an amazing man. *A gentle giant, only trying to protect his family.* I felt rage consume my whole body. I grabbed the sword Raven had dropped; pushing myself out from underneath Paul and running into the same direction they had left in. *I will avenge Seth.*

I ran through the back door, finding myself to be surrounded by trees. The moonlight shone brightly before being covered by clouds once more. I saw a shimmer of metal in the distance and ran after it, sure it was them.

Chapter Twenty-Five - Betrayal

$\mathcal{I}$ searched over the gloomy trees running through thorn bushes that scratched at my legs, as I hurriedly tried to catch up. My running was faster, my endurance was exceptional, and I could feel Misfeata's presence from within me giving me strength.

I skidded on the red dirt searching for Lucas, as my hair stuck to the back of my neck from sweat. I searched past the trees, listening to the rattling of the wind that brushed past my scratched legs, stinging them sharply. I jumped into one of the trees as I felt myself being pulled into a specific direction. I felt my hand pulse and itch at whatever was calling for me. Something was enticing me; something that my body desperately wanted. The unknown entity whispered to me, and I felt as though it was a part of me. My hands sweat and itched with pulsated desire. I demanded to obtain something they have longed for. Something I had never felt before yet I was immensely looking forward to seeing.

I lunged out of the trees like a cat, projecting my Shield into purple ripples and knocking Raven to the ground. I jumped on her back before quickly jumping back into the air. My feet grazed to a stop before I fell over a ledge. *Is it Raven that I feel the pulses drawing me to?* Trees wrapped around everywhere I looked, blocking the woman and myself into a small ring. Behind me was a huge waterhole where water flooded in from a small, rocky gully. Who would have thought a cliff and waterfall would be so close to the old warehouse?

Raven growled as she rose to her feet. Her blue crystallized eyes shot at me like darts, and her pale skin was grazed at where she had plummeted into the ground. My hands twitched and pulsated for control. I have never wanted anything so bad. But I didn't know what it was that I wanted so badly. My hand clutched and released excessively over the sword I held. *What is this feeling of desire?*

Raven smiled with pleasure, understanding my uncontrollable urge. "They're nice, aren't they?" she said, tormenting me with the blade in her hand, drawing my eyes to the reason for my uncontrollable reaction.

'*Aeisha,*' Misfeata's voice was as dominant as ever as she announced the name of her blades. Raven put the blade in front of her face where she could see the reflection behind her. She licked the blade cutting her tongue and letting the blood drip down the blade. Any other time I would have looked away in disgust, but I found that I couldn't. My body surged with desire for Aeisha. *My Aeisha.*

Why does Raven have Aeisha? Is it because she is high ranked amongst the Starkorfs like Lucas once said she was? Those are my Blades. I threw my sword to the ground, disgusted with the blade I held. *I cannot use this; I must have and use my own Blades.*

I lunged for Raven's chest, feeling the sharp graze of Aeisha cutting past my arm. *I must have her.* I lunged again for Raven, catching her off guard with the time of my recovery and tore at her arm until I twisted it behind her back. I heard a sharp snap. Raven howled like a dog, crying in pain. Aeisha grazed past my leg, and I fell. I felt for the handle of Aeisha.

I quickly found my footing, watching my Shield turn from red to purple and lunged for Raven again. *Aeisha is mine.* I skidded between Raven's legs, kicking her in the back and then wrapping my leg around her ankles forcefully. She lost balance before she could jump into the air. I jumped on her, letting my right foot jam her head into the ground so that she struggled to move. Our Shields fought for dominancy, tearing and fighting against one another for protection.

Aeisha shimmered in the moonlight, guiding me to her. I greedily snatched it. The feel of Aeisha, the touch of her, instantly gave me a burst of power and strength. Raven smashed her elbow into my nose and knocked me off of my feet. I found my footing once again, ready for another lunge.

"Lucas!" Raven bellowed as she groveled. I had forgotten all about Lucas's presence until I looked up at him to see cold eyes. He walked out from amongst the trees. Lucas's whole body tensed like a statue. *How could have Lucas betrayed us? Has he truly done so? He said his brother and father were dead.* I looked away from Lucas, ashamed at my conflicting thoughts. *Lucas could never betray us.*

I lunged at Raven, angered that she would ask him to protect her.

"Lucas!" Raven yelled again as she struggled to her feet, holding her broken arm. I was thrown off mid-air as I rebounded off a wall. I lifted my head to see Lucas standing between Raven and I. I had never felt his Shield so strong and dominant.

"What are you doing?" I asked, coughing through breaths of coarse dirt. Raven used Lucas for support to get up before he shrugged her off. He stared down at me with pained eyes.

"You know, for someone that keeps coming back from the dead I have no idea how you're so stupid," Raven said, with a small triumphant laugh. She made Aeisha's presence known again as she played with the sais in her hand. I wanted Aeisha so badly, my body begged for her to be in my hands, but I couldn't get up as Lucas stared me down with an unreadable expression.

"Ah yes, that look," Raven said smugly as if she had read my mind. "That is the look of betrayal." She laughed, her damaged figure poised defensively as she held Aeisha.

"Lucas?" I whispered, pained at the truth of the words. I tried to understand. I tried to see how it was possible. I had trusted Lucas so much. I believed I was so strongly drawn to him, that I could rely on him. *Was it only that my body instinctively knew what he was—that I was drawn to him because I was meant to fight him? Is this the betrayal Misfeata spoke of?*

"You're one of them?" I asked in a wounded tone. Lucas flinched under my words, his jaw tight and his dark brown eyes staring at me, hurt. It all sharply clicked into place, it all made so much sense. That's why he was always going for walks, to tell Raven of Kurt's plans. I gasped to myself in shock. It was his brother who was at Max Jacket's cottage when we got ambushed—Lucas knew it would happen. Everyone was in so much danger, and now Seth was dying because of Lucas's brother.

"Seth is dying because of you," I said, now finding my anger once again. My rage burned through me so strongly that I wanted to see Lucas hurt. "I hate you!" I yelled. "I hate you so much!" *No. I wanted Lucas dead.*

I jumped to my feet, anguished by the betrayal. Yellow ripples tore from my chest, burning into red and then again to yellow with the flames of my Shield. It wanted to take my pain and fury out on Lucas who I had once trusted the most. I thought it was need but it was simply his mark of drainage that connected us; the birth defect he relished in that differentiated him from man; the curse that labeled him a Starkorf. My body was torn between the desire for Aeisha, and avenging Seth by fighting Lucas. My body didn't feel as if it were my own. It now ran from the energy my Shield projected. My Shield was so angry. It had such terrifying energy surrounding me and it was encompassing my thoughts.

Before I could force my hatred on Lucas, Raven stood in front of him to protect him. *Because he was her kind.* I could not detect Lucas's Shield, I couldn't sense it or feel it anymore. *How dare he not try to fight me!* He had no desire to face what he had done to me—to everyone. *He chose their side so he should defend it and stand against me. I want Lucas to acknowledge what I am capable of and what I will use against him.*

My defense dropped as I realized the enormity of what I was contemplating—hurting Lucas. My Shield weakened instantly at my own saddened thoughts. I was thriving off the raw energy my Shield created but now with my own thoughts being projected, I realized I was still far too weak to use my ability against Lucas. *How could he betray us all?*

My tears spilled as I was thrown off by Raven's Shield, falling in silence over the ledge. My long, light hair flickered past my sight covering the image of Lucas's cold face as I fell towards the water. In the few seconds I had of drifting through the air I strained to produce my Shield.

I hit the water hard like a balloon bursting under a heavy amount of pressure. *But my balloon didn't burst.* My Shield covered me in a bubble of protection against the hard fall; keeping the water out so I only drowned in the tears I wallowed in. My Shield kept a small amount of oxygen in the bubble so I could curl myself within it. I slowly sank to the bottom; watching the crystallized shine on the water's surface disappear into darkness.

Ripples tore through the water, shattering my clear sight of the moon. The water tore at my chest and then my waist, as I was dragged back to the surface, breaking the darkness that overtook my sight. My body was ripped through the sparkling surface of the water and thrown onto the hard ground beside it. My chest was pounded forcefully and I felt a pressure in my lungs.

I spluttered water across the mud, choked out a coarse cough and then flopped back into the mud like a fish out of water. The water was bliss; it was quiet and magical. The outside was cold, dry, and unforgiving, inflicting more pain and ache on my battered body.

My vision slowly focused on Paul as he looked down at me relieved. He raised me to his chest, hugging me, as I lay there limp. I looked back at the water, understanding I had not at all projected my Shield when I plummeted. I was drowning.

Paul lifted me from the cold ground and began carrying me as my hand flopped around numbly. My body felt so numb and my mind could only rest on one thing: *how could Lucas betray me like this?*

Chapter Twenty-Six - Expenses

$\mathcal{P}$aul carried me to the warehouse as I had flopped into his arms, numb and shocked. I was cold as the night's breeze licked at my wet skin. I began to realize I had almost drowned. I looked up at Paul's face, feeling the heavy jolt of his every step. His big arms carried me effortlessly. His brown hair seemed almost black but the tips looked blue in the moonlight.

How so much has changed. How did any of this come to be? With both Paul and Lucas, I wondered. *How is Paul protecting me now? Why has Lucas betrayed me? And why did I not have the strength to fight Lucas? Why would my Shield falter on protecting me?*

We walked through the big back doors to the warehouse after Paul slowly let me down to my feet. I still had my hands wrapped around his neck for support. I was looking over to the other side of the warehouse where Helena's mourning echoed throughout the large room, pinching at my every nerve. I took one step forward as my knee faltered. Paul lifted me, not letting me drop to the ground.

How could he have killed Seth? I took another step slowly as Paul helped my rattled legs to find their balance. Step by step I got closer to Seth's pale face and closed eyes. His hands were still entwined with Helena's. Ashley sobbed by his father's side as Chris and Suzumiya hugged one another, also crying. Kurt leaned against the wall near the door, staring up at the moon. His grey eyes also looked wet from crying. I caught glimpses of Max and Trish shuffling about outside the warehouse, leaving us in our grief.

I dropped to my knees in shock beside Ashley. Seth had always looked so big, and now the Englishman was cradled by his loved ones like a small infant. His eyes looking so peaceful but his lips already were turning blue.

I put my hand over Ashley's, showing my condolences. Paul's hand never left my shoulder as we all simply sat with our heads bowed in grief; for Seth was now dead. He was a father to most here and a kind man who had helped and supported me so much. And because of this war he was now dead, leaving Helena and Ashley behind in this bloody battlefield.

Paul's grip around my shoulder tightened as I looked up at him, clutching at his chest silently, my face pained. The five marks in his chest oozed with a red and black like ink.

"Your companion has been poisoned," Max's voice rang through the warehouse, breaking the silence. I looked over at Max gravely. Trish followed him with a cocky bounce, looking over all the Starkorfs that had been killed. All of them were dead around us, mouths open in shock: some from stab wounds, some from broken necks. Others had melted skin.

It appeared that only Raven, Lucas, and his brother escaped.

I looked at Paul, concerned as he angled himself away from me so I couldn't see the scratch marks any longer. *Poisoned?*

"Can you heal him?" I asked, desperate. *I cannot have Paul harmed at a time like this.* I looked at the back of his muscular shoulders that pulled away from me. His hand still rested on my shoulder. I put my hand on his, looking back to Max Jacket who was now by my side.

"I would give him about another twenty-four hours of life if I couldn't heal him. However I want to ask something of you. A trade of sorts: his health for something I want," Max said simply. Of course he wanted something. *Why are they even here helping us, it was only yesterday they organized an ambush against us. Or maybe Lucas knew of that all along. Of course he knew.*

"What do you want from me?" I said angrily, as Ashley's hand tightened underneath mine in frustration. Now was not the time to speak of this. "Let's go outside to discuss this," I said, pulling myself up and giving Paul steady eyes. I looked at the five scratch marks down his chest once more, saddened by the sight. *How did I not notice the pain he was in?* I cupped his face so he would now look at me instead of the warehouse's back doors. He gave me uneasy eyes before the corner of his mouth twitched.

Paul was so strong and selfless. He has only been introduced to this war tonight and yet it seemed as if he were managing it better than I was. He once said it was to protect me. *Could he really be going to all these lengths for me?* I thought in amazement.

"Stay here," I whispered to him, before dropping my arm and walking behind Max and Trish. Kurt gave me a hard look as I walked out. I dipped my head, not wanting to see his sad eyes. I looked up at the moon that was now covered by clouds once more.

190

"I was promised something by Nathanial," Max began, as his blind eyes focused around my face. "Whom you now know is Lucas's brother. He didn't hold his end of the deal and that I find intolerable."

"You knew," I said harshly. All of this could have been avoided if only Max had said something.

"Well, of course I knew," he said, unfazed. "It was of no real benefit for me to reveal anyone's identity. However I do think we can strike up a deal that can benefit both of us."

My fists shook furiously as I looked down at the old man. *How could he have risked our lives? How can he be so unfazed by all that has happened?* His eyes flashed black, and then back to his milky white. Trish began playing with her short red hair, pulling at a hard substance that stuck to her hair. She yanked at it in disgust. *Blood.*

"I know where they are retreating too," Max said, commanding my full attention. "You wish to avenge Seth—I can tell you the place. However there is much more over there than only Lucas, my dear. You might be saddened that Lucas has betrayed you but it goes far deeper than that."

"And why is that?" I asked, savagely. Hearing the name of Lucas left a bitter taste in my mouth. Once again it was not only I who felt betrayed; Misfeata stirred within me and the energy of my Shield wanted to project in fury.

"Well by now I am sure you can acknowledge that you're the last descendant of Misfeata; now able to tap into her raw energy, enhanced strength, and ability. I still don't know how this came to be as you are not Elisabeth's daughter, but her disappearance may very well be the answer you are searching for. But for now you cannot argue with me that Misfeata stirs within you, she is transported through her descendant's blood, using their body as she pleases. I am sure by now she speaks with you," Max said, giving a small smile as my body stiffened at this knowledge.

"Yes" he continued. "Elisabeth went through the same, although she had more control over Misfeata than you. Obviously she was born with the descendant's blood, unlike you who somehow managed to simply obtain it. There was a huge war a hundred or so years ago that bound all of those with ability in a separate world of sorts to the humans. That is where the young Elisabeth and I first met Nathanial. This was initiated to contain the Starkorfs, and in short, we planned to kill them. Easy enough. However the haven was infiltrated by

Lucas's brother, and eventually that wall between us and the humans was shattered, leaving the Starkorfs to escape."

I opened my mouth in shock, but nothing came out. *Over a hundred years ago both Max Jacket and Lucas's brothers were alive,* I realized. *If Nathanial lived that long ago, how many people has he drained and killed to keep the pretense of youth? Was Lucas alive then too? Has he been draining and killing people? I gave Max an alarmed look, feeing it all weigh heavy on my chest. How old is Lucas?*

"Yes," Max said, as if reading my mind. "You see, my dear, your dilemma is that Lucas is in fact third in line to inherit Tyran. He has his blood running through his veins and upon his father's and brother's demise, he will then slowly start hearing Tyran speak to him like you do Misfeata. When those two fall, then Lucas will one day be possessed by Tyran as well. Just like Misfeata tries to do to you." My stomach stirred as I felt Misfeata trying to take control of my body at the mere mention of her brother's name.

"Praytar is his father, who now has Tyran fully at his disposal. And he has something I want. When you were ambushed last night, I was promised Aeisha," Max said as my eyes sharpened on him at the name of my blades. Not mine: *Misfeata's.*

"However Nathanial betrayed me. I do not take kindly to betrayal," Max said as his eyes flickered with black once more. "So this is the offer I have for you. You may keep Aeisha for yourself. I, however, want Borac."

"Why do you want Tyran's Immortal Blade?" I asked inquisitively.

"I have my reasons. You have your own. I will, however, warn you. Upon confrontation it will not end well. I once watched Elisabeth and Praytar battle when that wall was dropped from our world one hundred years ago. It is not a battle of control; both of their entities were almost completely taken over by the two immortal Elders. You and he will both lose yourselves to the Elders that you both have locked inside you. In saying that, at this point I see no other option but for you to go," Max said, looking over towards the large warehouse doors. Ashley crossed his arms angrily with two swords as he listened in.

"You know he wants to go with you. And you can go now," Max said with a smile. "This way it puts no one else in harm's way except for Seth's son. But that is a path he has already chosen. I will look after your companion in there. We will heal him. If you really care for that boy, this is the only way you may save his life. You get to confront Lucas, and have the chance to obtain Aeisha. You will truly experience the mass of energy Misfeata contains. She will not be dormant inside you much longer. For all this I simply ask for Borac."

I narrowed my eyes on him angrily. I had no choice. It was the only way I could save Paul. And every other point he had, rang true. *I must protect Paul at every cost.* It saddened me that I had to leave him after being reunited with him only a few hours before. *I must obtain Aeisha. She feels a part of my being*, I thought, as I remembered how Raven teased me with her. *I must take my Immortal Blades back. Not mine*, there was a sharp reminder from deep inside me, *Misfeata's.* Ashley now walked over to me with the two swords in his hand.

"Karla. I want you to take me to this place," Ashley said sternly, staring at me with his pained blue eyes. Ashley looked so desperate. *How can I possibly protect him if I don't know if I will even be able to protect myself?* I looked back at the warehouse, thinking of Paul. *I must do everything I can to save him. As strong as he has been for me, I must do the same now for him.*

I gave Ashley a slow nod and looked down on Max's crisp smile.

"Excellent," Max said. He gave Ashley and I the location quietly. Ashley nodded vigorously before climbing onto his motorbike as I followed. I looked back at the warehouse where Kurt looked over us, unmoving. I frowned at him, unsure as to why he would let us go so easily. Or maybe he also thought I was the only one who had the strength to fight Lucas and avenge Seth. *But if so, how could he possibly know I have Misfeata inside of me?*

At the rumbling of the motorbike Paul had run out the doors, searching for me in a panic. I felt a tear slide down my face. He clutched heavily at his chest, holding himself up on the warehouse's doorframe. As Max and Trish approached him, he yelled out my name. Ashley drove us quickly away. *I am sorry Paul, but this I must do to protect you. It is the only gift I have to offer.*

After travelling until dusk, we finally found ourselves at a site with many trees. The last small town we had gone through was over an hour ago and we were now on a dirt road, which Max had foretold. I looked at the dead trees that trailed a path on the right, just as Max had described. We turned left into the dead trees and drove as far as we could, before getting off to walk the rest of the way.

Walking behind Ashley, I held my arms together, watching his bulky frame walk forward angrily. *Are we really going to make it in and out alive? Can I do this?* With no other option I had to step forward into this. My body was now fully healed but I could still feel the rawness of Lucas's betrayal. *Half a day is not enough to cover such a wound.* I searched over Ashley once more. *Will Ashley be okay?* He is led by such anger right now. *Will we be able to do this?*

All I have to do is obtain Borac and Aeisha, and get out. *But where would that leave Ashley? What do we do when we get closer?*

"I think we should stop when we get closer and watch their movements for a while," I said stiffly. Thinking of an approach of attack was foreign to me; and yet I felt like we needed something of a strategy instead of diving in blindly.

"We will talk about it when we get there," Ashley muttered as he moved a dead branch from his path, breaking it off and throwing it to the floor of the forest. We both held a sword firmly, and we were alert against the approach of attackers.

"Ashley, I understand you're hurt now. But we can't just barge in, we need a plan for this to work." I quickly ran in front of him, holding both his shoulders firmly as he dropped his head, hesitant to look into my eyes. His black hair covered his face so only the silver of his eyebrow piercing was seen. "Ashley. For us to go back alive I need your help. I've never done this before," I said heavily. It was the truth. I now walked a path I had no experience with. It would have been Lucas, the one I once relied on. Now it was only Ashley and I; both fighting to make up for what we have lost on this horrific day.

Tears began to drop to the ground as Ashley cried, his shoulders shuddering under my grasp. Ashley has lost his Father. He had even more reason to return to his mother now. I took a step back where I almost tripped over a log, and I grabbed at Ashley's leather jacket for support.

A dead man lay next to my feet, face down in the dirt. I looked away, saddened at the sight. His skin was pale blue and purple with a clear hand print mark on his back from being drained. *We are close*, I thought. I looked over my shoulder, peering further into the dead trees. Taking a few more steps forward, something changed and stirred within me. I searched around our surroundings with a banging throb of power itching at my hands. I let Ashley walk on.

I started walking back, feeling the pounding sensation of power twitch at my hands once again. I searched through the trees surrounding us, crouching to feel the ground's movement. I felt Misfeata stir within me again. *We are very close, I can feel Aeisha, but something else is present as well. Could this be Tyran's blood enraging me?*

Misfeata played me a memory in my head, insisting that I repeat the actions on display. I did so, holding my hand to the ground and projecting a small Shield to hover between my hand and the almost dead grass. The energy of my Shield pulsed and fed me movement. Using my Shield like this gave me an awareness of my surroundings that went beyond sight. The ground fed me footsteps: footsteps that were approaching quickly. The small patch of grass that my hand hovered over began blackening as it quickly died. I pulled my hand away from it, staring in disbelief. I was just draining the earth for information—it filled me with knowledge on my surrounding area. I looked from my hand to the ground, apologetic. *I have the ability to drain as well? And that includes the earth, it seems,* I mused. I rose to my defensive stance while clutching the handle of my sword, ready to fight any attacker. The burden of my uncontrolled power only grew stronger; throbbing over me with possession.

Ashley walked forward, leaping from tree to tree in an effort to search for hidden Starkorfs.

I heard the snap of a branch and I looked over to see a pair of red beaming eyes at me. Figures ran towards me, eyeing me hungrily. The power surged over me like a transformation, and I knew instantly Misfeata was very present in my every action and movement.

I cut at sections of them that weren't vital with my sword. I felt that Misfeata was angry with me as I still avoided killing them; even though it was her will to see them dead. Red stained the ground as mutated beings grasped at their arms and legs in pain. *Was there anything humane about these Starkorfs?* Another pulse of power surged within me, forcing my body to quickly cut down the few Starkorfs that remained in a circle around me.

I ran past Ashley who was chopping through his attackers, killing all of them angrily as they jumped for him. I ran faster than I ever had before, putting a distance between us in mere seconds. I broke out into an open space, looking for Raven. I knew she was there: *I could feel Aeisha.*

"Aeisha!" I shouted. My hands clenched around the sword I held, envisioning it to be my paired blades instead. I felt the desire to possess them run over my back, straightening my spine as I swung my sword behind me and brought it forward just as Raven appeared. My sword stopped as she held Aeisha across it, pushing me back with force. My feet skidded back as I took in her arm; it had now completely healed. I had only broken it hours ago.

I jumped towards her again. Our weapons clashed repetitively as we anticipated each other's strikes. As I struck more and more I felt the power rise and I began to enjoy every swing. I wanted Aeisha desperately. Raven fumbled to defend herself. No noise was heard, no movement was seen. My body pulsed and fought blindly. *No, not blindly—under Misfeata's command.* I felt a snake swirl within my stomach. I stopped attacking Raven to jump back and clutch at it. Through my pain I became aware that the wind whipped my hair from my face. I looked in the direction from which it blew and saw Lucas's figure standing on a small hill. He was hovering over the battle that tore through the little valley we fought in.

A brush of rage tore through my body as another two figures came to stand on either side of Lucas. An older man placed his hand on Lucas's shoulder. Nathanial, Lucas's brother, stood beside him watching over the battlefield, amused.

"Tyran!" I bellowed. *Not I. Misfeata.* It was the first I had heard Misfeata's voice corrupt my own, and she spoke so savagely. I felt my control fade as I could only hear, see and feel everything she did. She now carried me in her thoughts, as she possessed my body. I felt like I was trapped in glass, only gazing through a pair of eyes that did not feel my own. I had no control. My screaming and the itch for possessing Aeisha was no longer my own. My soul was now dormant; my body possessed.

"Brother!" Misfeata yelled wildly towards the hill. She began running towards where they stood. As oncoming Starkorfs tried to block her, she cut through all of them with clean and precise cuts, killing them all. Blood spurted across my vision as Misfeata tore through every moving limb that came within a two-meter range of my body. She was quickly sidetracked as Raven stepped in front of our path. Misfeata's thoughts rang clearly through my head, making her thoughts my own: *Kill Raven.*

Raven's insignificant Shield projected itself, which only angered Misfeata more as she glared at her. A veil of thick ice—her Shield—projected itself around my body, surging power through me as the energy bounced from my limbs to the interior of its magnificent wall. Although I had no control over my body, I felt the power crush me overwhelmingly. This iced wall was now my Shield too, and I could feel how impenetrable it was. The strength of it filled me with adrenaline and a lust for power.

"Karla!" someone shouted for me. I heard my name being called from the outside of my imprisoned cage. I was able to see the slowly running figure of Ashley, who ran towards us. Before my flickered vision was back on Raven, I saw a handsome figure stalk him: Nathanial, Lucas's brother, now hunted him.

My body started to change, to transform its figure into something bigger. I could feel it as it absorbed the energy of my Shield, trying to grow from within me. I took slight control of my body, clinging to the intense pain that engulfed my body—the pain that made me human.

'What are you doing Misfeata?' I shouted at her, collapsing to the ground as I felt shards puncture out of my skin. Within seconds, my control over my body had vanished. And it was now Misfeata who screamed back at me.

'No Immortal is without a curse, stupid girl,' she replied angrily. A small shard of green gem pierced through my arm and I bellowed in pain. I can't take this. The ice of my Shield shattered, taking my mind with it as I reached the edge of death in total darkness.

"What was that? What did you do to me?" I asked of Misfeata as I was engulfed by a trance of black. I felt as if I was simply floating. I could see nothing and it was only Misfeata and my words that claimed my consciousness.

"You silly little girl," she spat out angrily. "I told you it is my body."

"What was that back there?" I asked, ignoring her rage and remembering the green shards of crystal gem that burst through my skin. In this place I did not hurt, I felt nothing but calmness and serenity. I liked this place a lot. Those green shards had felt like the beginning of a transformation from human to beast.

"Being immortal we must pay a price, girl. Power always costs something," she sighed. "The gems on our Immortal Blades retain our souls. Our blade is our attachment. This is how without my body I am still immortal. My soul is bound into Aeisha, keeping me grounded on this land. My true being is a reflection of that gem. With Aeisha so close I could attempt transforming into my true being. But your weak body had little time for me to change. You're human and sick, poisoned blood, cannot cope with the power I need to illuminate."

"That's why Aeisha means so much to you," I realized, understanding why the search for her blades was so important, and why both her and I were so drawn towards them. "So if the gem in your blade was destroyed...?" I asked with complete serenity.

"Our mortality would be lost, as would our power," Misfeata answered grimly. If her gem were destroyed then her soul would be as well. Meaning she would no longer be in my head and would be forever gone.

"That's right," she answered. "Stupid girl, your thoughts are my thoughts. I can hear every word you are thinking. However it is not as easy as you think. If it were, then Tyran would have done so long ago. So never entertain that thought in your lifetime because it is out of your reach."

"So Praytar has Tyran in him? You yelled to him on that hill and I felt the urge you had to kill him. So, that was your brother?" I said calmly. This empty space was so calming I never wanted to leave it.

"I felt Borac, Tyran's Blade, on that man but yes I also felt him stir within Praytar. My brother resides in that man. That descendant of Tyran's on the hill will soon be possessed by him. If I continue to antagonize him Tyran shall show his true face and we will finish this war once and for all."

"But I don't feel like I can go back," I said feeling my mind drift with ease. "I like it here. It is so peaceful."

"This is not a place for you, young one. I have already begun regenerating your body so it is fit to go back," Misfeata said.

"When you yelled for your brother and ran towards him..." I remembered the urge and the rage that pumped throughout me, "You had no control over yourself. Did you?"

There was a long pause, forcing me to think that Misfeata had left my side and I was now in this serene place alone.

"When you are around for centuries and your path is nothing but destruction and death..." she sighed. "When your true being is that of a beast filled with rage and hate, a chain can only hold the power back for so long. When that beast is let out, nothing can stand in its way. Not even your soul."

Chapter Twenty-Seven - Answers

*M*y eyes fluttered in the dim light surrounding me. I woke in a small cell where silver walls surrounded me with open metal bars on my right side. It looked like a prison. Red gems surrounded me, intoxicating me with what felt like poison. It was weakening me. I tried moving my leg but I could only stare at it as it remained still.

Misfeata was no longer with me, which made me wonder if we were cut off from one another as soon as I was thrown into this room. *This red gem looks awfully similar to the one on Borac, Tyran's Blade. Maybe this is somehow keeping Misfeata at a weakened state and silent,* I thought.

Someone walked at a fast pace towards me, and I tilted my head weakly as I waited to see whom it was that came to bother me. "Finally, you're awake," Praytar said. He looked no older than fifty, with a beard that trailed down to his chest. The tips looked a dark red, like stained blood. My eyes glided across him but all I saw was silver shiny walls.

He had deep brown, almost black eyes, very similar to Lucas's. I twisted my lips and looked away as the resemblance was a painful reminder of the betrayal.

"Am I talking to Misfeata or Karla?" Praytar questioned, as he dropped his head down to my level, searching my eyes for an answer. My head flopped lower, catching a glimpse of the long sword that adorned his waist. The red gem glowed from the Blade. *Borac.* It was Tyran's Immortal Blade, the bearer of his soul. And this man carries it.

Heavy footsteps were approaching while the older man prepared to interrogate me.

"Father," Nathanial said, as he made his appearance known, giving me a charming smile. Now that I searched for it he did look very similar to Lucas, perhaps five or so years older. I wondered how old he truly was, or Lucas really was for that matter. I winced at the reminder of Lucas. *I must stop thinking of him,* I told myself, for it brought up such a bitter taste and a pain in my chest.

Last I saw of Nathanial he was stalking Ashley. I looked behind them once more, hoping to find another cell of some sort so I could see if Ashley were safe. *Please be alive, Ashley.*

"Yes, Nathanial?" Praytar gave him an annoyed glance. I looked at Nathanial evenly. Even if I was successful in making it out alive and getting rid of Praytar like Misfeata wanted, it seemed somewhat pointless: *because Nathanial would be next to inherit Tyran.* And then, last in line of the inheritance was Lucas, and yet there was only one of me.

"Raven, is having difficulties recovering: her powers of rapid healing are nowhere near powerful enough to deal with wounds like this," Nathanial reported to his father in a whisper.

What happened to Raven, did I hurt her? She was one of the stronger Starkorfs I had met; if any damage had come to her she should have been healed by now. *Not all Starkorfs heal rapidly, if I ever get out of here alive I should ask Kurt if there are any that can't heal rapidly.* There was a silent pause, until he spoke again: "If something happens to Raven, this one is mine." Nathanial gestured angrily towards me.

"I would not waste such a meal as this on the likes of a weak son like you. She can go to your younger brother. She is not going anywhere. The gems are strong within this cell and I cannot feel Misfeata stirring which means it is working. These walls drain her constantly," Praytar smiled proudly.

I looked into Nathanial's eyes and saw the jealousy that tore through his dark brown eyes. Praytar let out a sick cough, and clutched for his chest in a frenzied motion. He looked up in bewilderment at my smile.

"You are cursed too," I said sadly, knowing that feeling oh-too-well. Although he had stopped Misfeata doing much within myself, he could not block Tyran from feeling her presence and stirring within him.

"He lives and breathes in you, doesn't he? Tyran tries to possess your worthless body doesn't he?" I taunted, almost amused. I had finally met someone who understood my suffering, yet I only wanted to see him dead. *Was his death now my own desire or that of Misfeata's?*

"I am Praytar!" he bellowed, angry as his hands clutched around the bars tightly. "I have many years experience of controlling him. I am in charge of Tyran and all the beings around me."

Another small smile of amusement spread across my face. There was no controlling Misfeata and whatever he thought he had over Tyran, it was not that. "You are weak," I said simply, dropping my head as I looked at him in an antagonizing manner. This I could say truthfully,

I had experienced his weakness. *We are the same: both weak against the Elders. This is a curse.*

Praytar flushed red before clutching at his chest as he let another coarse cough out. He looked back at me bashfully; his dark brown eyes showing anger at himself because he was exemplifying the truth I spoke. Praytar left the room with Nathanial, who glided behind him obediently.

I dropped my head to the ground, looking at my hands. *What am I going to do? How will I get out of this cell, find Ashley, steal both Aeisha and Borac, and return to Paul? How will I do this when on my own I am sickly and weak?*

After sitting numbly for hours exhausted by the red gems that depleted what little energy I had, I heard the approach of someone. I had fallen asleep into the depths of darkness and when I woke up, hardly anything has changed. I reassessed the red gems, sighing to myself as my neck felt too heavy to look around my cell now. My body was too weak for a confrontation. I still have not thought of a plan as my body forced sleep upon me.

Dark brown eyes stared at me through the bars. I pushed my face away in disgust as my heart ached at the sight of Lucas. "Lucas." I said bitterly. "Son of Praytar, descendant of Tyran, Starkorf, and traitor." All these words ran off my tongue with contempt. "Have you come to feast off me, Lucas?" I asked sarcastically, sadly thinking of what he truly was: *a Starkorf*.

"I wanted to see you," Lucas admitted sadly, looking over his shoulder to see if anyone else was coming.

"You knew all this time..." I said, hurt. "You knew that I had Misfeata within me. You knew of the struggle I was bearing and yet, you said nothing. You knew all the answers to the questions I needed but you let me suffer instead," I whimpered, surprised at the lack of control in my tone.

"I triggered it," Lucas said honestly. "When we met at the shopping center and I nudged you with my bare shoulder bumping yours; that was what triggered Misfeata within you as she felt Tyran's blood present within me. I didn't realize she would do all these things to you though, Karla. Please, you must believe me," he pleaded.

"Believe you?" I repeated in shock. "You have betrayed everything you ever meant to me."

The air between us stood heavy as Seth's face appeared in my thoughts. I winced away from the sight. "Seth died because of you."

"No... I never meant for any of this to happen," he said desperately, looking as if he was about to cry. "This is what I was raised for and I have kept to that. But then when you came along, everything changed. You were the first person I have ever met that was dependent on me, that didn't see a monster in me. You saw something else within me—something I had never recognized myself. I never wanted harm to come to anyone, especially you."

"But that was never you," I said harshly. "That was all a lie." I thought of the many years he must have been preparing for this; remembering Max Jacket speak of Nathanial existing over one hundred years. *Is Lucas also over one hundred years old?*

"How old are you really?" I asked gravely, scared of the answer. *How many years has he been lying and killing...*

"Ninety-eight," Lucas confessed somberly. I choked at his answer, looking over his youthful body once more. He looked no older than nineteen.

"Karla, we don't have much time but I want you to know that I want no harm to come to you; also, I know how all this came to be... how you contracted this curse."

My eyes narrowed on him beneath my long, brown hair. *How it all came to be? Is he speaking the truth? Does Lucas really have the answers as to how I have Misfeata within me when neither of my biological parents have the ability?* I winced at the thought of them.

"Do you know where my parents are?!" I said, panicking. Lucas looked at me sadly as he slowly slid down the bars himself and sat next to my cell.

"I do not," Lucas replied with a disappointed tone. "Although I can tell you what Raven has told me; an encounter she had with Elisabeth about seventeen years ago and I think it explains much of your body shutting down on you and how you came to be in possession of Misfeata."

Hesitantly, I looked away and up to the ceiling. *Will this be the truth or just another lie?*

"When your mother was pregnant, you lived in a small community that had only a few people living in a deserted area amongst the woods," Lucas began, looking behind him once again to make sure no one approached.

"Raven and a few Starkorfs had killed everyone in that area.

They were originally hunting for Elisabeth as she was the last descendant of Misfeata, but decided to feast instead. Eventually Raven reached your parents' home. Your father and another man tried protecting your heavily pregnant mother and another woman."

I closed my eyes, remembering the last I saw of my parents: when Misfeata had reached out to me in my unconscious state. She wanted me to feel the same pain and suffering as she had; showing me the image of my parents burning alive instead of Sebastian and the princess who had died. It pained me to remember such a horrific dream. Thinking of it as them, I felt all the horror that Misfeata had on the same day. *I can now relate to such memories*.

"At first they began draining your father and the other man but then Elisabeth interjected. She had been close after all. She had come to save the remaining humans of the small township—she had come to protect your family.

She killed many of the Starkorfs instantly using Aeisha against them. However, to Raven's delight there were too many Starkorfs for Elisabeth to handle. She huddled in the same corner as the four humans, projecting a large Shield to keep the Starkorfs out. However one of the women was not within complete protection and one of Raven's followers killed her.

Raven waited for hours knowing Elisabeth was weakening. Elisabeth's energy was slowly draining by projecting it constantly for so long. She was reaching her limits. Raven said Elisabeth cut her hand, and then the hand of the pregnant woman's; then held them together.

Elisabeth kept apologizing to her before bandaging up your mother's hand and making a deal with Raven: if Elisabeth was to leave, the humans were to be left unharmed. At the time, Raven didn't think much of it but now it is apparent what Elisabeth was creating.

Elisabeth was weak by then and Raven agreed. She considered it an honor to be the one to kill the last of Misfeata's bloodline and to possess her Immortal Blades. Raven said that Elisabeth reached for your mother's stomach after wrapping her hand with a cloth and said '*Karla*'. Raven remembered it instantly about a month ago when we sensed your presence and found that to be your name. Our theory was confirmed when Raven recognized your parents. Your mother presumably went into contractions shortly after contact with Elisabeth.

It was Elisabeth who gave you Misfeata's blood, transferring her blood into you, an unborn babe. When an unborn baby of Shielder blood is infected with the ability they are able to either overcome the virus, or have the ability infused into their blood in acceptance.

You were never a Shielder; you had no Shielder blood in you. You were normal.

But after Elisabeth infected your mother's blood stream it contaminated you in the womb.

You never had the chance to fight or accept it. Instead you were born with the mixed blood. Your human blood and Elisabeth's blood— The descendant blood of Misfeata.

Since you never had time in the womb to fight it, you fight it off now; which is the reason your body shuts down on you. It's trying to rid itself of the mixed blood. The two different bloods keep fighting each other at random times. Your human blood fights Misfeata's blood. When we touched, it was that which triggered Misfeata to awaken within you. This is something your body will always be fighting," Lucas explained in a hushed tone.

I stared at the ground, trying to envision the story. *Is Lucas speaking the truth? But why would he make such a story up, even if he were a traitor? Is Elisabeth what my parents thought I would turn into? Were they scared of this very day in my entire upbringing? What if I really die because of it, will there ever be a cure for this?* A loud horn echoed through the silver walls disturbing my jumbled thoughts. Lucas looked behind himself once again making sure we were alone.

"I can never make up for what I have done and this guilt will bear heavy on me always, Karla, especially for what I have done to you, and to Ashley and Seth. I don't have the strength to go against my father, especially when Tyran is entrapped in him. Only you can. Ashley is down this hall on the left," Lucas said, as he stood staring at me sadly and stroking his hand through his sandy blonde hair. "That horn was to call us forth to a meeting that we must attend."

Lucas swiftly dropped a small piece of silver from his pocket, flicking it towards my feet. A small, red gemmed key was near my foot. *Lucas is giving me the chance to set myself free,* I realized. *That is why he told me of the meeting and Ashley's whereabouts.*

Lucas still looked at me sadly, his jaw tight as he took a step to walk away. He hesitated and then looked back at me once more.

"One day we are destined to fight, and when that happens I will do everything I can to not hurt you," He said quietly, staring at me intently before quickly walking away. *We are destined to fight. After his father and brother are gone, Lucas is the last descendant of Tyran.*

Chapter Twenty-Eight - Humanity

I slid myself across the floor, looking down at the red key in my hand. I felt the intensity of it drain my energy. I pulled my gaze away from it and looked up at the large red gems embedded along the wall; I felt fatigued at the very sight of them. The power they emanated kept me exhausted, but I gripped the key in determination. *I must save Ashley and we must escape. That is my priority. While Misfeata is not disturbed, I will leave Aeisha and Borac here and then flee with my life.* I slid over to the metal bars, ignoring the sting of the key's material against my skin. I slowly pulled myself up using what little strength I had left, while holding firmly on to the key. The gems surrounding me had the effect of a drug, and it took all my will power to focus on where the keyhole was, as I was seeing double. Finally, it clicked and the heavy door slowly opened. I dropped the key and instantly felt the release of tension.

Looking down the silver walls of the hallway on my right, I was relieved to find it empty. I listened intently but there was no sound of approaching footsteps. My hands traced along the bars as I walked towards where Lucas had suggested. I felt relief as I got further from the room. Slowly, my sight cleared, and I felt myself replenishing. I walked around the corner only to be confronted with Raven as she stood there panting weakly against the wall. I looked across and saw Ashley locked in a similar cage as my own, with a cut across his eyebrow close to his piercing.

"You left me with quite the wound," Raven said angrily, her short figure no longer leaning against the wall. Next to her was a Starkorf who was slumped in a chair with a long sword sticking out from his stomach. She smirked in the direction of the dead man: "He told me I couldn't stay. I didn't like that."

I took in her appearance as she spoke. She wasn't wearing the usual leather jacket: only a dress that revealed her injured right shoulder. The bandage that she wore didn't conceal the festering wound that seeped through, staining the material green. It was the same green crystals that had pierced through my own skin. "and besides, his orders were from Lucas. I knew he wasn't trustworthy," Raven said savagely as she lunged at me with Aeisha in both hands. I dodged her first strike, throwing myself into the wall on the right as I quickly scurried around her. My energy rapidly increased as I relished the freedom from the cage.

I pulled the sword from the Starkorf's dead body, swinging it around and holding it strongly in front of me as Raven stood before me with Aeisha's blades forming a cross. Swiftly, she took aim for my chest with one hand. I easily flicked Raven away as her injured shoulder gave way under the pressure, and the force of my blow sent one of Aeisha's blades in the direction of Ashley's cell.

Misfeata began stirring within me again as she felt the presence of her Immortal Blades. Raven clutched at her shoulder briefly and looked over at me angrily. I remembered the first time I was confronted by her—mistaking her for an ordinary twelve-year-old girl. *That was before she tried to drain me. She has killed many humans. She had even tried to kill my parents.*

I could no longer differentiate between my hatred and Misfeata's, and I lunged at her, quickly closing the distance between us. As she slammed to the ground, I looked down into her surprised, crystalized eyes and searched them for a sign of humanity. I punched into her injured shoulder and she let out a hideous wail. My weight was still on top of her as I hovered over her stomach. I stole Aeisha out of her hand in one fluid motion.

If I do this I will have to kill someone, I thought.

'Not someone—a Starkorf' Misfeata answered internally. I felt her step away from my thoughts and feelings. This was now *my* desire. *She will hurt and kill everyone I love if I allow her to live.* I felt Raven's Shield tickle at mine as she tried to gain power, despite her weakened state. *I must protect those I love—and all other humans—from her kind. I have a gift that enables me to do so: I am a Shielder.*

I brought my lips to her ear and whispered gently: "You are no Immortal." I plunged Aeisha into her chest as she struggled and screamed beneath me. I pulled my blade back out grimly as I watched her face contort in pain; her tongue poked out of her mouth, past her pointed, cannibal-like teeth. She had a grotesque fit and then her body stopped moving. Her eyes—though lifeless—stayed open, staring at me, as she lay soulless on the cold ground.

I looked down at my hands that held Aeisha. I had just taken a life.

'...One that had been in existence for over one hundred and fifty years. She was a monster,' Misfeata said, defending my actions. I heard noises from down the hall and I quickly rose to my feet.

Looking around I could see no one nor hear anyone. This was where the Starkorfs stayed; this was their hideout. There seemed nothing humanly or normal about the place—there was nothing but metallic walls. It seemed like a metal cage to keep everyone trapped.

I placed my hand on the lock to Ashley's cell, concentrating on my hand to project my Shield within the lock. It broke apart, opening the door for Ashley. He quickly gathered the sword from the ground, as I picked up Aeisha's partner blade, looking at her mesmerized. Finally I had my Immortal Blades.

I heard noises. I looked to the end of the hall that stopped after Ashley's cell, thinking of no other way out. I searched over the metal wall, projecting my Shield into a combusting bang where it blew a hole through the thick silver and lead us into the cold and rainy night.

That wall I have just blown apart is the difference between my imprisonment and my freedom. It is now night again. For how many days were we enclosed in the Starkorf's hideout?

Looking down on the wet dirt beneath us, we jumped outside through my man-made hole. We rolled into the night, free at last from our cages. Ashley and I ran into the direction that the wind pushed us to. *Where are we?*

I was grabbed by the back of my hair and slammed to the ground, awakening Misfeata. On my back, I looked back up at Praytar. I was surprised that I didn't feel his presence sooner.

"I'm awake now, sister," Praytar said, smiling down on me.

"As am I, brother" Misfeata beamed back, mirroring his deadly smile.

Once again my body was no longer my own. My soul was dormant—I was once again possessed.

Chapter Twenty-Nine - Reckoning

I was an onlooker as Misfeata twisted in disgust at her brother.

Will this be the end of this war or only the trigger of a new one? I could die in this fight.

My hand grazed over where Praytar held my hair firmly. Misfeata dug her nails into his hand as I felt an overwhelming squirm of power release from my fingers. A green crystal slid and extended out of my nails, digging deep into Praytar's hands and forcing him to pull his hand away. My screams of pain were silenced as Misfeata pushed me further back into my own being and mind. I looked down at my torn and extended crystal-like nails. Looking over the transformed sight I recalled Misfeata speaking to me of her true form—a beast.

Within seconds, Ashley was surrounded by Starkorfs; fighting them off with the large sword he had picked up. Rain was dripping off his face as his black hair stuck heavily to his neck.

Lucas jumped out of the same hole in the wall that Ashley and I had run from, and was looking around over the fight that had erupted before we had made our escape. Starkorfs surrounded Lucas as he held a large sword and a small knife in the other hand. He held one in front of him and the other behind his back, slicing at them as they approached him.

Praytar looked at us steadily as he swung Borac over his fingers teasingly. Within seconds the rocky ground had lost any distance it held between Praytar and I. Aeisha aimed for his face as quickly as my blades were thrown into my chest in defense, as Borac tried to plunge down on me. Praytar's movements were so quick I could hardly understand how my body counter attacked everything he charged with.

My body was moving with precise and strong hits as Misfeata held possession over it. Praytar hovered Borac over my side as I reached Aeisha above me in defense. One of my knees dropped under the pressure of Tyran's strength in that moment as his Shield dominated mine. He punched me hard in the ribs, making my arms drop slightly as I winced. Borac sliced at my right blade, knocking it out of my hand as he punched with his other hand into my other side. His knuckles were covered in a red gem as he punched twice and then sliced Borac over Aeisha, knocking her out of my other hand as well.

Both partnered blades of Aeisha were out of my grasp as I looked up at him annoyed. Misfeata hardly cared that she was now defenseless. Another surge of power swept through my arms and burst green blades through my elbows. The gemmed blades were forced in front of my face once again in protection to hold off Borac.

"It seems your strength has weakened over the centuries, Misfeata," Praytar hissed spitefully, as his head hung over Borac, applying more and more strength. It was not the same old man's voice that spoke to us. It was no longer Praytar.

"Or perhaps it's this pesky human's body that can't handle your being," Tyran said, laughing as Borac grazed past my arm, slicing a deep cut into it. Misfeata growled in anger as I felt her rage rise, and pain swarm to the wound. The blood that wept from my arm froze into little shards and glazed over into a sparkling green gem. *Can this green gem be created and used for anything Misfeata needs it for?*

As Misfeata concentrated on healing and covering that wound I took slight possession of my body. *This is my body.* Only my thoughts were to be controlled, and that meant contact with Misfeata. Her own buildup of anger and rage was tearing through my body and ripping it to shreds.

'*Misfeata,*' I quietly whispered. My eyes gazed at Praytar as he licked over where Borac had indulged in my blood.

"I forgot how sweet your blood was, sister," he said with sickening pleasure. "A little too sweet because of the girl, however!" Praytar leapt on us once again, and Misfeata used the same gem-like blades that pierced through my elbow in defense. Before Praytar's feet hit the ground I felt another set of crystal shards pierce out of my knees and into his stomach as he fell onto them awkwardly. I could only let a bellow of a cry rip through my body as I took possession for a moment until my soul was then recaptured, and I was locked in my own head once again. Misfeata's anger was literally tearing my body apart. As I possessed my body for only a moment I felt how far gone she was, what little control she had.

My body balanced as Praytar's figure thrashed back and forth, as his body was pinned to mine.

Misfeata can use the green gem and manifest it into anything she wants: into any weapon from any part of her body. No, from my body. Just as quickly as Misfeata's gems had ejected, a pair of red-gemmed blades pierced into my shoulders. Misfeata did not yell in pain. She hardly even flinched. I felt another shard of crystal tear through my stomach as she continued to create shards.

"Misfeata!" I cried out to her in my mind. "You are killing me!" I screamed into the wind, as the clattering of weapons engulfed me at the same time as the throbbing pain of my body. I had taken possession. The shards of gem retreated as I took complete control. The energy that kept my Shield materialized as those green-gemmed blades were gone. Holes were left in the places they once were. I bled from my elbows, knees, stomach, and nail beds.

I concentrated my Shield onto my shoulders where Praytar had me pinned. I projected it quickly and harshly, pushing his red shards of gem out of my shoulders and pulling my body away. Praytar dropped to his knees as I steadily stumbled back, crouching near the ground in exhaustion.

I forcefully projected my Shield again as Borac tried to crush down on me. I gazed up at Praytar's face, where half of it was now covered and misted with a red shard like skin. It slowly expanded and grew, ripping apart any skin that was once under it. I stared up at the horrific and slow transformation. *That's irreparable.* Tyran's transformation is tearing apart Praytar's body.

'The more I antagonize him with my true self, the further he comes forth. I can control the lust of my beast but Tyran has never had that strength. He is always consumed by it; always destroys the Starkorf's body he is using and creates it into some form of beast... whatever form or shape he finds to be of most use or convenience to him. Who knows what he is turning into right now? With this restraint I have a much better chance,' Misfeata said. I felt her strength within me as if I were back to back with her physically.

Flames wrapped around Praytar's figure as he jumped. He took five big jumps back. Trish walked away from Ashley as she was waving her hands, forming circled flames that struck at Praytar as he continued leaping back. Paul was pushing Max Jacket awkwardly in his wheelchair over the bumpy rocks as they hurried towards me. Any Starkorfs that came towards them were hit with a bolt of lightning, dropping them dead instantly with blackened smoke. I could hardly see them through the thick rain and I was surprised when Paul ran towards me.

"Karla!" Paul shouted, as he snapped me out of my dazed Shield. The Shield shattered, letting the outside noise of the battle overwhelm me. Next to Paul sat Max Jacket in his wheelchair, gazing directly over where Lucas still fought his own kind. *Was Lucas fighting for us or had the Starkorfs turned on him?*

"Why are you here?!" I shouted at Paul and Max over the pounding rain. The speed of the frenzied wind tore at my hair. Trish kept Praytar distracted for a moment as Max looked at me with black eyes. No others had come: only Max, Trish and Paul.

"I came to make sure our bargain was staying true: Borac for this boy," Max said gesturing to Paul "He is now fully healed. I see Praytar has lost full control and will have no redemption of his current body. You must kill him."

I looked back over at Trish as she now jumped further and further away from Praytar as he tried killing her with Borac.

"I know," I said raising myself to stand and clutching at one of the elbows that still bled. Paul cupped my face, looking worried as he held my face so closely to his own.

"Please don't do this. You don't have to," he said pleadingly. His face got closer to mine as I looked up at him, weakened by the intense stare of his stunning green eyes.

"I must, Paul," I said, placing my hand over his. "I am so sorry to have involved you with all of this."

"Don't apologize," Paul said, resting his forehead on mine. The rain that dripped from his nose washed over my lips as I looked up into his eyes. "Please don't go. Let me protect you from these creatures."

I closed my eyes, ashamed that these 'creatures' that he spoke of were now a part of who I was. *I can no longer be scared nor cry. This I must do.*

"I am sorry," I said pulling myself away from Paul and running with Aeisha in my hands.

For some reason Praytar could not control his own body over Tyran. His physical appearance had changed so much and like Max had said; there would be no going back from that. *How have I found control over Misfeata?*

Another loud crash of thunder hit the ground, sending unbalanced shakes through the gravel that I slipped on. Finally I was able to focus on the flames that ripped at the dead trees. Trish jumped away from Praytar who was chasing her. She continued throwing back flames until she was struck in the chest by Praytar's red-gemmed hand, forcing her to fall and hit the ground awkwardly.

I ran as quickly as I could, finding my place by the deformed creature that frothed foam from the mouth. The red gem had spread down one of his shoulders, and Praytar's tailbone had begun to extend out of his skin, forming a spiked tail. *Is he creating some form of tail so he can cover more distance to reach Trish?*

I jumped through the rising wall of flames until I balanced on top of the creature, striking it with Aeisha in my hand. I was thrown off the creature by its rapidly growing tail that wrapped itself around my foot and threw me to the ground. I flipped myself backwards but my body was dragged along the rocks, and I glided on the dirt. Finally my feet stopped dragging as I shot back at him and broke into a run.

He has turned himself into a beast, I thought in horror.

His long tail tried to wrap itself around me again. I dodged it, jumping into the closest flaming tree. I jumped from branch to branch until I was near the top. Praytar swept his tail through the tree, forcing the tree to groan in pain as it crashed to the ground. Never had I imagined that such a creature could manifest, that this was the shape Tyran would decide to use.

My focus fell on the next tree, but his unseen fist found my stomach and plummeted me to the ground, where a massive explosion of impact bombed the ground underneath me. I choked for air as my Shield was projected.

His tail slammed down my chest, once more obliterating my Shield. I caught one quick breath before I jumped to my feet, retreating away from him. I looked at his tail, noticing the tipped blade. The end of his tail was Borac. *He has entwined himself with Borac.*

'He has a weak spot in the front of his Shield, near his chest,' Misfeata said, as I felt her align herself within my body's frame. 'He is focusing all his energy on his tail. You must aim for his chest.'
I felt Misfeata trying to break the control I had over my body. *I cannot let her in. She will kill me.*

I have very little time. I must finish this quickly; the raw energy of his red gem is draining my own. I have to get close somehow.

An arrow was shot towards Praytar's face. He knocked it away with his tail angrily, searching over the direction it had come from. I too looked, watching Lucas leap to the side as his father had tried to kill him with his tail. Lucas shot an arrow once again, missing as he began to run, dodging the attacks from Praytar.

Praytar was sluggish because of the form he had chosen. He lacked the control and strength that Misfeata possessed. Lucas gave me a small, determined nod before running towards his father with a large sword. Praytar swung his tail vigorously at him. I was running towards

Praytar like a blur from behind, tracing Lucas's steps.

The tail wrapped itself around Lucas's waist, catching him as he miscalculated his next jump.

Avoiding the touch of Praytar's red-gemmed skin and tail I leapt over him, now confronting his surprised face.

Praytar's eyes have now completely vanished and were replaced with red crystal. I focused the energy of my Shield on Aeisha, feeling her quickly take to my energy. With as much pressure as I could, I plunged Aeisha into Praytar's Shield, shattering it and piercing into his chest.

Praytar's smile cracked in sick delight as I coughed blood onto his face. I looked down to find Borac piercing through my stomach. *When did he…?* I looked behind me; Lucas was now lying on the ground, dazed and looking back up at me in horror.

I delivered Aeisha's partnered blade into the side of Praytar's head. There was a silent pause: his face dimmed without the pain of death. "I shall see you in the next body then, sister," Praytar said, coughing blood coarsely. Still, he smiled as red crystal flaked from his lips and dropped to the ground. "If your *only* body can survive that is." Tyran was right; in this fight he still had Nathanial and Lucas's body at his disposal. Misfeata only had mine. *And I will not let her have it.*

I panted, feeling the edge of Borac thrive inside my stomach. "I will survive, Tyran." It was both Misfeata and I who spoke strongly.

It was then that Praytar's head rolled back—only half of his face was now recognizable. The crystal gem tail that held firm around Borac shattered, leaving only the remains of Praytar's body behind. I stood there for a while, letting the rain wash over me after committing such awful sin. I held my hand to my bloodied stomach and wobbled a few steps to collect Aeisha. I looked down on the beautiful blades, honored. *You did great.*

One of my knees buckled as I was quickly caught, breaking my fall. I looked into Lucas's dark brown eyes while still clutching at my waist. I projected my Shield forcefully to push him off and let myself fall to my knees weakly. "This changes nothing," I said to him angrily, still poisoned with his betrayal. *Lucas is Tyran's descendant*, I thought. He had betrayed me and everyone else; and he watched as Seth was murdered.

Lucas looked down on me, wounded and hurt, as his jaw tightened. There were numerous bleeding wounds on his face, and cuts through his leather jacket. I closed my eyes, letting the rain's heavy noise and water wash over me. When I opened them Lucas was gone and Borac was still lying on the ground next to his father's corpse.

Perhaps Lucas really had no interest in Borac. Was he speaking the truth when he said when we fight, he will try not to hurt me? I collected myself, mustering the strength to walk over to Borac. I felt its potent energy. I grabbed it, feeling it slowly seep into me, intoxicatingly.

My walk was long, but it was a walk of triumph. The battle has ended, and the rest of the Starkorfs have retreated as soon as Praytar was killed. Ashley, Paul, Trish, and Max now gathered unsteadily towards one another. Paul and Ashley ran towards me as soon as they saw me staggering in the distance. I fell into both their arms, exhausted. I offered Borac to Ashley so he could walk with it in my stead. Paul's green eyes looked saddened as he took in my wound. He looked up at me, pressing his lips to my forehead.

"Thank goodness," he said, as he swept me quickly off my feet and carried me, not struggling in the slightest under my weight. I looked at his large arms in surprise at how content and easily he could lift me. Small cuts littered his face and his shirt had been cut open, revealing a small wound across his chest. Other than that Paul was alive and safe.

"He got her through and through, father," Trish said, looking at my stomach as Paul carried me over to them. Ashley was at our side throwing Borac to Max's feet. Trish's nicely sown and hemmed dress was torn to shreds. Trish wrapped her hand around Borac slowly, looking at it in amazement, before passing it over to Max.

I screamed out into the wind, feeling my body shut down on me as painfully as it always did. My body quickly dropped in pain, rolling out of Paul's large arms. All feeling and sound was blocked. *I can't die like this. Not again. Not now.* My face hit the ground, landing in a small puddle and stifling my ability to breathe. My face was lifted out of it and I was turned onto my back. *My body is shutting down on me again. I am dying.*

My vision became clear once more as I felt a serum creep through my arm and spread throughout my body, relieving my pain. Max held a syringe in my arm and was rubbing over it as he pulled it out.

"What did you do to me?" I asked, clutching my arm.

"It very well might be your solution. I thought it might work," Max said coolly. "It's adrenaline. I know of your case, child. I injected you with adrenaline because it speeds your heart up and forces the blood to spread faster. Your conflicting bloodlines will not have the time to fight, if your own blood dominates your veins and quickly spreads throughout your body. I will throw this information in for free on our deal. After all, you did kill the man who betrayed me."

"Lucas and Nathanial have survived but they have fled," Max lectured. "You know what this means, young one. Now that his older brother Nathanial is next to inherit Tyran's rage, he will seek you again. Lucas is one step down from that. It may be almost impossible for him to control himself near you. Who knows, all hosts of Elder blood are different. Elisabeth was very strong and fought Misfeata on everything. She avoided her body being taken over at all costs. But now that you hear Misfeata and she is within you, it would seem my old friend Elisabeth has passed." Max looked into the sky as another flash of thunder hit the ground, shaking it beneath us. His black eyes changed into the milky blue once more. "Praytar was weak, for any chance of survival you must strengthen yourself."

I looked up at Max, understanding. "Why was I never told of their true being?" I asked, annoyed and horrified at the sight and sensation it had over my body.

"Energy is an entity. For it to materialize it must turn into a crystal gem form. The three Immortal Blades carry the souls of the Elders and are the reason for their large and powerful mass of energy. When connected with their weapon, they can use the entirety of their energy and manipulate the gem into any form they wish or desire. That is the true being of the three Elders and the three Immortal Blades. And your body has been cursed with it. Only a few have witnessed it and not many of the bodies possessed by them survive. If they do, slowly they weaken from their inflicted wounds," Max spoke wisely, while peering blindly over me.

I looked down at the hole where blood seeped from my stomach, feeling the wind rush through me. Heavy wounds covered my body, and blood smothered my skin and dripped. Everywhere Misfeata had released her gems from tore my body apart, leaving gaping holes in their place.

"Please heal me enough so I can find my way out of this place," I begged, and then turned to Ashley. His soaking, black hair almost completely covered his blue eyes. He looked at me exhausted, slumping his large shoulders as the fight was finally over.

"Ashley, I am not coming back. We have all lost a lot from this fight," I said, picturing Seth as a tear pricked at his eye. "I need to find my parents now," I said, my decision already made.

Max Jacket slowly took in my wounds with great difficulty. Elemental Breathers were able to reverse the damage done to them and heal others, but an injury of this magnitude was a challenge, even for him.

"This won't be enough. You'll need constant healing for months even with your own healing abilities. If it is your own raw energy that has inflicted this onto yourself; it creates a lasting injury that you will struggle with. You will need to come back with me so I can perform the procedure properly; I'm purely guided by instincts here. Not to forget the rehabilitation," Max warned.

"Just please..." I said raising my hand to him. "Just for now, do what you can."

After hours of quiet healing from Max I was able to conclude that Misfeata was chained in the back of my mind, where she could only see pure darkness; she was once again dormant. *For now.* The rain had finally cleared up as both Trish and Max's eyes found their pupils once again. I was impressed at how Max was able to create such a rainstorm in just mere moments.

Ashley tried fiercely to convince me to come back with him but I declined. *I will search for my parents now. Who knows how much longer I had to live.* As powerful as I was now, I knew there was more to come. This was only the beginning.

As dawn started to stir and arise over the bloody battlefield we once fought in, I had made up my mind that it was now time to go. I slowly rose to my feet with the support of Paul, who was holding me up from underneath.

"I will come with you," Paul said, resting his forehead onto mine. "Wherever you go." He was breathing his sweet scent of fresh breath into my own.

"I can't protect you," I said ashamed. *I should have never brought Paul into this.*

"You don't need to, Karla. I told you that I was here for you and that I want to protect you. Please don't take that right away from me," he said grimly, cupping my face. I looked into his deep green eyes and saw desperation. *I don't want Paul to leave my side but it is selfish to keep him in danger.* I placed my hand on his, nodding my head in agreement. *If this is what Paul wants then who am I to take that right away from him?* In truth I wanted him by my side more than ever as I feared every step I would take after this. I reminded myself that now wasn't the time to be weak. *I can no longer cry. I have changed and transformed. I am a part of something bigger now.*

Paul let a little smile pull at his lips, before he kissed me gently on the forehead and embraced me tightly. I looked over Ashley's sad face once again, and held my hands out to him. I hugged Ashley thinking of Helena and Seth. Ashley had lost so much because of Lucas, and although he fought bravely in this fight, it would never bring back his father.

I turned to say goodbye to Max and Trish but they had gone. Paul tried collecting me under his weight but I shook my head instead. I grabbed his hand so I could walk as his equal, next to him. *When I find my parents I don't want them to think they have lost the daughter they once had. I have just transformed into something I was always meant to be. My childhood has been lost amongst this war, and with it, I am entrusted with this curse. If I can't put an end to it, then no one can. I am the last of Misfeata's descendants.*

I know it will be a long recovery even with my rapid healing, but with Paul by my side I am positive we would find a way. We walked together into the dawn that broke, washing away the sins we had dealt with and the lives we had taken. For the moment, I was alive. Paul was alive. Lucas was alive.

Misfeata is dormant—for now.

Sneak Peek of Possession Of My Heart

"*A*re you ready?" I questioned Paul as we both looked at the entrance of the hospital in front of us. We were only in a small town this time, one that stated 'Darby Welcomes You' as we drove in.

"Yea." Paul reached into the back of the car and grabbed a small backpack. His green eyes turned almost gray in the thundery weather, and the dark lighting only emphasized the dark bags that were under his eyes from lack of sleep.

"Okay," I said. "Let's go." I jumped out of the car and slowly closed the door as two nurses came out of the hospital entrance for their lunch. I scurried to the side of Paul's door and opened it. I quickly retrieved the bag he gave me and threw it over my shoulder, giving him a glance that prompted him to nod in confidence.

He quickly stumbled into my arms, feigning weakness. I held his weight with my shoulders and half-carried him to the hospital entrance. As the two doors opened, Paul kissed the top of my head and whispered into my ear: "Good luck, Karlz." I could feel a smile pull at my lips but I somehow managed to keep my face expressionless.

As soon as I saw the first doctor I kicked my acting skills into gear, as did Paul.

"Please!" I yelled over the tranquil music that played in the waiting room. "Someone help!"

Paul started coughing violently into my shoulder, and within seconds the first nurse had rushed to our side.

"I don't know what happened," I exclaimed. "He just all of a sudden—…" I started to tremble. "He just got sick! Please you have to help him!"

"We will," the nurse confirmed, before she called over her shoulder for reinforcement.

I let Paul fall into the doctor's arms. "I'm sorry, but I can't do this anymore!" I said dramatically, running away toward the toilets. The doctors made little fuss over me, as I had hoped. I paused at the entrance to the toilets, quickly glancing back at the small huddle of nurses bent over Paul. One nurse turned to look at where I had been standing until Paul grabbed her arm, distracting her from searching for me. *This is my chance.*

Instead of entering the toilets, I scurried down the hall, searching for some form of medical room. A small room that matched the criteria came into sight. I quickly ran to it, using my powerful sense of sight to see where everything was. I couldn't switch on the light because that would draw too much attention.

I fumbled through the labels until I finally found the one I was after: Adrenaline. The heavy door opened slowly behind me, leaving me with just enough time to jump to the roof and plunge my hands and feet into the side of the walls. I forcefully projected my Shield to keep myself in place, pushing against the walls so I didn't fall.

The bottle I was holding fell to the floor. I quickly strained to project a small Shield over the spot it fell to. With a little pulse from my shield it bounced back up toward the ceiling, where I quickly caught it with my mouth. After my confrontation with Tyran I was now able to project my Shield within a short physical range... *another* new skill I had to learn how to control.

The light flickered on and a nurse walked in and began searching over the labels. Her hands tightened over what she was after and she walked out just as quickly as she had come in. When the light was switched off at last and the door was closed I quietly dropped to my feet, retrieving the bottle out of my mouth. I opened the zipper on my backpack and placed the bottle in the bag. When I went to retrieve the other bottles also labeled 'Adrenaline', I found to my dismay, only another three. Indeed it was a small hospital but this would only last me a few weeks, maybe two at the most.

Soon Paul and I would have to go to another hospital and steal more bottles just so I could sustain life. Pumping myself with adrenaline was the only way to keep myself alive when my body next had a fit and shut down. *At least I now know it shuts down because it is trying to fight the Shielder blood that runs through my veins that continues to curse me,* I thought, thinking of Misfeata's blood inside me.

I checked the corridor to make sure nobody was around and then ran down to the toilets near where I had left Paul fumbling and coughing in a show of sickness. When I finally drew his attention he nodded and pulled a tight face, causing the doctors to look up at him in concern.

Paul let a huge fart out. I looked away in embarrassment. How men found it so easy to fart at any time was beyond me. The doctors took a few steps back before searching over Paul, who simply patted his belly. I held my breath and ran in to hug Paul.

"Oh baby, you're alright!" I smiled happily.

"Sorry guys." He scratched his head, messing up his dark brown hair. "Guess I shouldn't have eaten all that cheese, huh?" I couldn't hold my breath any longer and started tugging Paul out the door as he wrapped his hands around my waist.

"Oh, you're alright!" I cried out again. My voice was high-pitched and false. To be honest, it was annoying. Paul and I both kept walking to the car, not bothering to look back at the nurses as they looked at each other in confusion. Finally, we got into the car where I could breathe normally again.

"That one stunk bad," Paul said, smiling as he put the key in to start the engine.

"Don't they always?" I joked, carefully putting the bag down at my feet and catching a glimpse of myself in the review mirror. I adjusted it, disgusted at the sight. I looked the same as I always did: fair skin, green eyes, and light brown hair—which I noticed had lengthened over the last few months. Now my body was fitter, more toned, and adapting well to the training Paul and I did together. But regardless of what others might see, I saw a hideous beast.

I hardly dared look at myself in the mirror now in case it was Misfeata who looked back. I stopped myself from getting angry to avoid allowing Misfeata to stir within me. I hated myself and avoided acknowledging my existence, for if I thought of it for too long, I would question how my existence could be good for anyone. *I am now a thief; stealing from hospitals.* It was Paul's idea after Max Jacket had told us that injecting my body with adrenaline would keep me alive, but now I questioned how far he was willing to go to save me at the cost of his own sense of morality.

Paul's hair had also grown over the last two months, giving it a wild, messy, untamed look. His olive-colored skin now had a lot more pink scars; the worst being the three scratch marks ingrained in his chest. I caught his eye. His expression was hard and his green eyes flickered in the storm. *How far will Paul go for me? Does this make me a terrible person to let him destroy himself for me? Is he really happy with all this running, stealing, training, and searching for my parents? Is this a reality anyone can come back from?*

"How many did you get this time?" Paul quietly asked, looking back at the hospital as he reversed into the dimly lit street.

"Only three," I sighed. I couldn't take them all. I had to leave at least one just in case someone needed it more than I did. It was hard to steal from hospitals as it weighed heavily on our conscience. We always looked out for cameras, at any moment we could have a criminal record on our hands. I couldn't walk up to a doctor and say: "Hey, can you prescribe me adrenaline as this is the only way forward? Sorry, no, I can't explain." We now constantly played with a double-edged sword. In trying to keep myself alive, I risked a future for us both of running from the law. *How selfish of me to let Paul do this.*

Projecting my Shield still strained me after my confrontation with Tyran. Although I was the victor, I had survived with much physical and mental damage. Slowly my Shield was regaining its strength, but only because I worked on it tirelessly every day. I had nowhere near the power that Misfeata had, but I was slowly building myself up to have enough strength to at least defend Paul.

I lifted my long black shirt and looked over the scabby marks on my elbows. It only projected the memory of the green shards piercing out of them. *If Misfeata ever tried to possess my body like that again, I wonder how far she would go. These wounds are taking too long to heal and I have them all over my body. It's been two months now. They should have already completely healed.*

"You had to use your Shield didn't you?" Paul asked, looking over my stomach. I searched over his face as the flash of lightning behind him flickered the night with color, turning his hair from dark brown to silvery gray. He looked across at me with saddened eyes. A depressing sight; I recalled the ghost of the cheeky smile that had once stretched over a face that was now stricken with worry. I slid my long shirt over my knees and looked out the window at the rain that had now started to pour.

Paul turned into a large driveway, before stopping the car outside a derelict looking building. We bought this car for $460. It was old and rusted, with paint scratched off, leaving patches of white all over the two-door car. I didn't know what type of car it was. I didn't even care; all that mattered was that it got us from place to place.

"We will stay here tonight. The hospital shouldn't know anything is missing for another day or so. We can afford to stay here one night." Paul left the car running as he grabbed his wallet and walked into the small office on the right to book a room. The light flashed on and off, stating there were rooms available. No doubt there were. The roof was rusted with clumps of brown and the pool had taken a green tinge to the water.

The hotel room was only tiny, freezing as well. Paul and I slept in our separate single beds next to one another as the lightning flashed color through the room. Rain beat relentlessly against the windows.

There weren't any curtains for privacy—only brick walls surrounding us. With only the one blanket to keep me warm, my teeth chattered as I tried to fall asleep.

I quietly tiptoed to the small cupboard that was in the corner of the room. I opened it, hoping to find at least another blanket, but was greeted only with an ironing board. I clutched my body as I shook uncontrollably in the cold. I looked at the small gap that came between Paul's bed and my own. Not even a thirty-centimeter ruler would come between. I grabbed the thin blanket off my bed and wedged myself next to Paul in his. His body heat was so much warmer than mine—like a hot water bottle. I fiddled with the blanket until Paul fidgeted and rolled over so he was facing my back.

"I wondered how long it would take you," he said with what I could imagine was a sluggish smile. He lifted his blanket and I squeezed

under it, fumbling with my blanket so it wrapped around me. He moved his arm around my stomach. I allowed that small comfort and his gentle snoring to soothe me to sleep.

I woke up to the smell of scrambled eggs, finding myself to be alone in the small single bed. A trail of fresh blood soaked the pillow I laid next to; droplets and splatters of blood crossed the floor, tracing around the corner and into the kitchen. I instinctively clutched at my waist in search of Aeisha—she wasn't in her usual spot. *Where are my blades?* I searched around the room, finding the lantern next to me to be the closest thing to a weapon. Slowly walking to the edge of the wall dividing the kitchen and bedroom, I strained to hear what was around the corner. I stopped, holding the lamp tightly. Taking a deep breath, I leapt across the room in a roll, holding the lamp above me and landing in a crouched position. To my dismay nobody stood in the kitchen. Only a bloody figure lay on the floor, and dull green eyes stared up at me.

Paul.

I froze as I scanned over his body—all the cuts and stabbings— my eyes finally resting on Aeisha. My very own blade was now embedded in Paul's stomach. I only had time to cough out a shocked cry before I turned around and was confronted with Lucas. He raised Aeisha's other blade to my throat. I only had a brief second to look into Lucas's cold face: his angular jaw, his tight lips, his dark golden hair—all stained with blood. Lucas stared at me with piercing brown eyes that I no longer recognized. He looked at me with the same contempt I felt for myself — as though I were a beast. As Lucas's eyes tormented me, I felt the cold ooze of life pouring out of me. Slowly, I looked down to see Borac gliding out of my chest, causing me to slump onto my knees, struggling for breath. A flash of green gem streaked past my sight as I heard Misfeata's laugh echo through the room. I screamed as green shards pierced through my skin, breaking apart the shell that kept my soul intact.

My head flung to my knees as I panted, choking for air. Perspiration covered my whole body as I searched over the blanket that concealed my feet. I heard a creak and opened my eyes to find a pair of piercing blue eyes staring back at me.

"Another nightmare, ey?"

A familiar voice. Ashley stood still as he looked over me.

I straightened myself, forcing my hard face to slightly soften as I looked over the single bed beside me where Paul loudly snored. Thank goodness. It was just a dream.

"It's been a while, Ashley," I said. He leaned against the wall with one leg bent back, arms crossed against his chest.

"Still carrying around your little pet?" Ashley slowly took one of his legs off the wall, as he stood strong before me. "I wonder what he dreams of as you perish in your own nightmares," he said contemplatively as he glanced over Paul. "I imagine his obsession with you actually is returned in his dreams. Instead, in reality he walks around with someone who isn't willing to show him a quarter of the affection he displays…. I imagine."

"You speak out of line. If you came to die, say one more thing of the journey I have chosen to take," I spat.

Ashley let out an exhausted sigh. "Come, I have someone I need you to meet. Someone whom I think will benefit your cause." He walked out the front door that he had easily broken into. As I grabbed Aeisha, I winced and clutched my stomach, finding red on my hand as I retrieved it. My wound had reopened. I grabbed my jacket that hung on the end of my bed, slowly getting up to put it on to cover the visible signs of my bleeding stomach. I quietly closed the door behind me, casting one quick glance at Paul who was still sleeping peacefully.

After hearing the click of the door behind me, I looked up to see Ashley standing beside a man I had not yet met. The first thing that captured my attention was his dominant features—starting with his florescent pink eyes. His smooth baby-soft skin, white hair, plump lips, and thick eyelashes, gave the impression of a man in his mid-twenties. I squinted at him, quickly glancing over his bold red suit that certainly condemned him to be out of place at a cheap motel like this. Then I recognized the detail in the material — the little ripples.

"Material of an Elemental Breather," I said hesitantly, straightening my back in preparation for conflict. The man simply laughed at me maliciously, forcing a hand over his mouth until his mirth lightened into a giggle. I met Ashley's eyes to see him roll them in exasperation.

"Oh my," the stranger said. "We are certainly paranoid."

I searched Ashley's eyes once more, annoyed at being mocked. I resented this meeting with the stranger he had presented. "Are you serious?" I questioned Ashley. Ashley sighed, letting the awkward silence roll on.

I peered over the stranger once again, waiting. "Who are you and why are you here?"

"Oh how you have changed, young one," he said, his piercing eyes looking through me.

"I've never met you," I said coldly.

"In truth, you have," he said. The man before me shrunk into a wolf within seconds. Although there was not much shrinking to be done, the wolf was enormous. I stared at the wolf in front of me, recalling the same thick fur and features of the one at Max Jacket's home. This was the same wolf.

"Sam?" I asked in astonishment. Sam was the pet wolf of Max Jacket. The animal and I had bonded before the ambush Max Jacket had organized against us. I gazed at him in amazement as he transformed again into the young man that previously stood in front of me.

"Actually, my name is Scott," he said as he made a funny face and a clicking noise. He waved his arms in the air dramatically. "You know, code names, secret names… Awkward," he proclaimed flamboyantly.

"I don't understand," I admitted, still astonished.

Ashley stepped forward to speak: "Max Jacket and Trish abandoned their home not too long after the encounter with Tyran. Scott came in search of you, coming across me instead. Mum's still in hiding with Chris and Suzumiya, but Kurt hasn't been found. He's just vanished. Everyone is staying quiet until we find Kurt again, but Scott found our hiding place and demanded to see you."

I nodded at Ashley, taking in what he had stated and then looking over at Scott once more. "And you've come to me, why?"

"I wanna help your little group thing that you've got going here. It seems like a little bit of fun and, well, my father hasn't much time for me, even if I did find him." He sighed to himself with a small giggle. "Wasn't quite accepting of his own son, but balderdash, I'm a free man now," he said, glowing as he gazed at nothing in particular. I glanced up at Ashley, who was looking the other way. This man before me had literally stunned me; I didn't know what to say.

I heard the click of the door and looked behind me as Paul came out shirtless, rubbing his eyes as he looked at us all sleepily. Scott only took a second to start giggling to himself and then he clicked his fingers. "And aren't you cute!" he said, absolutely beaming.

About The Author

Kia grew up in the Darling Downs Region in Queensland, Australia. Graduating High School, she pursued a career in freelance journalism. In 2014, having always had a passion for writing fiction, she decided to follow her dream of becoming an accomplished author.

Now living in Edinburgh, Scotland Kia has a can do attitude, a strong will and the touch of kindness that makes it hard not to fall in love with her. Announced 'The Best New Author of 2015' by AusRomToday, and being awarded numerous awards, she has no intentions of stopping. Kia Carrington-Russell is definitely the new author to be looking out for.

Learn more about Kia at www.kiacarrington-russell.com and follow @kia_crystal on Instagram.

Also Available

The Three Immortal Blades
Possession Of My Soul
Possession Of My Heart
Possession Of My Fate

Phantom Wolf Series
Phantom Wolf
Sia
Phantom Eye
Phantom King

Token Huntress Series
Token Huntress
Token Vampire
Token Wolf

The Shadow Minds Journal Series

My Escort Series
My Escort
My Exception
My Expectation

Taming Himself Series
Aroused
Taste

www.ingramcontent.com/pod-product-compliance
Lightning Source LLC
Chambersburg PA
CBHW030642110726
47901CB00002B/543